****

"Have done, lass," Gordon said.
"No matter what you do,
I shall come after you. You are <u>mine</u>."

"This isn't a game, is it?" Constance asked quietly.

"Who said it was?" his conscience made him admit. "You have my word that you will be treated well, provided you do as I bid."

Her jaw tightened. She looked up at him, reproach in her eyes. "That was my first kiss."

He didn't know what to say. It had been a long time since a kiss meant anything to him. Their kiss had been a means to an end.

"A first kiss should mean something," she whispered.

Dear God, had he ever been that innocent? He couldn't remember.

"They rarely do," he answered, and kicking his horse forward, he set off for Ben Dunmore, where his clan waited.

Cathy Maxwell

IN THE HIGHLANDER'S BED

AVON

An Imprint of HarperCollinsPublishers

This is a work of fiction. Names, characters, places, and incidents are products of the author's imagination or are used fictitiously and are not to be construed as real. Any resemblance to actual events, locales, organizations, or persons, living or dead, is entirely coincidental.

AVON BOOKS
An Imprint of HarperCollins*Publishers*
10 East 53rd Street
New York, New York 10022-5299

This one is for you, Samantha.
May your world be filled with adventure,
laughter, and, of course, love.
Always, always love.

One

Ollie's Mill, Scotland
November 1808

Desperate men resorted to desperate measures.

Or so Gordon Lachlan reminded himself as he raised his hand, an order for the three men he traveled with to halt on the moonlit road.

His plan was to kidnap Miss Constance Cameron, a pupil at Madame Lavaliere's Academy for Young Women, and the Duke of Colster's sister by marriage. The price of her ransom would be the Sword of the MacKenna, a weapon revered throughout the Highlands. The man who wielded that sword would have enough power to lead his countrymen into the very bowels of hell.

Gordon didn't want to go that far. He just wanted to throw the English out of Scotland, and he needed the authority of the Sword of the MacKenna to do it.

Unfortunately, Colster wasn't of a mind to hand it over to him. The fine duke had forgotten his Scottish loyalties. Upon accepting his title, he'd sworn allegiance to the king. So Gordon knew he was going to need coercion. He didn't want to kidnap Miss Constance Cameron, but His Grace left him no other choice.

"Dismount and lead your horses up across the ditch into the trees," he ordered softly. "We'll walk from here. The school is about a mile through that pine forest. Wait until your eyes adjust to the darkness before you move. I don't want any stumbling around."

Horses and riders crossed the ditch by the side of the road. They had just melted into the shadows of the trees when a rumbling vibration beneath their feet warned them they were not alone.

Gordon and his men raised their hands to their horses to keep them quiet just as a large party of men came galloping on the road, heading toward the Academy. *English soldiers.*

Mostly officers, by the amount of gold braid on their uniforms. Moonlight turned the red of their military jackets to black and their wigs to silver. They were obviously from the garrison at Edinburgh, and riding as if eager to reach their destination.

The four Scots waited until the soldiers had safely passed. Thomas was the first to break the silence by spitting his opinion of the English on the ground. He was a giant, a bear of a man, with black hair he wore pulled back in a queue under a wide-brimmed gray hat. A scruff of whiskers always darkened his jaw. "Did you not say this road dead-ends at the school? What business would they have on this road this night?"

"You don't think they know about *us*, do you, Gordon?" Robbie asked.

"They couldn't," Gordon assured him. This plan was too new and had been kept too secret to have been compromised.

"Are we going to continue?" Brian wanted to know. "They outnumber us three to one."

"They could outnumber us a hundred to one and we'd go forward," Gordon said. "Follow me."

Enough of the rising moon's thin light came through the trees to guide their path. Gordon wouldn't show it, but he was concerned about the English.

Madame Lavaliere's Academy for Young Women catered to the daughters of the wealthy, the privileged. There could be a number of reasons a party of soldiers could be rushing to the school.

What Gordon didn't want was to delay his plans. Winter was upon them. He had a camp of five hundred men, women, and children who depended upon him to see them safe. He needed the Sword of the MacKenna. It would give him credit to purchase gunpowder and shot as well as food for empty bellies.

The soldiers might complicate matters a bit, but they would not deter him from his quarry. He had traveled a long way to kidnap Constance Cameron, and kidnap her tonight he would.

When he estimated they were close to the school, he motioned for Brian to hold the horses while he and the others took the climbing ropes and made their way to where the forest met the edge of the school's vast manicured lawn.

Gordon's plan was simple and expedient. They would wait until the students were settled for the night. He would then climb the wall to the second-floor window where Constance

Cameron slept. He'd tie her up and carry her away. His horses were fast and his men traveled light. They could outride anyone pursuing them, even a party of English soldiers.

After all, they'd done it time and time before.

However, as they came into sight of the school, Gordon came to an abrupt halt in surprise. The school was ablaze with light. Grooms walked horses along the front drive, while the faint but distinct sound of fiddles and drums drifted in the air toward them. Among those grooms were several of the king's soldiers holding some very fine horses.

They were having a bloody dance. Gordon swore in disbelief and ordered his men back into the shadows with a curt gesture.

"What now?" Robbie whispered.

Gordon didn't answer immediately. Madame Lavaliere's academy had been an abbey back in Scotland's Roman Catholic days. Over the centuries, towers and buildings had been added. "Her room is on the second floor by that far garret." He'd paid a maid for the information. Obviously, the puss had forgotten an important detail—*like the dance.* "I was to be in and out in ten minutes."

"After dancing all night, they'll be sleeping all the better," Thomas said. He leaned against

5

a tree, making himself comfortable. "At least now we know why the Sassenachs were in such a hurry." He referred to the English soldiers. "They've come a *woo*ing." He drew out the syllables of that last word, making Robbie smile. "They want to catch a rich man's daughter. We should go dancing, too."

Gordon scowled.

"*Och*, come on, Gordon," Thomas chided. "You are too serious. We'll take her. We just have to bide our time, or have you forgotten the price on your head?"

"How can I, with you reminding me of it every time I turn around?"

Thomas grinned, unrepentant. "You're just lucky it's such a pittance or even I might be tempted."

"As if you'd dare," Gordon shot back good-naturedly. He and Thomas had been boyhood friends. Many a time, each had trusted the other to guard his back. "You aren't so big and ugly I can't still take you."

"What? And mark your pretty face? The lasses would never forgive me, would they, Robbie?" Thomas settled himself more comfortably against his tree before continuing philosophically. "Then again, such golden looks are wasted on Gordon. He's practically a monk."

He rolled his eyes heavenward. "God, why couldn't you have given that face to me? I'd have put it to good use. Instead, it's my lot to console all the lasses Gordon rejects. Sometimes it's more work than one man can stand."

Robbie's teeth flashed white in his smile. "I'm always happy to help if you need it—"

"I can manage," Thomas assured him quickly. "Some tasks are a pleasure."

Gordon only paid half an ear to their banter. He'd never enjoyed cooling his heels, although it seemed as if he'd been waiting forever for that moment when he could avenge his father's death.

What *would* his father have said? *What advice would he offer in circumstances such as this?* He'd been a prudent man, an honest one. *He* would have waited.

"I'm going in," Gordon said.

"Later?" Thomas asked.

"No, *now*." Gordon turned and headed back toward where they'd left the horses. "I'm going to the dance."

Thomas and Robbie hurried to catch up with him. "What are you planning to do?" Thomas asked furiously. "Walk in there and ask Miss Constance for a dance?"

"Yes. That's a good plan," Gordon answered.

The more he thought about it, the more he liked it. He rubbed a hand over his chin. "I need to shave. Any of you have your kit with you?"

"I do," Robbie said. It stood to reason. Robbie was the dandy of the group.

"Let me have it. And your jacket, too. It's better than my own."

They'd reached Brian, who appeared confused that they'd returned so quickly and without Miss Constance. But before he could ask questions, Thomas blocked Gordon's path, saying, "Have you forgotten you are a wanted man?" There was no teasing in his tone now.

Gordon laughed, his spirits rising at the challenge. "Those soldiers won't recognize me," he said with confidence. "Or even my name. Most likely they haven't ever heard of Nathraichean. And if they have, they've forgotten, especially when there are heiresses to court. They are thinking about themselves. But someday soon, lads, they will know our names, and they'll never forget them. As for now, I'm going to the dance. I want to see this Miss Constance up close, and perhaps, with a wee bit of luck, I may pry her away from watchful eyes and save us a climb up a wall. Or were you looking forward to that, Thomas?"

The giant grumbled his answer.

"What was that?" Gordon prodded.

"I said, come here, and I'll shine your boots," Thomas answered with little grace. "If you want to play the gentleman, then I won't stop you. I might even come to your hanging so I can laugh."

"I'd appreciate that," Gordon replied, slipping on Robbie's coat. "Now, what do you believe the odds are that I can steal one of those officers' fine horses as I'm leaving?"

"Grab the gray," Thomas advised. "It will show up better in the dark when they come chasing you."

Gordon grinned.

Desperate women resorted to desperate measures.

That's why Constance Cameron had decided to run away tonight. She'd had enough of Scotland, enough of England, and enough of her overbearing sister Charlotte. She wanted to go home, to return to the Ohio Valley, where she could talk to folks without wondering who was introduced to whom, dance without being "taught" steps, and *read* a book instead of walking around with it on top of her head.

She didn't need poise or deportment—and she especially didn't need, or want, a husband.

The husband part had been Charlotte's dream,

not hers. What Constance longed for was the freedom of the valley. She was homesick, and if she didn't get away from dreary Britain soon, she feared she would turn into a vain, silly creature like all of Madame Lavaliere's other pupils.

To that end, Constance had been feverishly planning her escape ever since she'd learned that the *Novus* was leaving for New York from Edinburgh harbor. It was a stroke of luck that the ship's departure was timed around one of the monthly dances held in the academy's sitting room. The day of these dances, everyone was too preoccupied with themselves to care what anyone else was doing. In the midst of all the preening and furniture moving, she hadn't had any difficulty hiding a bundle of clothes under a shrub out in the garden.

As soon as everyone was involved with dancing and men and all the petty dramas of women, Constance was going to steal out the garden doors, grab her precious bundle of belongings, and head for Edinburgh. The ship would depart in four days. In that timeframe, she could *walk* the distance to Edinburgh harbor if necessary.

She had no worry about paying her passage. Charlotte's new husband, the despicable but very wealthy Lord Phillip, was overly generous with her allowance. Constance had no qualms about using it for this purpose. After all, it was because of him she'd been sent to Madame Lavaliere's. The money was tied away in a scarf in her bundle.

But first she had to slip past Headmistress Hillary's eagle eye.

She'd thought the task doable, until Captain Jonathon Ardmore, the man who sent half the hearts at Madame Lavaliere's swooning, decided to fix his attentions upon her.

Really. The man was worse than a bloodhound in tracking her down. Constance had spent the past half hour attempting to avoid him and failing, since once again he was blocking her path.

"Captain, we have already danced," she said, dropping her voice, hoping no one overheard his second request.

Of course, she knew better.

Off to her left, Lady Mary Alice Herrington was fuming. Captain Ardmore was *hers*, or so she'd told everyone before this evening's event began. She was not taking his defection well, especially his defection to Constance.

And, in spite of her urgency to run away, Constance *did* take a measure of pleasure out of that. Lady Mary Alice needed to be knocked down a peg. She'd made Constance's life miserable . . . that is, until Charlotte had married Lord Phillip.

Evil brother-in-law or not, that marriage had been a powerful tonic in Constance's life. Before it she'd been the butt of every nasty little jest or prank. They'd laughed at her American accent and simple, straightforward ways. But now she'd been raised to Lady Mary Alice's rank and given all the privileges due the daughter of a wealthy and important family.

Of course, Constance wasn't certain that she didn't prefer her earlier ignoble state to the tender-hook scrutiny of the staff at Madame Lavaliere's. Headmistress Hillary had doubled her lessons in deportment and behavior, admonishing her to work harder now that she was to make a brilliant match.

If that wasn't enough to make a girl want to escape, Constance didn't know what was. Especially if it meant being polite to the likes of Captain Ardmore.

"I defy all approvals and disapprovals," Captain Ardmore declared. He was in his late twenties, with sloped shoulders and a rangy build that reminded her of a scarecrow her neighbors back in the Ohio Valley had used. "I could no more hold myself back from you than I could refrain from charging enemy cannons."

Constance remembered having a very different reaction that moment when their eyes had met across the room. After hearing Lady Mary Alice and the others carry on about him, hers had been one of disappointment. She didn't understand why he wore such a fussy wig, with its tight row of curls across his forehead. In her opinion, any man worth her interest didn't wear other men's hair, or douse himself in scented water when he should be drinking it to sweeten stale breath instead. A man who couldn't use soap or tooth polish was not one she could enjoy.

She flipped open her fan, the movement a smooth twist of her wrist as drilled into her for hours. "Certainly I am not as dangerous as a cannon," she suggested, wondering what he would think if he knew she had a knife strapped to her right thigh. She always wore it in spite of Headmistress Hillary's reprimands.

"You are, where my heart is concerned," he answered with so much false sincerity Constance had to stifle the urge to gag. It would have been unladylike.

Instead, she said, "Or could it be I am more attractive to you, dear captain, since my sister married the Lord Phillip Maddox and I am now a relation to the Duke of Colster?"

His eyes widened at her bluntness.

She continued, enjoying herself. "You see, we've met two other times and I never impressed you then."

"I must have had other matters on my mind," he murmured. "My responsibilities at the garrison are quite rigorous—" He stopped at the eyebrow she raised over his excuse. "Or I was a complete fool," he amended before smiling, an expression that reminded her of a tinker pushing inferior goods for too high a price. "Please, let me make amends for my slight now." He reached for her gloved hand, boldly lifting it to his lips as he whispered, "I shall never be so remiss again."

He was going to kiss her hand. Panic mixed with annoyance.

Constance had never been kissed by a man in any form. She had avoided it. Her first kiss was going to be special. She wasn't going to waste this rite of passage on a hand peck by someone who irritated her.

Closing her fan with military precision, she rapped him on the head before his lips could touch her kid gloves.

The startled man pulled back.

14

"I beg your pardon, Captain," she said, reclaiming her hand. "My fan slipped."

"Why you vixen." His sudden anger was a bit startling. "Do you think to embarrass me?"

"You are doing a perfectly acceptable job of that on your own," she answered. Perhaps he intimidated other women, but not her.

His lips curved into a harsh smile. He took her arm by the elbow, pinching it tightly as he leaned close to say for her ears alone, "If you thought to set me off, you're wrong. You were right earlier. I *was* interested in your family connections, but now it is *you* I find intriguing."

"And I find you a bore," Constance replied calmly even as her chest tightened with alarm. She didn't need this. Didn't want it. He'd have his eye on her all night, and she'd never be able to run away—

"Captain Ardmore, you have not yet danced with Lady Mary Alice."

Headmistress Hillary's intervention could not have been more welcome. The headmistress was a dour Scottish lady who was no one's fool, as Constance had learned repeatedly, much to her regret.

Apparently the captain also had a healthy respect for Headmistress Hillary. He released his hold on Constance's arm, glancing around and realizing he'd been in danger of creating a scene.

"Yes, I do believe I owe Lady Mary Alice a dance. If you will excuse me?" he said with a bow.

"Of course," the headmistress answered.

Dismissed, Captain Ardmore turned to find a very anxious Lady Mary Alice waiting for him a few steps away. Headmistress Hillary watched until the couple was walking toward the dance floor before asking, "What was going on?" Her pleasant manner belied her keen interest.

"I did not encourage his advances, Headmistress Hillary," Constance said in her defense.

The headmistress's smile said she knew better. "The next time you deliver a set down, please don't resort to violence. A fan is for attracting, not attacking." Her clipped, Scot accent gave the rebuke even more weight.

"Yes, headmistress. I shall be more docile in the future."

Headmistress Hillary met her eye. "I doubt that, Miss Constance. However, I shall endeavor to remember how uncivilized you were when you first arrived. Almost a savage. If I succeed in taming you, then the success will be my life's reward."

It was going to give Constance great pleasure

to disappoint her. She bobbed a curtsey. "I pray that I may become a model of propriety, Headmistress, the better to prove the importance of your educational methods."

"Sarcasm is the lowest form of humor, Miss Constance. I don't like you any more than you like me. But understand, I shall succeed."

Constance thought of the clothing bundle waiting for her beneath the bushes. "Yes, Headmistress." She was tempted to punctuate her words by wiping her nose on the puffed sleeve of her dress, but refrained. The dress was a sore spot between them. Constance had wanted to wear one of emerald green, a color that would not be noticed in the night when she made her escape. Headmistress Hillary had insisted that all the girls be dressed in white, as befit their unmarried state.

Constance had protested, but as always happened in her battles at the school, Headmistress Hillary won. She held all the control, which only fueled Constance's determination to run away. She hated being portrayed as some American rustic who was all but a lost cause save for English manners.

"Now, let us find you another dancing partner—" Headmistress Hillary's voice broke off as her gaze went to the door, where a new guest had arrived. Constance turned to see who it was that had caught the headmistress's attention.

A gentleman handed his hat to a servant, a gentleman with the looks of Apollo come to life. A tall, golden-haired god blessing their poor assembly with his radiant presence.

Even the musicians put down their instruments to gape, and Constance found herself staring as well.

His coat had seen better days and the riding gloves he removed were exactly that, riding gloves, used and abused. But no one cared. His shoulders were broad, his limbs long and strong, his manner confident. Candlelight caught the gold in his hair, the hollows in his cheeks, the aristocratic, masculine line of his nose and jaw. There wasn't a person in the room who hadn't marked him for a gentleman.

Feminine interest stirred. Breasts were lifted higher, lips were licked, fans fluttered. His appearance raised the stakes of their country dance. He was the Unknown. The Stranger. The evening suddenly promised to be a night like no other. Captain Ardmore was vanquished from all minds. This golden gentleman had now become the prize.

"Who is he?" Constance whispered, speaking her thoughts aloud.

"I don't know," Headmistress Hillary said, sounding dazed herself. "But I shall find out." She moved forward to greet him as the mysterious gentleman walked into the room with the fluid grace of an athlete.

And Constance realized that although this stranger was handsome, she had no time for weak knees and heart flutters. *Here* was the distraction she had hoped for. While everyone else's wits were man-addled, she would make her escape.

But before she could take a step toward the door, the gentleman looked right at her.

His sharp eyes took in everything about her, from her new kid slippers, to her silk stockings and demure debutante's dress in virginal white muslin and lace, to the lock of hair that had been plaguing her all evening by threatening to tumble out of its hairpin . . . and she had the uncanny sense that he'd come to search her out.

Unsettled by the disquieting thought, Constance knew that if she was wise, she'd best leave now.

Two

Gordon immediately knew which young woman in the room was Constance Cameron.

When he'd last been in London, the three Cameron sisters' names had been on everyone's lips. They were the long lost granddaughters of the disgraced Earl of Bagley and had been raised in the American wilderness. They'd come to London with scarcely a shilling to their names and taken the *ton* by storm. The eldest, Charlotte, had just made a brilliant match with her elopement to Lord Phillip Maddox, one of London's most eligible bachelors.

Gordon had seen Charlotte from afar and thought her indeed beautiful, although he'd heard she was extremely outspoken. He wasn't fond of outspoken women and hoped the youngest Cameron was more malleable.

In truth, Constance shared her sister's same blue, jewel-bright eyes framed by thick dark lashes, but there the differences seemed to end.

Constance was taller, more slender. Her honeyed brown hair was several shades darker than her sister's and her mouth wider and more expressive.

However, what caught Gordon's interest was the air of purpose around this young woman. There was an energy to her, a confidence that every other woman in the room lacked. It was as if she stood apart and unafraid. He had the unsettling notion that here was a warrior, a female warrior, and it was *that* vitality that drew him to her—

He stopped, surprised by the direction of his thought.

There was no place in his life for a woman. The Cause was his mistress. He was here to kidnap Constance Cameron, not woo her.

However, courting gave him an excuse for searching her out. The problem was, he sensed that he might be wagering more than he wanted to stake in this matter.

Gordon shook his head. When had he become fanciful? He wasn't a man given to doubts. He couldn't afford them. He wanted the Sword of the MacKenna and this lass was the key. The time had come to put his pretty face to good use.

But before he could take a step toward his goal, a matronly woman with the protective air of a mother hen placed herself between himself and Constance Cameron. "I beg your pardon, sir?" she said crisply.

Gordon immediately realized his error. This was the headmistress the servant by the door had directed him toward. He'd almost walked right by her.

Giving his best bow, he attempted to recoup lost ground with flawless manners. "Mistress Hillary, please forgive my intrusion. I'm Gordon Lachlan." He used his name. Every ear nearby was cocked in their direction. He dared the English to recognize him.

No one overhearing stirred. Not even the few soldiers. So much for Thomas's worries.

"I had an interview with Mr. Fryson last week about sending my sister to your excellent school," Gordon lied smoothly. Fryson was the school's owner. There had been no such interview the week before, however, a few quick questions of the servant at the door had re-

22

vealed that Mr. Fryson was not in attendance that evening. He'd been called away and the servant had been gossipy enough to mention the headmistress always had her hands full when left in charge. Gordon gave the headmistress his easiest and most charming smile. "He invited me to the dance, but I didn't know if I would still be in the area. However, business has detained me and I thought to pay a visit and see this part of your program for myself."

"Ah, yes, Mr. Fryson spoke of your visit," the headmistress said, giving truth to the servant's assessment. "Social skills, as well as a thorough knowledge of the gentle graces, such as dancing, are an important part of our program. I hope your sister will one day join us."

"I'm certain she will," Gordon said, praying Fiona never found out he'd so used her. She'd be furious at being cast as a schoolgirl, but then, lately, any emotion out of her, even anger, would be welcome.

He pushed concerns over Fiona out of his head as Mistress Hillary asked, "Are you from this area, Mr. Lachlan?"

"No, Speyside," he said. "My father was Sir John Lachlan."

"The magistrate?" The stiffness dropped from Headmistress Hillary's manner. "The man courageous enough to stand with the crofters against the Clearances?"

Pride would not allow Gordon to deny it. "He was my father."

"He lost his life for it." She shot a glance at the soldier standing some six feet away and lowered her voice. "The Clearances are destroying my beautiful country. And what is left behind? People who don't care. Look at my charges, so wealthy and so empty-headed. Their parents want nothing more from me than to make them elegant. I was a vicar's daughter, sir. I was raised with a conscience. I have intelligence. I have seen for myself how the poor suffer. If we are not careful, everything we once valued will be gone."

"Not as long as I draw breath."

A sad smile came to her lips. "I'm older than you, Mr. Lachlan, and I think, perhaps, wiser. Sometimes we can't stop the changes that are happening."

"We must always stand for what is right."

Her eyebrows rose and she released her breath with a sigh of resignation. "You are a crusader. Good. The world needs a hero, even if it doesn't know what to do with him." She offered her hand. "However, welcome to our small school. I pray your sister will someday be one of our number."

"Thank you, Headmistress," he said, genuinely meaning the words. Here was another supporter of the Cause.

Raising her voice, a signal that confidences were finished between them, she said, "May I introduce you to some of the young women who are my charges, Mr. Lachlan? I assure you, they are most eager to make your acquaintance. You can see how they are gathering around." It was true. Girls had been inching forward, covertly jockeying to be the first to receive an introduction, while the men in the room stood back with arms crossed and frowns deepening.

"As I am theirs," Gordon replied dutifully. He couldn't help but take a secret delight in upsetting the other men's plans of conquest for the evening, especially those of the Sassenachs.

"Your father was a magistrate but what of yourself . . . ?" the headmistress asked.

"I studied law."

"In Edinburgh?"

He smiled. "No, London."

Mistress Hillary's own smile widened. "All the better. My charges live for talk of London." The feminine faces around her nodded enthusiastic agreement.

"It's been several years—" he started apologetically, but a young woman with silvery blond curls cut him off.

"That's fine. We are interested in whatever *you* have to say."

Headmistress Hillary frowned at the chit's forwardness, but she ignored her. She offered her hand. "I'm Lady Mary Alice."

Gordon bowed over the gloved hand. "It's my pleasure, my lady."

Lady Mary Alice did not pull her hand away. For a second Gordon had no choice but to hold it until Headmistress Hillary cleared her throat and brought the young woman back to her senses.

An English officer wearing a ridiculous wig of tight ringlets across his forehead cut right in between her and Gordon. "Lady Mary Alice, do you not remember? This next dance is promised to me. The musicians are ready to play now."

Lady Mary Alice's lips puckered into a moue of protest. "Was it promised, Captain Ardmore? I remember you ignoring me—"

"It was," Headmistress Hillary interjected.

"Yes. I almost forgot," Lady Mary Alice said. She placed her hand on the arm the officer offered with an obvious lack of enthusiasm.

"Perhaps I may have the next dance?" Gordon suggested, pleased to see the Englishman receive such a snub.

Lady Mary Alice brightened. "Of course—"

"*I'm* open for this dance," a bosomy redhead said, jumping in to fill the void and beating two other of Madame Lavaliere's pupils to the opportunity.

"I beg to differ," a lieutenant who had been standing close to Captain Ardmore said. "You promised this dance to me, Miss Heloise."

"Did I?" the redhead wondered. "I don't remember."

"Miss Heloise," Headmistress Hillary said sternly.

The corners of the redhead's mouth drooped. "I really don't remember," she protested. "But if I did, I suppose I'll *have* to dance with you."

"You did," the lieutenant said, offering his arm while frowning at Gordon.

Before another young woman could claim the dance, Gordon said to Headmistress Hillary, "Please, may I beg an introduction to the young woman standing behind you—" He broke off in surprise.

Miss Constance Cameron wasn't there.

He looked around and caught sight of her attempting to slip unnoticed out a glass-paneled door leading into the darkness of the garden. Headmistress Hillary, noticing his hesitation, turned just as Miss Constance glanced back to see that she was safe.

She wasn't.

Caught, she attempted to cover her actions by making a great pretense of opening and closing the garden door as if there had been some difficulty with it she needed to fix. But Gordon knew differently. So, apparently, did the headmistress.

"Excuse me," Headmistress Hillary said. Without waiting for a response, she marched over to Miss Constance. Gordon followed, too aware that if he stayed, a half-dozen girls were lined up to jump on him.

"I just wished a breath of fresh air," Miss Constance quickly explained as the headmistress approached.

"We have guests, young lady," Headmistress Hillary said with the irritation of one who has had to repeat herself too often for patience. "A gentlewoman does not leave the room when she has guests to entertain."

"One breath—" Miss Constance pleaded.

"No—" Mistress Hillary answered as Gordon cut in.

"I fear I've created a contretemps," he said. An apology was always the best reason to set aside manners.

It worked. "Oh, Mr. Lachlan, I'm sorry for leaving you alone," Headmistress Hillary replied, a bit rattled by his presence. "Believe me, this is none of your fault."

"But I fear it is so," he pressed.

Mistress Hillary forced a smile. "My pupil was feeling a bit faint but she has recovered completely, haven't you, my dear?"

Constance Cameron murmured an unintelligible answer. Her side glance toward the others standing close by told Gordon that she did not appreciate so much unwanted attention.

But he had what he wanted. "Please, Headmistress, may I beg an introduction?"

Headmistress Hillary frowned, but did as he asked. She had no choice. "Miss Constance Cameron, may I introduce to you Mr. Gordon Lachlan of Speyside. His father was an important magistrate in this country. Miss Constance is related to the Duke of Colster."

He had the right woman. "Miss Constance," he murmured with a slight bow.

She didn't want to play at manners. Her hands stayed at her sides. She was angry that her desire to go outside had been thwarted, and he wondered what waited for her there. Most likely a gentleman. All of London knew the Cameron sisters were opportunists.

Now, how could he play this to his own advantage?

"Miss Constance?" Mistress Hillary prodded. "Perhaps you are not feeling well and wish to be sent to your room?"

A reluctant gloved hand came up and was offered to him. "It is a pleasure, sir." She even bothered to give him a curtsey, although it was the very swiftest bob of her knees.

Gordon wanted to laugh. Now that he had her, he wasn't going to let her go. "Please honor me with the next dance," he begged.

A frown formed between her brows. She blamed him for her being caught, but before the word "no" formed on her lips, she cast a swift glance at Mistress Hillary and changed her mind. "I'd be honored, sir."

Thomas and the lads would be proud of him, Gordon thought. Now all he needed was to discover why she wanted to go outside and promise to escort her. This was going to be far easier than the original plan of scaling a wall and stealing her from her bed.

Gordon offered his arm. She accepted it with all the grace of a princess being paired with a peasant, not even bothering to meet his eye— and he felt challenged.

Women chased him. It was rarely the opposite.

"If you'll excuse us, Headmistress?" he said.

The headmistress nodded her assent, her lips pursed in concern.

Gordon waited until out of earshot of the headmistress to confide, "She is not happy with you." Offering sympathy was often the easiest way to a woman's heart.

"She rarely is." Miss Constance kept her gaze forward, her back stiff.

And Gordon realized he was going to have to work harder. His sister Fiona had often said that women came too easily to him. He wondered what she'd say now.

"I'm sorry I upset your plans for a lovers' tryst," he said, taking a stab at her motive for going out into the garden.

Her chin lifted. "I wanted a breath of fresh air. Nothing more."

"Liar," he said.

Her head whipped around and her gaze met his. "Snitch," she responded.

Startled, Gordon came to a halt.

He reassessed his original impression of Constance Cameron. She was young but not defenseless. He'd best be on his toes.

"You are a bit older than the other girls, aren't you?" he said.

"You are a bit rougher than the other gentlemen, aren't you?"

"I know my manners," he said.

"I do, too," she answered, but then capitulated with the truth, "Well, sometimes I do. It seems every time I turn around, Headmistress Hillary makes up new rules for me to obey. And I fear I've been a bit gruff. It's not your fault I received a dressing down."

Her directness, her honesty, caught him off guard. She *wasn't* like the other preening women in this room.

And for a moment he could imagine himself in another time and place. For a moment he found himself wishing he was nothing more than a country gentleman come to flirt a few hours away at a dance. For a moment he wanted to live in those precious carefree days of what seemed to be long ago.

"Let us start this again," he offered. He bowed. "I'm Gordon Lachlan of Speyside."

Her clear eyes searched his face before dropping to the ungloved hand he offered. He gave no apology. Not for not having gloves nor for the calluses there, a sign that he was accustomed to hard work.

She placed her gloved hand in his, and this time her curtsey was flawless. "It is a pleasure to meet you, sir. I'm Miss Constance Cameron, formerly of the Ohio Valley." She said this last with pride.

"I had thought your family was from London."

"My sisters chose to live there. *I'm* an American."

It was as if she was declaring herself and daring him to find fault.

Gordon didn't. As a Highlander, he understood being an outsider. "I understand American women are of an independent spirit."

"Yes," she said, her lips curving into a smile. "We are."

And for a second Gordon was transfixed.

No one smiled like Constance Cameron. It lit her face. Her skin even seemed to glow. A man would perform any feat to see such a smile, especially if it was directed toward himself—

"Are you two joining the dance or not?" Lady Mary Alice interrupted. "We are waiting for you."

Her shrill voice broke the moment between them. Miss Constance—*Constance,* he amended, dropping the fussy "Miss" from his mind, because her name sounded more independent, *more* American, without it—broke away as if suddenly realizing they were not alone. She hurried past him to take her place among the line of women ready for a lively reel.

Gordon moved to stand across from her, finding himself between Captain Ardmore and the young lieutenant. He could feel the tension in both men. They wouldn't look at him, but were aware of him.

Across from them, Lady Mary Alice and Miss Heloise were giving Gordon their best dimpled smiles. He couldn't help but savor the moment, capping it off with a wink at Lady Mary Alice.

Constance's stomach hollowed with disappointment.

Mr. Lachlan had winked at Lady Mary Alice, her nemesis, and he'd done it right in front of her.

The music started. She moved her feet with the rhythm. She was too proud to let anyone know she'd witnessed the wink.

Of course, what bothered her most was that Mr. Lachlan almost had her fooled.

Yes, she found him physically attractive—what woman with two eyes wouldn't?—however, in those brief, private moments between them, she'd thought she'd discovered something *more* in him. He'd not looked down his nose at her as so many others did when she mentioned her American upbringing. He'd actually appeared to respect her for it, to understand her pride in it . . . to accept her.

Unfortunately, that wink evaporated all good-will she had toward him.

And when Captain Ardmore and Lieutenant Nelson sought retribution for Mr. Lachlan's flirting in the form of a well-timed shove out of the line, Constance didn't bat an eyelash as the captain took the Scotsman's place. She even smiled brilliantly at Ardmore as they reeled their way down the center of the other clapping dancers.

Mr. Lachlan was left to partner Lady Mary Alice.

In fact, Constance thought it would be poetic justice if Mr. Lachlan ended up marrying Lady Mary Alice and had to wait on her hand and foot forever. That would teach him to keep his winks to himself.

Nor did she balk when the dance was over and Captain Ardmore led her to the punch table on the other side of the room.

Mr. Lachlan was stuck with Lady Mary Alice and Miss Heloise.

Not that she cared, Constance told herself.

She'd mentally drawn a line through Mr. Lachlan's name. Let the other girls fight over him. She was running away. She'd best not forget it.

Unfortunately, Captain Ardmore had decided she was now his, and his comrades had gathered around, each begging for a dance. They would keep her busy all night. She'd never have a moment to slip away.

Constance took a sip of the punch Captain Ardmore offered her and decided the time had come for extreme measures.

She dropped the cup, groaning loudly as she did so.

"Miss Constance, is something the matter?" he asked.

"Yes, I've suddenly taken—" She hesitated. "—*violently* ill. Please excuse me." Dramatically, she threw her hand over her mouth and charged through the ring of soldiers, heading for the stairs leading to the upstairs living quarters.

As she suspected, considering her exit, Mistress Hillary followed close behind. Constance lingered at the staircase for her.

"Miss Constance, have you become ill?"

Constance sucked her cheeks, leaning against the banister. "I fear so," she said in a small voice.

"Oh, dear," Mistress Hillary said, lifting her skirts to come up the stairs to attend her.

"Please," Constance said, warding her back with a frail hand. "I shall be fine. I just need to lie down a bit. You must see to our guests, especially since Mr. Fryson is not here. One of the maids will help me."

The reminder to Mistress Hillary that she was the only one in full authority did the trick. The headmistress stepped off the stairs. "You are right. I need to stay down here. Let me send Miss Esmay up to you." Miss Esmay was the French teacher and very well liked.

"No, she's busy at the punch bowl," Constance said. "But I need to go to bed . . . "

She didn't wait for a response, but started climbing the stairs as if the weight of the world rested on her shoulders, a weight she threw off the moment she'd rounded the corner of the upstairs hallway. She counted to forty-five and peeked back down the stairs.

Headmistress Hillary was gone. At last, she was free to leave.

Constance walked to the end of the hall and the stairway that led to the kitchen. She wondered why she hadn't thought of feigning illness sooner. No one would bother a sleeping sick person, and she could have been well on her way to Edinburgh by now.

The kitchen was deserted. All the servants were busy with the dance. Constance hurried across the room and slipped out the back garden door.

Light poured out from the ballroom windows onto the lawn. Conscious of her white dress, she stayed to the shadows, making her way toward the bundle of clothing she'd hidden in the shrubberies and congratulating herself with every step toward freedom.

Her skin tightened with the cold of the damp night air. The bundle contained a shawl, her beloved moccasins, and a sensible dress. She would change as soon as possible.

She'd also thought to pack a book to while away the tedious days of sea travel, a novel by Maria Edgeworth, *Castle Rackrent*. Miss Esmay had lent it to her on the sly since it wasn't approved literature for the young ladies of Madame Lavaliere's. Constance couldn't wait to read it. In fact, her only concern in running away was that she wouldn't be returning the book. Perhaps, when she reached the valley, she could send some money to the French teacher for its replacement.

Her eyes had adjusted to the dark, and the path was well marked. However, it took a moment to discover the exact location of her bundle. Pulling it out from under the shrubberies, she tossed aside her fan, kicked off her silly dancing slippers, yanked off the irritating silk stockings, and put on her deerskin mocs.

Mistress Hillary and Charlotte had refused to let her wear them. But now she didn't have to listen to them, or anyone. Her toes wiggled in pleasure as she retied her bundle, placing her dancing shoes on top of her clothing. Her money and the book were at the bottom.

Her fingers had just finished the knot when she sensed that she wasn't alone.

Her heart went still. A pair of booted feet walked up to stand beside her.

Relief flooded Constance. It wasn't Mistress Hillary.

"Are you gardening, Miss Constance?"

Mr. Lachlan's soft burr surprised her. She looked up. His face was in shadows. She couldn't tell what he was thinking, what he wanted. She considered making an excuse—and decided not.

She was too close to freedom to give up now.

So, doubling her fist holding the bundle of clothing, she started to rise to her feet. And, as she did so, she swung at him with all her might, aiming for his groin.

Castle Rackrent gave a nice heft to her attack and it was all that was needed.

The Scotsman doubled over in pain, and Constance took off running.

Three

Gordon had not expected the attack. He had anticipated anger, perhaps a tear or two—but an attempt to neuter him?

He dropped to one knee. For one sharp, dizzy moment he couldn't breathe let alone think. She had a surprising amount of strength and determination for a woman, not to mention that he felt as if she'd struck him with a brick.

Meanwhile, she'd taken off running in the opposite direction of the school.

Through the haze of pain, Gordon realized the contradiction.

Where the devil was she going? There was nothing surrounding the school but woods—

She was running away.

The moment he had the thought, he knew it to be true. The question now was where was she running to, or to whom? Young girls didn't take off on their own. There had to be a secret lover waiting in the forest. He knew that if she reached him, he would lose his best opportunity to reclaim the sword.

Gordon stood and took off after her. Although he ran like a lame bear, his longer legs outpaced her before she reached the treeline.

This side of the house was dark and deserted, so there was no one to shout out when Gordon tackled Constance around the waist just as she was turning to see if he'd followed. He fell on top of her, his body weight pinning her down. For a second the air was knocked out of them both, but Gordon was taking no chances. He slapped his palm over her lips.

"Don't," he warned. "Not one word."

She put up a struggle, hitting him again and again with her bundle.

These blows were not as mortal as the first had been, and he easily fended them off, yanking her bundle out of her hand.

"What do you have in here?" he snapped, shaking the bundle so the knot came loose. The contents spilled out, clothes, shoes, money—

"A book?" he said in disbelief. "You almost neutered me with a book?" He tossed it aside and came to his feet, bringing her up with him. She twisted her arm and pulled, bending this way and that, trying to escape. He held fast. "Miss Constance, I don't know where you were running off to but you are mine now—"

Gordon broke off as he realized she held a knife in her other hand. Moonlight glinted off a blade sharp enough to skin a rabbit.

She slashed out at him. He registered her movement in time to jump back, just barely keeping his hold on her. He grabbed the wrist of the hand holding the knife and used plain, brute strength to force her fingers to drop it.

He kicked it aside. With an angry sound, she lunged for it, but he yanked her back.

Her carefully coiffured hair now tumbled down around her shoulders. Her eyes were bright with fury. She attempted to kick out but he whipped her around to hold her firmly.

"Where did you keep that knife, lass? Do you have other weapons?" He made no apology as he subdued her with one arm while his other hand ran along the contours of her body in a quick search.

His purpose was the sexless one of survival, and yet he was aware of her womanly curves.

Too aware. He went hard, a reassurance that she, thankfully, hadn't gelded him . . . however, she also felt the movement.

She drew a sharp breath.

He could feel the pounding of her heart. Her breasts were tight and full from their struggles. The curve of her buttocks nestled his hardness.

This was more dangerous than her attack.

Colster would want the girl back with her virginity intact. Still, it had been a long time since Gordon had felt this strong a need. He had a strong, almost overwhelming urge to bury himself to the hilt inside Constance Cameron. The sooner he handed her off for someone else to take care of, the better—

A sharp elbow in his side brought him back to attention.

In God's name— The girl had the strength of ten men when she decided to use it. Gordon lost his hold and she took off running—this time *toward* the house.

He cursed his own male nature and ran after her. Once again he caught her handily. She opened her mouth to scream but this time he didn't waste time on niceties. He pulled a kerchief from Robbie's coat pocket and stuffed it in her mouth.

Miss Constance almost gagged, and he didn't

blame her. He heaved her over his shoulder and started walking toward the woods. She tried to buck herself off his shoulder, to free an arm and hit him, but Gordon wasn't letting go of her again.

He no longer feared a lover was close at hand to save her. Whoever she'd been running off to meet couldn't have witnessed him manhandling her and stood by. He either wasn't there or he was a coward.

Gordon reached the shelter of the forest, then gave her a good, hard smack on her rear. "Stop it," he whispered furiously. "You will only make this more difficult for yourself."

Her response was to shove her hip at his head. He ended that nonsense by resetting her on his shoulder so her head hung even farther downward.

As he moved in the direction of the horses, Thomas and Robbie fell in by his side.

Thomas's eyes glittered with savage amusement. "Enjoying yourself?" he said.

Gordon dumped Miss Constance into the giant's arms. "You carry her," he ordered. "Did you see her attempt to gut me?" He should have known. They probably had a good laugh at his expense.

"With that wee knife?" Thomas asked. "Aye,

we watched a good bit of it. We would have helped but you appeared to be having a good time." Miss Constance was finding it harder to free herself from the giant. Thomas's arms were longer and he proudly used his superior height and strength. "You are out of practice with the ladies, Gordon. If you are having trouble with a wee lass—"

His words were cut short as Miss Constance freed her hand and smacked his chin with the heel of it.

Caught by surprise, Thomas dropped her. "*Hellion*," he hissed. He never could take a blow to the face.

She landed on her feet like a cat and would have been off if she hadn't taken a moment to pull Robbie's kerchief from her mouth. She made a face. "That is the nastiest thing—" She spat on the ground with the grace of a guardsman, giving Gordon the opportunity to catch her again. He grabbed her arm at the wrist.

By now they were far enough away from the school so he could talk without keeping his voice down. "Stop it," he ordered.

Her answer was to whip her head around, her flying hair a weapon. She wasn't one to give up easily.

Gordon took her by the shoulders and gave

her a shake. "Miss Constance, you can make this difficult or easy. It's your choice."

"My choice is to leave," she said defiantly, and would have pushed away, but Gordon held tight, wisely keeping an arm's distance between himself and her knees.

"You can't, lass," he said. "You are a prisoner of the Clan MacKenna. You will be our guest until the Duke of Colster meets our demands." He braced himself for her to fight harder, expecting more scratching and kicking.

Instead, her struggle ceased. "A prisoner?" She glanced at all of them in the dark. "Are you kidnapping me?" she asked as she pushed her hair back from her eyes and righted her dress.

"Aye," Gordon answered. "And you will stay with us until your ransom is paid."

"By whom?" she wondered aloud.

"The Duke of Colster," Gordon answered.

"I barely know him."

A fit of vapors he would have understood. This cool, logical response put him on guard. "His brother is your brother-in-law Lord Phillip."

Miss Constance shook her head. "I don't know the duke but I don't like my brother-in-law *at all*. I doubt if either of them will pay a ransom. You'd best let me go."

"I will," Gordon said, "*after* the ransom is paid."

"Well, don't ask for much, because you won't see any money," she said as cool as you please.

"I'll take my chances." The Duke of Colster had once been part of the clan. Gordon knew what sort of man Colster was. He'd pay any price for a kinsman.

A horse nickered from where Brian waited.

Miss Constance's head turned in the direction of the sound. "Horses," she breathed, as if discovering the Holy Grail. "They are yours?"

"Aye." Gordon didn't trust this new eagerness in her voice.

"We should go, then," she said, her words a command. "My disappearance could be discovered." She would have walked off, Robbie and Thomas at her heels, except Gordon still held her fast.

She glanced at his hand on her shoulder. "Are we leaving?" she asked impatiently. "Or are we going to stand here yammering all night?"

Yammering? Gordon had never heard of such a word. "We will leave, but when *I* give the order." He wasn't usually this prickly. He preferred for all of his men to show leadership. However, that didn't mean he wanted his captives to take over control. Especially the female ones.

Unfortunately, at that moment a shout went up from the direction of the school. "I found a book," a man cried, "and shoes and clothing!"

Miss Constance made an exasperated wound. "They've discovered I am missing. Mistress Hillary must have checked my bed."

"There's money here, too," another man shouted.

"Oh, bother," Constance said. "All my money was in my bundle." She frowned at Gordon. "Are you ready to give that order to ride yet?"

Thomas and Robbie went bug-eyed. No one spoke to Gordon that way.

No one had ever dared.

And the worst was, there was nothing Gordon could do about it. They did have to leave.

"Mount up," he said, his eyes not leaving Constance's. It was her saving grace that she didn't smile or react in any way that would make him want to throttle her.

Thomas led the way, and within seconds they reached Brian. "We've got to go," Thomas told him. "An alarm's gone up."

"Robbie," Gordon said, "take our prisoner up on your horse. She'll ride with you." He would have preferred Thomas to take care of her but feared the extra weight on top of his friend's bulk would be too much for his horse.

Robbie hopped up into the saddle, but Miss Constance balked. "I must have my own horse."

"Not for the kind of riding we'll be doing," Gordon said. There was more shouting coming from the house. They were probably preparing to search the woods. "I'll not risk your neck." He put his hands on her waist to lift her up, but she'd have none of it and dug in her heels.

"What if *he* breaks his neck?" she asked, referring to Robbie. "You know it will be safer for each of us to have a horse."

"I don't *have* another horse," Gordon replied. And he wasn't about to give her another chance to escape. Constance was far more brazen than any other female of his acquaintance. "Now, climb up."

Calls were going up from the school for horses. The woods would be searched shortly and the roads cut off. There wasn't time to waste.

Miss Constance heard, too, and at last exercised good sense. With a soft sound of protest, she allowed him to lift her up to sit sidesaddle in front of Robbie, something she did with enough confidence to tell Gordon she was comfortable on a horse.

He took his own reins and climbed into the saddle. With a nudge of his leg, he set Tempest off through the woods. The others followed.

They reached the road and set off at a gallop. Gordon glanced over at Robbie. He had one arm around their captive. She leaned over the horse's mane, riding with him.

At last, Gordon felt he could breathe easier.

They'd done it.

The moment he reached the clan's camp in the mountains, he would send a messenger to Colster. Within two weeks, at the most three, he would have the sword.

And perhaps it wasn't such a disaster that the soldiers were here this night or that Constance had been discovered missing. All this would confirm the ransom demand.

After several minutes of hard riding, Gordon turned Tempest off the road, cutting across the open moor, heading west. He rode at the head of his men, proud on this moonlit night to be their leader.

They'd all waited a long time for action. Laird MacKenna had once amassed an army, he'd had the sword and a mandate from the Highlanders, but now, looking back, Gordon could see that the chieftain had lacked the conviction of their Cause. He'd been more interested in the trappings of power than freedom.

In the end, the laird and his other officers had betrayed the clan. They'd taken the money that was raised to support a rebellion and run off to Italy. Gordon hoped their stomachs shriveled on sour wine.

The night air was crisp against Gordon's skin. He'd keep them riding at this speed for a few more miles and then it would be safe to walk. Traveling across the countryside, avoiding the main roads, they would reach their camp by late afternoon.

Gordon counted himself lucky that Miss Constance was headstrong enough to *want* to run away. He had rope in his saddlebags. He would have tied her up. Her cooperation had saved them a great deal of time—

A shout behind him interrupted Gordon's thoughts.

Alarmed, he reined Tempest sharply and turned in time to see Robbie's horse go charging off in the night, traveling in the opposite direction.

"It's Robbie," Brian shouted.

"His horse has run away?" Gordon asked.

"No, he's back here and hurt bad," Brian answered.

And what of Constance Cameron? Gordon was afraid to ask the question, riding back to where Thomas stood beside Robbie stretched out on the ground. Gordon didn't see a second figure.

"The lass pushed him off the horse," Brian said, answering his unspoken question. "Shoved him hard when he wasn't expecting it. Then she threw her leg over the saddle and rode away as if she was a man."

Robbie moaned. It was a welcome sound and allowed Gordon to breathe again.

"See to him," he ordered the others as he pulled a rope out of his saddlebag. "I'm going after her."

"When you catch her, put her over your knee," Thomas said.

"*If* you catch her," Brian said. "The lass is riding like the wind. I've never seen Robbie's horse move so fast."

"Oh, *I'll* catch her," Gordon said.

Constance rode with her heart pounding in her chest and her spirits high on freedom. For the first time since . . . well, before her father died, she felt alive. She felt *powerful*.

She would be in Edinburgh before morning. She'd lost her money and her clothing but she didn't care. She'd manage. She always had in the past. She'd be on the *Novus* because she was going home.

The horse was not as wild as the ponies she'd grown up on. She'd frightened it when she pushed his rider off, which was fine. A frightened horse was a fast one.

She was so involved in giving the animal his lead and her own unfettered happiness that she didn't realize Mr. Lachlan had followed until he was upon her.

His hand reached for her bridle. He was a better horseman than herself. He leaned so far in the saddle, he could have fallen, and yet his legs held tight.

Her horse protested the yank of the reins. He tried to veer, wanting to take his head back. Mr. Lachlan jerked the rein and the horse kicked out, struggling to keep from stumbling.

Constance lost her balance.

She fell to the ground and barely missed being stepped on by inches.

The earth beneath her was spongy and damp. For a moment she feared she couldn't move. She wiggled her toes, her fingers—and then found a rock to wrap her hand around.

She was not going with Mr. Lachlan.

She had a ship to meet. She didn't have time to be kidnapped.

He subdued the horses some twenty feet from her and jumped to the ground. Dropping the reins on the lathered horses, he turned to her.

Constance clambered to her feet, prepared to

defend herself with the rock in her hand. "Stop right there," she ordered.

He didn't listen. He kept coming. He looked very strong, very tall, and very angry in the night, a rope in his right hand.

She threw the rock as hard as she could. Rock throwing had worked for David against Goliath.

It didn't work for her.

Her rock bounced off his chest and he kept coming.

She turned to run, but in a blink he was beside her, his hand closing around her wrist like a steel band. "You could have killed my man back there," he said. "Or yourself with that wild riding."

Constance had a stab of conscience. She had been rough on Robbie. "I have the right to escape," she defended herself.

"It's unfortunate for you that you didn't," he answered, his voice silky tight.

His men, Robbie on the back of Brian's horse, came riding up to join them.

The giant, Thomas, said, "I'm tired of this merry chase. Tie her up and be done with her."

"Aye," Mr. Lachlan agreed. "We'll not trust her again." He walked toward his horse, dragging her when she refused to follow.

Constance was furious at the amused faces of the men on the horses. Mr. Lachlan was going to carry her off to wherever he wished and she'd miss her ship.

She decided to tell him the truth. "Please, I mustn't go with you," she said. "I have a ship to board. It's leaving from Edinburgh in four days." She twisted her arm, to no avail. "I want to go home. I don't want to stay here any longer. I *hate* Britain. I hate *England*. I hate *Scotland*. It's cold, it's damp, and it's ugly. And I'm not too fond of *you*, either."

Mr. Lachlan stopped, a tall, golden-haired warrior of a man in the moonlight. "Then we have something in common, lass, because I'm far from finding you attractive. As for leaving, you can go anywhere you like, *after* Colster gives me my sword."

"Your sword? What sword?"

"The Sword of the MacKenna. Colster has it and I want it back." He looked to his men before saying, "And it is not just the sword. I'm ransoming you for the freedom of my people. Now do you understand, lass? I don't care what you hate or what you think or what you feel. I have hungry mouths to feed and a need for justice burning so deep within me, I'd go to hell and back for the sake of it. So resign yourself. You are staying with me. When Colster gives me what I want, then you are free to go. You can set sail to the moon for all I care."

"Once he claims me, he won't let me leave," Constance protested. "My sister Charlotte will make me stay."

"That's not my problem, Miss Constance Cameron." His accent clipped the syllables of her last name, infusing it with complete dislike.

Constance threw aside all pride. "You can let me go and *tell* him you have me."

"I won't lie," he said. "I'm a man of honor."

And that's when she realized she was nothing more than a chore to him.

She didn't matter . . . any more than she mattered to her sisters Charlotte and Miranda now that they were married. No one understood what she wanted, or cared.

That didn't mean she had to swallow their disdain. Not as long as she had any fight left in her.

Constance curled her hands into claws and went after Mr. Lachlan screaming like a banshee.

But her resistance was a pitiful thing in the face of his superior strength. He took her by both wrists, easily keeping out of reach of her kicking feet. He was going to make her do as he wished. She was going to miss her ship. She was going to miss her chance to return home, and instead be trapped in England forever.

Worse, his men were laughing at her. Her anger amused them.

Constance lost all reason. She reacted. She spat at Mr. Lachlan, the most deadly insult a frontiersman could pay.

His men's laughter stopped.

Her aim had been true. She'd hit his jaw.

A glint sharper than the point of her knife came to his eyes. He rubbed the spittle off with his shoulder before yanking her close, her hands against his chest. His body was hot with anger. He smelled of the night air and male.

"That's the way, Gordon. Don't take that from her," Thomas said. The others growled their agreement.

Constance shut her eyes, holding her breath. This wouldn't be the first time she'd been hit. Her father had struck his daughters religiously. She knew how to take a slap.

Gordon Lachlan ordered, "Open your eyes."

She didn't want to see the blow coming, but refused to take the coward's way. She raised her lashes, meeting his gaze with a steady one of her own, even though her knees threatened to buckle from fear.

"You've made me very angry, Miss Constance," he said. "No one disrespects the name Lachlan. Not without paying a price."

And then he did something she had not anticipated.

He kissed her.

Four

Gordon could taste Constance Cameron's astonishment, her shock, her inexperience—and he used all three to his full advantage. This wasn't so much a kiss as a moment of locked lips. There was no passion, no spark, no energy. It was just pure expediency. He could have beat her or kissed her into submission. He chose the latter—*except* he hadn't anticipated he would have a reaction to this kiss.

Especially when Constance leaned into him, as if needing him for support, her breasts flattening against his chest. His hands had no choice but to come down to her waist and pull her closer.

Nor was he satisfied with pressing their mouths together.

Since they were going through the exercise, the very least he could do was show this young woman how to kiss. He ran his tongue along the line of her pressed lips. The sensation tickled and her lips parted.

Gordon took full control. He breathed her, tasted her, enjoyed her.

His men had gone silent. It crossed Gordon's mind that they probably wondered what had come over him. A part of him wondered, too. He only meant to subdue her.

But another part of him, the *hard* part, understood his motive too well. It was more than just bending her to his will. He'd wanted to know how she'd feel against him.

She "fit."

In fact, he didn't think he'd ever met a woman who "fit" him so well.

And yet, he could not forget she was one of the enemy. He'd never let himself do that. He was the last leader for the Cause and he would not fail . . . but that didn't mean he wasn't a man, and every "man" fiber in him yearned to take Constance Cameron.

Here was the edge of desire. One step more and they'd be lost.

But Gordon knew better than to take that step. He held both her hands in his left while his mouth explored hers. Her initial surprise was followed by a searching exploration. Constance Cameron had a bright, inquisitive mind. He could tell she had not been kissed often, but she was a quick learner.

However, someone should have warned her that the curious always paid a price. She paid her price now when he broke off the kiss and stepped away to reveal that he'd tied her hands together with the rope.

His men noticed before her kissed-muddled brain could grasp what had happened. They burst into cheers so loud and so raucous, Gordon almost felt sorry for her.

Almost.

Constance Cameron had proven herself to be more of a trial than he'd anticipated—and he didn't have time for trials. The number of his followers was dwindling daily. People were losing faith that they could win their Cause. He needed the sword, and he wasn't about to let one headstrong young woman stand in his way.

He was just thankful it was dark enough for Thomas and the others not to notice how tight his breeches were. He was ramming hard.

"You have no one to blame for this but yourself," he said. "You should have been a more willing captive."

"You tricked me!" she accused.

"I *kissed* you," he clarified. "There was no trick in that." He leaned closer to say, "But it is a lusty temperament you have, Miss Constance Cameron. There's a fire in you."

He anticipated another attack, expected her to attempt to kick him. The moonlight caught the glimmer of tears. She looked away, blinking, not wanting him to notice. But he had, and he felt like a complete scoundrel. He'd taken advantage of her innocence. He used her inexperience to his own purpose. He'd accomplished what he'd wanted . . . but at what price? He'd not want some other man to use his sister this way.

Then again, one already had.

He hardened his heart. "Mount up," he ordered the lads.

Thomas roared his delight. "You appear the one ready to mount up," he said, and Robbie and Brian laughed.

Apparently, the tightness in his breeches had not gone unnoticed.

Gordon shot a look at Miss Cameron. Her head was bowed, her lips pressed together tightly. Her defiance was irritating, but he found he preferred it over this quiet submission. "Fetch our horses," he told Brian. Tempest and Robbie's horse had stopped a few yards away and were grazing. "And the rest of you mind your manners."

"We're just following orders, Gordon," Thomas said, his grin still ear-to-ear. "I'm just relieved to see your pecker still works. We'd all been thinking it had dropped off from disuse a long time ago."

The crudity of the remark, as if Constance wasn't present, irritated Gordon. "I have other matters on my mind right now," he said pointedly.

The giant snorted his response. "God made man able to do two things at once—one is to exercise his pecker, and the other is to do everything else while thinking about exercising his pecker. Isn't that right, lads?"

"Enough," Gordon said before Robbie and Brian could respond. "This gentlewoman is our guest. We don't want her returning to London with stories about what savages we are. Mount up and save your clever remarks for the English."

Thomas laughed and did as told. Constance was still looking away. The moon's light caught the path of one tear that had escaped down her cheek. Gordon realized she stared in the direction of Edinburgh. He refused to feel guilty.

Instead, he climbed into his own saddle. Without so much as a by-your-leave, he reached down, grabbed her by her waist, and pulled her up in the saddle in front of him.

She arched her back, ready to fight.

"Have done, lass," he said. Her wiggling wasn't making *anything* easier. "No matter what you do, I shall come after you. You are *mine*. At least until Colster hands over the sword. A wise woman would conserve her strength." He couldn't help a tight smile as he added, "The better to tear me apart limb from limb later."

Her struggle stopped. The tear was gone now, dried by the wind. "This isn't a game, is it?" she said quietly.

"Who said it was?" His conscience made him add, "Don't pay attention to all that Thomas says. You have my word that you will be treated well, provided you do as I bid."

Her jaw tightened. She shifted her weight to make herself more comfortable, something that was awkward to do with her tied wrists. The others had already gone on. Gordon started to urge Tempest forward when she said, "That was my first kiss."

He sat back, not knowing what to say.

"A first kiss should mean something," she whispered, not looking at him.

Dear God, had he ever been that innocent? He couldn't remember.

"Kisses rarely do," he answered, and kicking his horse forward, he set off for Ben Dunmore, the mountain camp where his clan waited.

Constance sat on the saddle's pommel. The only way she could keep her balance and be comfortable was to sit on his thighs, her shoulder against his chest. The hardness of his body surrounded her—and she hated him for it.

Galloping through the night was madness, but gallop they did. She feared that his horse would stumble, fall, and they'd break both their necks, but she wasn't certain she wouldn't welcome that fate now.

She couldn't believe she'd let his kiss distract her. She should have fought harder. Fighting didn't cost her anything, whereas that kiss had cost her pride . . .

Until that moment the only kissing she'd done was with her pillow. There had also been a moment at Madame Lavaliere's where several of the girls were demonstrating on the back of their hands and she'd secretly tried it herself. If she ever returned to the academy, she'd tell the girls that the feeling of a man's mouth was completely different than the back of one's hand.

A mouth moved. It took. It *claimed*. A good kiss, a powerful one, drew you to its will.

Mr. Lachlan's kiss had mastered her . . . and Constance sensed it wasn't just the kiss. It was *him*.

Sitting in the haven of his strong arms, surrounded by the heat of his body and that clean, almost spicy male scent that was all his, she knew her wisest course would be to put space between them as quickly as possible.

In fact, she was going to stop referring to him with a courtesy title. He was Lachlan to her from now on. Lachlan the Rebel, the Insufferable, the Annoying.

Kidnapping was nothing compared to the unnamed threat she sensed from him. Her body responded to him in ways her brain could not control, and if she wasn't careful, he could crush her pride.

Fiercely, she vowed, "I will not be a docile captive."

His lips were close to her ear as he answered, "I wouldn't have it any other way, Constance. I don't want to like you."

He liked her? It wasn't the response she'd expected.

"You don't know me," she challenged. "If you did, you'd know I don't make idle threats . . . *or* give up."

There was a moment of silence, as if he were mulling her words. He brought his horse down to a walk, obviously feeling the animal needed a rest. The men behind grunted their approval. They lagged behind, seemingly lacking Gordon Lachlan's determination.

"I saw the knife you were carrying," he said to her. "You handled it well, lass. I imagine if you'd had a mind to, you could have carved out my liver."

"I had a mind to."

He shook his head. "You are no murderess."

No, she wasn't. However, with one shove of her shoulder she could unseat him from his horse as she had done with Robbie.

She shoved.

He didn't move.

Instead, his arm came around her waist. He jerked her back against his chest. His thighs could have been formed from steel. "I'm no fool, girl, and you'd be unwise to believe so. If you unseat me, we fall together. Is your defiance worth breaking your neck?"

"My freedom is," she answered, although she wondered how she found the courage. This man threatened her more than any she'd met before. She couldn't control him. He played by his own rules.

"*I* know about wanting freedom," he answered. "You'll have yours once Colster pays the ransom."

The man was so single-minded, he was irritating. "I told you there is no reason for him to pay a ransom. He doesn't know me. We aren't even truly related."

"Your sister is married to his brother. You are one of his. He's the duke. He'll take care of his own. He'll pay my price."

"And what if he doesn't?"

There was a beat of silence. Soberly, he said, "You'd best hope he does."

For the second time in her life Constance was speechless. The first time had been when he'd kissed her.

Who was this man? *And why was he ruining her life?*

She'd grown up on the frontier. She'd learned how to judge a man quickly. Gordon Lachlan wasn't one to speak carelessly.

Behind them the others laughed and talked. They were in good spirits. They almost seemed a completely separate party of riders, one out for a lark. It wasn't to Lachlan . . . and she knew then how to pay him in kind for disrupting her life.

"They don't share your passion," she said.

He all but flinched. She'd discovered his weakness.

"They care," he said, an edge to his voice that his soft burr could not hide. "But a man likes to talk to keep awake when he's riding hard."

Constance was tempted to call him a liar. Fortunately, common sense intruded. Baiting him would give her satisfaction but not what she wanted.

Inspiration struck. "What if I *paid* for my freedom?" There had to be a way for her to find money. She'd lost everything she had during the escape, but once she reached the valley, she might be able to borrow some. She'd heard that people borrowed money for all sorts of things.

Or, once she was safely home, she could write and petition Charlotte for the money. "You could craft another sword out of the money and no one would be the wiser."

He glanced at her as if she'd grown horns out of her head. "I wouldn't do that. 'Twould be dishonest."

"Oh, yes," Constance commiserated, "kidnapping is far more honest."

The moonlight caught the flash of anger in

his eyes. "I don't expect you to understand. The power of that sword goes back a century and more. It's the clan's pride. Colster doesn't deserve it. *We* are its rightful owners. He must return it."

"And then?"

"And then I'll use it to chase the English into hell."

The vehemence in his voice made her uneasy. The men riding behind them had fallen quiet, not because they were listening but because they were tired . . . just as she was. The only one of their number who seemed indefatigable was Gordon Lachlan. He was driven.

"There are thousands and thousands of English on this island," she said soberly.

"I know."

"You can't fight them all. It's a losing cause."

"I'll do what I must."

He didn't prevaricate. She respected that. He believed that deeply in his purpose.

The moonlight made the planes of his face look hard. There was a fire in this man. She'd seen it before, but not here. In America.

"Do you have an army?" she asked.

"My clansmen drill now at our camp. There are others who yearn for justice but they don't believe we can succeed. The Sword of the MacKenna will give them a voice. Then, they will join us."

She shook her head. "I know something about war. I've seen Indian battles and witnessed how ruthless men can be when the blood lust is upon them." She didn't want to think of Gordon Lachlan that way. He was her kidnapper, he'd tricked her, but there was something humane and honorable about him, too.

He seemed to read her mind. "Don't judge me harshly, Miss Constance," he said. "I have cause for my actions. The English allow a nasty habit to occur here, one they wouldn't allow in their own country. It's called the Clearances. Landowners have discovered the profit in sheep and want grazing pastures. These men who were once chieftains of their clans have gone English and shoved aside their responsibilities to the crofters and yeoman who have given them allegiance for centuries, all for the sake of money. They no longer accept their responsibilities to their people. They are forcing them from their homes, often with no more than the clothes on their backs, and using the land for sheep. It's not right. It's not the way things are done in Scotland. People should mean more than beasts."

Constance shook her head. "It sounds as if it is the Scottish with whom you have a complaint, not the English."

Disgust laced his voice as he said, "Aye, these landowners have English titles and prefer London to their own country while English troops set fires to burn the crofters out. They've left thousands of people with no homes, no land, and no way to feed their children."

"Isn't there a magistrate or someone who can use the law against this practice?" Constance asked.

"The English make the laws, lass, and they make them in their favor."

"Then change them."

He made an impatient sound as if finding her naive. "The landowners are powerful. They won't change a law that works for them. And they'll stop at nothing to silence a good man who speaks out for justice. My father was such a man. He believed in the law. Taught me to believe in it. When he spoke against the Clearances, when he stood up for his countrymen, he was murdered. Stabbed by an assassin on his way home from court. The people took to the streets to protest his murder. They even caught his murderer, who confessed that he'd been hired. However, the man conveniently disappeared before he could be tried."

"What do you mean, disappeared?"

"He escaped . . . or so they say." The twist of

Lachlan's mouth said that he had doubts. "The man was never seen or heard from again. I know. I've searched for him."

Now she understood what drove him. This quest for a sword was personal for him. He wanted vengeance, even if it meant rebellion.

And she didn't want any of it. She wanted to go home. To return to her beloved Ohio Valley, where she understood the rules and didn't need to be anyone other than herself.

She also realized something else. "If you plan to use this sword to lead a rebellion," she said, "then the Duke of Colster must not give it to you. To do so would be treasonous."

Lachlan frowned. "That's his problem."

"He won't give you the sword," she said with complete certainty. She didn't know the Duke of Colster, had only met him once, but she knew his brother. She might think of Lord Phillip as evil and mean . . . but he was famous for being incorruptible and proud of it.

"You'd best hope he does, lass," Mr. Lachlan replied.

"Because if not . . . ?" she asked. "What will you do then?"

He looked down at her, meeting her eye. "'Tis the sword or your life."

Panic choked her. He said it so casually.

73

She forced herself to be calm. "I know what it means to desperately want something. I want to go home. It's where I belong. There is a ship that is leaving Edinburgh harbor in four days time, sailing to New York. Perhaps there is a way we can both have what we want. You can pretend you have me. I'll even write a note, but please, let me go to Edinburgh. I must be on that ship. I *must* go home."

He shook his head. "When Colster gives me the sword, I shall turn you over to him. It's what must be done. I am a man of my word. You for the sword."

Constance's temper exploded. "I despise you," she said, putting every ounce of her frustration and anger into those words.

"Good," he answered, spurring his horse, increasing its gait to a gallop. "Keep it that way."

Five

The movement of the horse and her tied hands forced Constance to lean against Lachlan. She didn't hide her bitterness, little that he cared. She'd never reach that ship before it sailed. Not now. He was taking her farther and farther east. She could tell by the location of the moon.

Her heart heavy, she struggled with tears of disappointment. He must have sensed her movement and misinterpreted it—either on purpose or out of guilt; she hoped it was the latter—because he reined his horse to a stop to pull a swath of tartan wool from his saddle-bag.

"Wrap this around you."

"I don't need it," she informed him proudly. She knew this tartan was his clan's colors. Well, she didn't want to wear it.

His response was to impatiently wrap the tartan around her anyway.

They rode on.

At some point she surprised herself by nodding off. Right there in his arms. She slept deeply, too.

When she did wake, she did so in stages. Her joints were stiff and it took her a moment to remember she'd been riding a horse, and even a few seconds more to realize she was still on the same horse and still in Lachlan's arms, albeit a bit more cozy and familiar with him. Her head rested in the indentation of his shoulder. The warmth of his body kept her relaxed. His jacket against her cheek smelled of damp wool and the pines they were riding through.

She didn't move. She didn't want him to know she was awake. Not quite yet . . . because this half dreamy state was pleasant compared to the problems of the real world. Once she opened her eyes, she'd have to battle him again. For right now, she'd rather conserve her strength.

However, curiosity eventually overcame her good intentions. Lifting her eyes just enough to take in her surroundings, Constance took in dawn's murky light and the fog that hung from the fir branches of the forest and rolled across the ground.

The Scots were all quiet now. She imagined some napped lightly even as their horses kept going. She'd known frontiersmen who could travel in that fashion for days without stopping to rest.

She was certain Gordon Lachlan wouldn't close his eyes. That would mean losing control, allowing the world to move upon its own accord, and he wasn't that sort of man.

He confirmed her suspicions when he said, "So you're awake, Constance."

She opened her eyes wider. "You may refer to me as Miss Constance," she replied, aping Lady Mary Alice's hauteur. She wanted to stretch her muscles, but she didn't, fearing it would bring her even closer to him. She wiggled the fingers of her bound hands, needing to circulate the blood in them. The bonds were not too constrictive, but resting her hands in one place for hours had given them cause for complaint.

"*Miss* Constance sounds foolish and fussy," he countered.

"It sounds proper," she answered.

He made a dismissive sound. "Why stop

there, lass? Why not have us call you Queen of All She Sees?"

She pretended to consider the suggestion. "That would be fine . . . and aren't you touchy when you don't have sleep."

His brows came together in a frown. "I don't need sleep."

She hummed thoughtfully and his scowl deepened.

"I wasn't being sarcastic," he replied. "I thought that was how you did consider yourself."

"Humor, Mr. Lachlan?" She shook her head. "It's not your strength, especially when you haven't had sleep." And then, before he could comment, she instructed him primly, "I don't mind being plain Constance. I'm a free-thinking woman. An American."

She liked the sound of her declaration, and realized that even though she was kidnapped and going in the opposite direction of her ship, at least she wasn't stuck in that overbearing school. She was wearing her moccasins, and when she had the chance, she'd free herself of this fussy ball gown. She could slouch her shoulders and laugh loudly and speak her mind . . .

Suddenly, her situation didn't look that difficult. She was on her own. Freedom was a heady thing.

Of course, there was the pesky problem of Lachlan and his band of Scots, but certainly she could think of a way to escape. With the dawn came a new day and a host of opportunities—

"Why are you smiling, lass? What mischief are you cooking up in that balmy head of yours?" Mr. Lachlan asked.

"What makes you believe I'm thinking of anything?" she countered.

He shook his head in disbelief. "Since my path has crossed yours, there hasn't been one second your mind was idle."

"Even when I was asleep?" she wondered, pleased with his assessment. She shook her head. "Please don't tell me you prefer women who lack nimble wit."

"Slow women are more amenable."

"But *less* entertaining," she retorted.

She startled a laugh out of him. The sound was obviously so rare, the others came alert and pushed their horses closer. Thomas the giant mumbled, "What is it? Is she being a pain in the arse again, Gordon?"

"Thomas," Lachlan said in warning. "Constance is our guest."

"No, I'm not," she said. "A guest may leave."

"Some women don't understand we don't want to hear them yap," Thomas said.

"That's not true, Thomas," Constance said gamely. "We understand. We just enjoy irritating you."

Robbie and Brian burst into laughter. But Gordon—because that's how she wanted to think of him—held up his hand. "We'll stop here for a spell."

"It's about time," Thomas grumbled, and the others agreed. They slid from their horses, stumbling a bit as their legs became accustomed to bearing their weight again.

Gordon didn't stop. He nudged his horse through the trees, moving away from his men. A minute later they came upon a trickling stream.

Constance wondered if he'd known it was there or if they had happened upon it by chance.

He dismounted. "You will want a moment of privacy to see to your needs."

Privacy. A magic word. "Thank you," she murmured, knowing here was her chance to escape.

Gordon took her by the waist and swung her down. Like Thomas and the others, her legs had trouble adjusting to being on solid land, while

Gordon seemed unaffected. Really, the man appeared invincible.

He kept his hand at her waist to steady her. It was a gentleman's gesture, a kindness. And yet there was something protective in his touch, too. But she was no fool. Gordon Lachlan was protective of her because she was his hostage. Nothing more; nothing less. She shouldn't read anything into it other than what it was.

Besides, in a few minutes she planned to give him a run for his sword.

His tartan was still draped over her shoulders like a shawl. Lifting her arms to show him her tied wrists, she said, "You will need to untie me."

With a grim smile he said, "You can see to your needs fine, lass, without my untying your hands. 'Twill be awkward but you'll manage, and save me the task of chasing you down later when you try to escape again."

That wasn't the answer she'd wanted. "You have a suspicious nature, Gordon," she informed him.

"Aye, and it is the reason I still have you, Constance," he replied.

"Yes, but you've obviously never had to see to your needs wearing a skirt and petticoats. It's not easy."

The argument worked. He gave her a suspicious eye, but pulled a knife from his boot and cut her rope. "Don't try to run."

Constance opened and closed her fingers. It felt good to move freely again. She looked up at him. "You know, if you let me go, no one would know you kidnapped me. I would go straight to Edinburgh and you wouldn't have to worry about your neck."

He raised his eyes heavenward. "You could try the patience of a saint," he said, with very little admiration in his voice.

"Why? Because I want my freedom?"

"No, because you are more annoying than a black fly, with your single-mindedness."

"Some would call being single-minded a virtue—"

"Not I—" he started.

"—because such a title could be applied to you," she finished, neatly cutting him off.

He opened his mouth to retort, then stopped. "Do you want a moment alone? Or shall we be on our way?"

"I'd like a moment alone," she answered.

"Then take it," he snapped. "I'll wait here."

Constance was tempted to bait him again. She liked verbally sparring with him. However, she *did* need a bit of privacy. And at some point he'd turn his back, and then she'd have a chance to run.

She began walking. At the stream's edge there were some shrubs and the shelter of tall grass. "That's far enough," he warned.

She glanced at him. He watched with guarded eyes.

"I thought you were giving me a moment of privacy?" she accused.

"That's private enough. And I want to see your head at all times."

"You can't," she protested. "I won't be able to do what I must do."

"Oh, you can do it," he assured her.

"You sound grumpy. You may need some sleep," she countered.

He growled an answer.

Constance knew better than to argue. As the youngest in the family, she knew when she'd pushed too far.

Happily, she set about her business.

When she was finished, she went over to the stream, taking off the tartan he'd given her as she walked. The pattern was a deep blue and green, with a bloodred line running through the plaid. She set it aside and knelt to wash her hands and face in the clear, frigid water. She'd grown up washing in cold water and the outdoors, but this time she discovered, to her surprise, that she didn't like it.

England was taming her.

She sat back on her moccasined heels and assessed her surroundings, something she would have done immediately back home.

A crow called. Beside her moccasins, Constance saw deer tracks. All was peaceful here. She closed her eyes, listening not just to the water in the stream bed running over rocks, but the sounds beyond. To her left a leaf fell and there was a scurry of movement. It was a squirrel digging an acorn.

There was another sound—a whisper. She strained her ears and realized Gordon was speaking to someone.

Constance opened her eyes, wondering what it was he didn't want her to overhear.

Now could have been a moment to escape, but she was curious. Gordon's low, soothing voice eased a tightness in her shoulder blades. It drew her to him as easily as a siren's song lured a sailor.

Gathering his tartan around her shoulders, she followed the edge of the stream a few yards before she caught sight of Gordon alone. He'd removed his jacket and was kneeling in front of a brush's maze of winter bare branches that formed a cage where a frightened bird was trapped.

He was trying to calm the bird. That was the whispering she'd heard. She doubted if he'd be successful. The poor creature was so frantic it couldn't notice that Gordon had broken some of the branches to give it a path to freedom.

The bird was a blue-gray dove, a fat one.

Constance waited, admiring Gordon's patience. Not many men had that . . . or, at least, not the men she'd known in her life.

The dove finally realized it didn't need to be afraid. It halted its panicked fluttering, eyeing Gordon warily.

"Go on," he crooned.

"She doesn't trust you," Constance whispered.

His piercing green eyes met hers. *"I'll win,"* he promised.

At that moment the peace was broken by the sound of a horse coming through the woods toward them. "Gordon, we're hungry," Thomas complained just as the dove realized there was a way out of the maze. It shot through the hole Gordon had broken for it.

"What's that?" Thomas asked. "A bird? Catch it! That'll be our breakfast."

The dove had been injured. It didn't fly well, and Gordon could have knocked it down before it managed to fly up to the safer branches of a tall pine.

"You don't want that bird," Gordon told Thomas.

"I like dove," Thomas insisted. "I'd like anything to fill my belly at this point."

"And I like seeing it have another chance," Gordon said. "You've got oat cakes in your kit. Eat that."

Thomas eyed the bird sitting on the tree branch over their heads. "I could shoot it through the head." He reached for the pistol in the belt at his waist. "It would be an easy kill."

"No," Gordon said. He didn't elaborate. He didn't need to. One word was enough.

The giant stared at him. Constance sensed the man ached to challenge Gordon. The giant had brute strength over Gordon . . . but he lacked Lachlan's quiet confidence.

Thomas drew his hand away from his weapon and took up his reins. "Damn bird's not worth the shot."

"That's what I said," Gordon answered.

There was the rustle of damp leaves. A beat later the other two, Robbie and Brian, rode through the woods to join them. "Thomas, have you found Gordon?" Robbie was saying as he approached.

"Aye, I did," Thomas answered easily. "Caught him freeing a bird. I wanted to eat it, but he's a soft heart. Wouldn't let me touch it."

Robbie and Brian both nodded, smiling. "You never know which way Gordon will go," Brian answered.

Constance thought those words true. And she'd seen the look in Thomas's eye. He didn't think Gordon soft, and it bothered him. She'd witnessed numerous of these standoffs among trappers and frontiersmen. Sometimes they were over ridiculous matters, and she'd learned they had more to do with one man's need to assert himself than who was right or wrong.

Gordon turned his attention to her. "Are you ready to ride, lass?"

She raised a distracted hand to her tangled hair, wondering if some of what she'd been thinking had shown in her expression. She hoped not. "Not quite yet," she said. "A moment more."

"Three minutes," he informed her. "Then we leave." He walked over to his horse. His men already moved toward the road. Thomas asked Robbie for an oat cake.

Gordon began seeing to his horse, an act he'd obviously been involved in before he discovered the trapped dove.

Constance began combing her hair with her

fingers and twisting it into a braid that she tied off with a piece of lace torn from her petticoat. She was glad now that she hadn't tried to run.

When she did make her escape, she'd best be certain it was at a time when Gordon couldn't come after her.

He glanced over at her, his expression serious, as if divining her thoughts. Like Thomas, Constance was tempted to take a step back. Instead, she stood her ground.

Overhead, the dove gave its low call, a warning if ever there was one.

Six

Gordon called Constance when he was ready to leave. She didn't hesitate, glancing up at the trees as she approached and noticing, "Your dove is gone."

He grunted a response, apparently a sign he wasn't in a good mood. She could have said something about lack of sleep but murmured instead, "Lucky bird to be able to fly away."

If he caught her barb, he gave no sign. "Here's something to break your fast," he said. He offered her an oat cake from his saddlebag and a leather flask of beer.

Munching on the flat-tasting oat cake and

washing it down with beer, Constance asked, "How much farther will we travel?"

"Far enough," he answered.

"Are you going to retie my hands?"

There was a moment's hesitation, and then he answered, "No." He took the flask from her, recapped it, and mounted his horse. He offered his hand to help her up.

Constance gave a heavy sigh of resignation but placed her palm in his. His fingers wrapped around her wrist and he lifted her as if she weighed nothing and settled her once again in front of him.

Her legs and bum wanted to protest against more riding. She'd grown soft since she came to England. However, this time, because her hands were untied, she didn't have to lean awkwardly against him. She could rest her back against the hard, flat plane of his chest, which was infinitely more comfortable.

He set his heels to the horse, his arm around her waist to keep her steady, and they were off.

They didn't ride with the urgency they had before. Thomas and the others kept up a light-hearted banter but Gordon was quiet. Constance listened to the men, picking up a name or two from their conversation but little other information. She couldn't help but lean her head against Gordon's chest. His strong arms prevented her from falling. She wanted to keep alert, but after a time, lulled by the safe, warm haven of his body, relaxed enough to doze off.

When she woke, the forest around them had grown more dense. There was a chill in the air though the sun was high in the sky. She pulled the tartan closer around her shoulders. Her stomach rumbled. She decided Gordon had been quiet long enough. "Are we ever going to eat?"

"You had an oat cake," he answered, not looking at her.

Constance frowned up at the stony set of his features. That little bit of sleep had helped restore her spirits. "I need something more than that."

The others had quieted, listening.

"We don't have time to stop for a meal," Gordon said.

"You don't need food?" she challenged.

As if in response, his own stomach growled.

Constance arched an eyebrow, daring him to deny his simple human hunger.

His first response was to scowl at the others as if they were the ones responsible for her questioning him. They fell back without a quibble.

"You act as if this is a game, lass," Gordon warned.

"Captives must be fed," she dared to remind him.

He whipped his horse around sharply. The animal heeled back, threatening to unseat them both. "Are you mocking me?" he demanded. "Because you'd best beware. This is no game."

Fear shot through her, but with it came anger.

He thought of her as some simple debutante, some pampered daughter of the *ton*, in spite of her actions to the contrary. She lashed out, "Oh, I'm wary, Lachlan. But you see, I've already faced danger and experienced terror the likes of which you'll never know. My mother and baby brother died at the hands of the Shawnee during a raid. They scalped my mother and smashed my brother's head into the trunk of a tree. Do you think you could be more bloodthirsty than that? Because that's the length you'll have to go to make me tremble."

He'd pulled back at her tirade as if physically struck by the flow of words.

Her hands had started shaking. She gathered the tartan around her, trying to hide them . . . knowing he'd noticed.

He was quiet, watchful.

She gritted her teeth. Pressed her lips together. She never spoke of that day. Ever. She and Charlotte had been in the woods collecting kindling when Miranda ran to tell them to hide, that the Shawnee were attacking the house, that their mother was dead.

And yet, now that she'd started, she discovered she couldn't stop. It all came back with frightening reality. "The three of us hid in the woods," she said, her voice distant even to her own ears. "We spent a long, cold night hiding by the trunk of a rotting tree. I knew better than to complain, because they were out there looking for us. We held each others' hands. I was so frightened, I squeezed Charlotte and Miranda's fingers to death and I wouldn't let go all night long."

Her eyes burned. She stared at a boulder beside the road, noticing everything about it from the crack through its center to the lichen growing in its grooves. Anything to keep from remembering, because after their mother's death had come the angry years.

Her sister Charlotte remembered when their father had been happy, but she didn't. He'd always been a bitter, mean-spirited man to her. From him, she'd learned not to show weakness. Not to anyone. Not ever. When one was weak, one was vulnerable. That was the lesson of the wilderness.

Lachlan sat quiet, not a muscle moving in his arms, on either side of her. She felt the horse shift its weight and paw the ground, anxious to move forward. Lachlan held him back, but he didn't speak. She could feel him waiting. It was as if he knew her better than she did herself.

And he was right. She broke.

"I'm not what you expected, am I?" She did not look at him, too aware of how weak she must appear to him, to the others. She held out her hand. "See? It trembles. I suppose I'm not a good captive."

There was a beat of silence, and then he said, "None of us are." He turned, bringing a protective arm around her as if shielding her from the others. "We'll stop for food at the first cottage we see," he instructed his men. "Brian, ride ahead and see what you find."

"Yes, Gordon."

"I'll go with him," Thomas offered, and didn't wait, kicking his horse into a trot.

"All right if I go, Gordon?" Robbie asked.

"Go on," Gordon replied.

"They must all be hungry," Constance said quietly after they'd left.

"Either that or they are uncomfortable around a woman's tears," Gordon answered.

"I didn't cry," she shot back.

He lifted his eyebrows, and she was honest enough to concede, "Do I look that bad?"

"The color is coming back to your cheeks, but you had me worried," he admitted.

There was a gentleness in his voice that threatened to unnerve her more than his earlier temper. "Well, now I know how to scare the lot of you. I'll threaten to go off in a fit of tears."

He laughed, the sound full-bodied and masculine. It changed him, eased years off his face, made him appear almost boyish. "I wonder if we can cry the English out of Scotland?" he said.

"I could lead the brigade," she answered.

Gordon shook his head, moving his horse forward. "Come now, you didn't shed a tear back there. You cried more over my kiss than any of what you just said."

She studied the weave in his tartan's plaid. "I think I like you better when I'm angry at you."

He threw back his head and roared with laughter. Constance glanced up, noticing the muscles in his neck, the shadow of his whiskers along his jaw, and her heart seemed to twist in a funny little way she'd never experienced before.

She didn't want to like him. At all costs, she *mustn't* be attracted to him. She wasn't staying in Scotland or England. She wouldn't.

And that quickening inside her, that consciousness of exactly how close his body nestled her, that awareness of his very scent, his every breath—that couldn't happen, either.

She had to be strong. For the first time, she understood what the prophets meant when they said, "Gird your loins."

Her loins needed protection now. She didn't know what a "gird" was, but an iron wall would be a start.

She didn't have an iron wall. She had words, and she used them. "If you aren't careful," she warned, "it will be hard to murder me if the duke doesn't give you the sword."

That sobered him. The camaraderie, the connection between them, vanished.

He looked away, frowned. "You aren't easy, are you, lass?"

"I just want to go home." She'd never meant those words more.

Gordon nodded as if he knew. "The problem may be that you can't. It's not easy to go back to what you've left . . . and that may be what scares you."

He'd summed up her doubts perfectly.

No one had ever paid this much attention to her. She was the youngest, the afterthought. Everyone was always too busy with important matters to think of her.

This man, her *kidnapper*, understood her better than her own sisters. No wonder she had to gird her loins.

"I just don't like making a fool of myself," she admitted.

"You didn't. I pushed you." He kicked his horse forward. They rode a bit before he said, "Sometimes we are all too hard on ourselves. But I'll tell you a secret. Often, when life takes us where we don't want to go, that's where we find what we truly need."

"And you need rebellion?"

He considered her words a moment. "I needed to stand for something. Six years ago, you and I would have met at a ball. My collar points would have been up to here"—he indicated a position halfway up his jaw—"and my boots would have shone with champagne blacking. Or at least, what was left of the champagne after my friends and I had a go at the bottle."

"You were a fop?" she asked, not able to picture him in the *ton*, let alone worrying about the cut of his coat or the style of his hair, which right now was wind-blown and sun-kissed.

"I was the dandiest of the dandies," he said. "I studied law by day and begged entrance to all the *ton*nish gatherings by night. I said I believed in justice, but I didn't even know what it was."

"Your father's death changed that."

"That, and realizing that everyone I confided in, everyone I had thought a friend, didn't give a care. The death of a crusading Scottish magistrate meant nothing when one was planning the next ball to attend and whether to wear a green coat or a red one. Some even warned me to correct my accent or change my name. That's when I opened those books and read them with purpose."

"You wanted justice," she said.

"Aye. And I couldn't have it. You asked earlier about the law. The law is expedient, Constance. The ones in power set the rules. But once I have that sword—"

"You make the rules," she finished for him.

"And I will make men who use the law to their own advantage pay for their sins."

He believed he would do it. He had enough conviction to save the world . . . but she knew better. "There was never justice for my mother and brother's death."

"Because the Indians who murdered them were never caught?"

"No, because of the nature of war," she said sadly. "Individual lives are not important."

"They are to those who loved them."

Before she could answer, they heard Thomas call out Gordon's name. A moment later he came riding up to them, excitement in his eyes. "I can't believe you haven't ridden farther," he chastised as he reined to a stop. "About a mile from here is a village beside a loch. Gordon, they've heard of you. They know who we are."

"And?" Gordon said.

"*And?*" Thomas repeated as if he couldn't believe his ears. "And they think you're a bloody hero. You are a legend to them. I told you we needed to leave camp more often, that we needed to be out with the people."

"Do you think it wise to be so free with my name?" Gordon asked. "The English will know where we are."

Thomas frowned. "The English don't think we are a threat. Not yet. But the crofters know us. They call you the Rebel Lachlan. They haven't lost faith, Gordon. They are waiting for you and for the army we are building."

"Well, then, let's go meet them," Gordon said, and both men urged their horses to a trot.

* * *

Thomas had not been jesting. As the road took them down toward a loch, they met small groups of people walking in the direction they were going. When the Scots saw Gordon, they put up a shout, cheering for "Rebel Lachlan."

A sprawling crofter's hut was around the next crook in the road by the loch. Gathered in the yard around Robbie and Brian were about thirty Scots.

The air was festive and alive. Women bustled around long tables fashioned from planks set up in the front yard, and benches had been created from logs and the same loose lumber. Breads, cheeses, sausages, and whatever the Scots had to offer was spread out on the tables. The men stood by the road drinking, while their children kept a look out for the Rebel Lachlan. When they saw him, they put up such an excited cry, even Constance had to smile and feel a bit proud to be a part of the moment.

A thin man came forward to greet Gordon. He removed his hat from his balding pate and fell to his knees.

"Welcome, Gordon Lachlan," the man said, "and welcome to my home. It is a glorious moment when I should meet thee."

"You don't kneel to me," Gordon answered. He dismounted, leaving Constance in the saddle. "Come to your feet, man. We are all free men here." He offered his hand. "What is your name?"

"William Gunn," the crofter replied, rising.

"William Gunn, it is my honor to meet you," Gordon said.

Gunn grinned his pleasure at such respect. "My Beth has thrown open her larder. What is mine is yours," he replied. He nodded to his wife, who had come to stand shyly by the door. Twin daughters of about four years of age held onto her skirts. She bobbed a curtsey to Gordon, who bowed an acknowledgment.

Mr. Gunn ordered his sons to take care of the horses while he set a table and chairs outside for the meal. Neighbors came, bearing what food they had to offer.

No one questioned Constance's presence. Gordon helped her from the horse but he was quickly engulfed by the growing number of crofters who had traveled to meet him. Her care was left to Robbie.

"What does that mean, 'the Lachlan'?" Constance asked Robbie. They stood by one of the makeshift plank benches and tables.

"It means they recognize him as a chieftain," Robbie answered. "Our Gordon is making a name for himself. And he is right. With the

Sword of the MacKenna, there will be no one who can stop him. Not since the Bruce, that greatest of all Scottish heroes, has there been such a leader."

"Does he receive this sort of reception often?" she asked.

"Aye, farther north. But this is the first time they've gathered for him around here," he answered. "It's a good sign. Our numbers will grow."

"What are the two of you whispering about?" Thomas said, coming up to where they stood. He carried a jug of hard cider hooked between two fingers of one hand and lifted it to his lips for a healthy swig.

"She was asking me a question," Robbie said. His eyes darted with disapproval at the jug.

Thomas sneered at the unspoken criticism.

"Your sweet Sylvie is not going to want you sharing confidences with an Englishwoman," Thomas said. "Best you let me watch her. I'd not be so soft on her the way you and Gordon are."

To his credit, Robbie stayed at his post. "Go on," he answered. "There are ladies enough here for you."

"But it's not one of them I've a mind to sample," Thomas said. "'Tis this English hellion. I'd like to see if she thinks she can pull the tricks on me that she has tried on Gordon."

"Thomas," Robbie warned, but Constance saw a chance to put him in his place.

The edge of the plank bench was beneath his jug. She sat abruptly on the far end. Her weight upset the balance of the plank and lifted it. Thomas's jug went flying.

For a second he didn't realize what had happened to it and looked around in comical surprise. The crofters who had witnessed her actions burst into laughter, which was when Thomas realized he'd been tricked.

"I'm *American*," Constance corrected him. "An American hellion."

Thomas grumbled something threatening, but Robbie said a few words in his ear and he backed away, his pride mollified when a pretty young woman fetched his jug of cider for him.

"I cannot like the man," Robbie muttered.

"Gordon does," she noticed.

A high spot of color rose to Robbie's lean cheeks as if, perhaps, he had not meant to speak aloud. "Thomas knows how to fight and can keep the men in line. Gordon needs that, just as he needs all of us."

Constance murmured her agreement but heard the discontent in his voice.

She glanced at Gordon. The day's earlier clouds had dissipated and sunlight glinted off the hard planes of the table and plates and the gold in his hair.

He listened as William Gunn and his neighbors spoke of how times were changing, about how they wished they could leave their hearths and families and march with him.

But they couldn't. Or wouldn't.

Constance thought it sad that these men so easily accepted the theft of their heritage. If this was her fight, she would have sided with the rebels. Sometimes, you had to fight for what you wanted.

These men would admire "the Lachlan," but they would not die for him—not unless he had a very certain chance of winning. The sort of chance this fabled Sword of the MacKenna could give him.

In the meantime, Thomas vied against Gordon for attention. The sweet young thing that had helped him earlier now let him drape an arm around her shoulder while she giggled her pleasure. Anytime the conversation became too exclusively on Gordon, the giant would interject his own thoughts.

It seemed to Constance that in spite of being relaxed, Gordon was keeping a watchful eye on this second in command. She wondered what thoughts were going through his head. She suspected that if Thomas didn't become more circumspect, he might soon find himself not as important to the clan leader.

It was when Thomas brought up the bounty on Gordon's head that tension openly rose between the two men.

One of the Gunn boys asked, "Is there a price on your head?"

Gordon shook his head as if ready to deny such a thing, but Thomas answered with a cheerful, "Aye, he has fifty pounds on his head, but I'll wager that number is multiplied by hundreds once we attack the English. We'll all have prices on our heads then."

The crofters were impressed. Fifty pounds would be a fortune to these people.

The giant opened his mouth to brag again when Gordon stood. "Enough, Thomas," he said. "We've overstayed Mr. Gunn's hospitality." He nodded to the crofter and placed some coins on the table. "You and your wife have been most generous. May you never rue the day our paths crossed."

Mr. Gunn rose. "You need never fear anything from me or mine. 'Tis an honor to meet you and one I shall tell to my grandchildren."

A few minutes later they were mounted and on their way.

Thomas was in high spirits. He rode beside Gordon, a cider-fueled grin on his face.

"You should be careful what you say, Thomas," Gordon said quietly. Riding on the saddle in front of him, Constance felt the tension in his body.

The giant scowled. "Are you talking about the bounty?"

"You know I am." He met Thomas's eye. "The more said, the less freedom we have to carry out our plan. Don't be so easy with your tongue in the future."

Thomas's eyes hardened. He looked away a moment. Constance braced herself for a battle. To her surprise, the giant begrudgingly conceded. "You are right, Gordon. But there is a part of me that wants action. They should know what we are doing for them."

"They already know. You saw them today. But just as they cheer us on, they could betray us."

"I'd kill the man who would betray you."

"I know you would," Gordon answered, and Constance understood then why he had Thomas at his side. She'd not thought to find such loyalty in Britain. She'd witnessed it on the frontier, but not here. In London and at Madame Lavaliere's, she had gained the impression that everyone looked only to their own needs.

Perhaps it wasn't such a bad thing to be kidnapped by these Scottish rebels. Perhaps she had something in common with them.

She was anxious to be done with the trip and tired of riding, but now she was curious about Gordon's clan. She wanted to meet the rebels and see if her suspicions were correct, if they were like her neighbors back home. Her desire to reach the *Novus* before it sailed faded a bit. She no longer felt so passionately desperate.

Questions rose in her mind . . . but everyone had grown quiet. The full meal seemed to have dampened their spirits. No one spoke. The men seemed anxious to reach the camp, each lost in his own thoughts.

They'd been riding for two hours, the horses moving steadily into the heart of the mountains. Constance had fallen asleep again. She woke to the sound of a dog barking.

Groggily, she looked around. There was no dog. They were riding downhill into a valley. Tall pines bordered a path wide enough for one horse.

The dog barked again, and then Thomas an-

swered it with a howl of his own. The bark had
been a signal. No wonder it hadn't sounded
natural to her ears.

They were coming to the rebel camp.

The pace of the horses picked up, a surer sign
than any that the end of the journey was in
sight. A scent drifted across the air. The smell
of a campfire.

Constance straightened and leaned forward.
She'd been to Shawnee camps and wondered
how this Scottish one would differ.

They'd just reached a bend in the road when
a pack of children came whooping down upon
them, calling "Gordon" at the top of their
lungs. Their clothes were homespun and they
appeared full of energy and life.

The children danced alongside the horses,
asking questions and staring at Constance. One
boy with hair the red of a ripe apple even boldly
said, "Is that the Englishwoman?"

"It is," Gordon said, and the children gave a
loud cheer, making Constance's cheeks flame
with the unwanted attention.

A few minutes later they came upon the
Scottish camp, and Constance caught herself
gawking.

It was like none she'd ever seen before. It was
huge and a veritable hodgepodge of humanity.

Tents, lean-tos, daub huts, and any other manner of makeshift quarters were haphazardly spread out along the shore of a silvery loch.

Gordon's followers weren't only young, strong men like Robbie and Brian. There were hordes of children and women of every size and age. A few goats, several sheep, dogs, and a pig wandered freely. Most of the men, many well past their prime, looked like farmers who wouldn't know how to shoot, let alone wield a sword.

These people reminded her of settlers who came to the frontier because they had nowhere else to go. They lacked direction and passion. They were the ones who couldn't survive.

"*This* is your rebellion?" she asked, realizing too late that in her shock and disappointment, she'd spoken aloud . . . and they were the wrong words to say.

Seven

The pleasure Gordon felt at accomplishing this mission, the pride he'd had that at last he was turning the tide of events in his favor, evaporated at her words.

Constance saw the camp with the unvarnished clarity of an outsider, forcing him to do the same.

It was a stunning moment.

He'd wanted to believe that only *he* had noticed the shortcomings of his followers. He'd told himself that he was too hard on them. His expectations were too high. He had to give them time to learn to fight. He'd wanted to believe he could teach them how to succeed.

Constance had just confirmed his deepest fear—that no matter how hard he tried, these people, the skeletal remains of what had once been a powerful rebellion, would never measure up to their deadly task.

At one time, at Nathraichean, he'd helped Laird MacKenna put together an army that would have fought well. However, when MacKenna stole the clan's money and ran to Italy, a good portion of that army lost heart. Many had left, scattered to parts unknown. Those who remained were the ones either afraid to leave or, like Thomas, who hoped for opportunity.

It was vital to Gordon that he keep the dream alive. They must fight the English and win. If they didn't, if they failed, not only would the Scotland of his youth be lost, but his father's death would have been for naught.

His clan's welcoming faces changed before his eyes. Constance's reaction made him notice what he'd attempted to ignore. His people depended entirely too much on him for guidance. Every day they pressed him, needing him to make decisions about even the most rudimentary matters.

They were also lazy, and it showed in the lack of orderliness in the camp. He knew without being told that while he was gone, they had taken the time off. They'd sat with their wives, played with their children, and waited for him.

That's why he needed the Sword of the Mac-Kenna. With it, he was certain he could rekindle the fighting spirit of the Scottish. And what Constance Cameron thought didn't matter . . . or shouldn't.

But it did.

It had been a long time since a lass had caught his interest. Constance Cameron's sharp tongue and sharper wit had accomplished the task almost overnight, and he knew he needed to keep his distance from her. She raised doubts, challenged him, expected to be his equal—all while not seeming to notice how hard he'd been riding with her bum against his crotch.

Well, he was no bloody eunuch.

Nor did she have a say here. These were his clansmen.

Gordon slid her off his horse so swiftly, she almost fell to the ground. He jumped down and steadied her. She flashed him a surprised look. Clearly, she realized he was angry. He ignored her. She was a hostage. He owed her no apologies or explanations.

"Robbie," he said, wanting the man's attention.

His young lieutenant didn't hear him. He was busy smooching his Sylvie. Thomas and Brian were boasting of how Gordon had walked into the school, which according to their stories was surrounded by a brigade of English and the fighting had been fierce.

They talked like they always did. Shoring themselves up. He knew it's what men did. They *lied*. He thought it harmless, except now they had a witness to those lies. Constance stood tall and slender, as regal as a princess—and with a mind as lethal as a barrister's.

"*Robbie!*" Gordon snapped.

No one ignored him when he spoke in that tone. Everyone went silent.

Robbie straightened to attention, practically in mid-kiss. "Yes, Gordon?"

Now that he had the lad's attention, he tempered his voice, "Take our Miss Constance Cameron to—" He hesitated, searching the crowd for the right people to keep watch over a young woman of independent sensibilities and who would be immune to her charms.

His gaze fell on Old Rae Reivers and his wife, Emma. Rae had been a sergeant in the king's army until he broke his back. But even hunched over as he was, he was tough as shoe leather and one of the most unrelenting men Gordon had ever met. His wife was just as callous. They'd be perfect wardens for Constance.

"Rae, you have charge of our captive until this matter is through," Gordon ordered. "I want her treated humanely. Let her have no complaint against us when she is returned to her kinsman. However, don't trust her for one moment."

Rae stepped forward, proud to be singled out for the task. Because of his back, Gordon had not found much use for him in the daily activities of the camp. However, this task was perfect. "You can count on me and mine, Gordon."

"I thought I could," Gordon answered. "Robbie, escort our hostage to Rae's. And bind her hands first," he threw out, as if it meant nothing to him.

Constance's back stiffened. As Robbie bound her hands, she glared at Gordon as if she'd been betrayed. Perhaps she *had* known her impact on him, he thought. Perhaps she'd been ready for him to play Samson to her Delilah.

Well, it was time she recognized that she was nothing more than a prisoner, a means to an end. Her opinion didn't matter. She was beneath his notice.

And he would keep his distance from her until Colster exchanged her for the sword.

Robbie took Constance by the arm to escort her to Rae's tent, but she shook him off. "I can walk," she said. "Lead the way."

Robbie glanced at Gordon, who nodded for him to do as she bade. Constance didn't wait. She turned to Rae and ordered, "Go on. I'm your charge. Take me where you will."

To Gordon's frustration, Rae dutifully did as commanded. His wife, Emma, and Robbie fell in behind Constance as the rest of the clan backed away, allowing them to pass.

There was no small amount of curiosity about her. Necks craned and there was a good deal of whispering. In return, Constance stared them down with just the right hint of disdain on her face.

Any concerns Gordon had about the impact of kidnapping her were laid to rest. She was a survivor, like himself. She'd never let anyone get the best of her.

But then Mad Maggie jumped into her path. Maggie's wild, unkempt hair was the color of the winter moors and her eyes burned with the fire of anger. She carried a rag doll under her arm wherever she went. 'Twas her "baby," and she spent her days cooing and rocking it.

At Nathraichean, Laird MacKenna had forced Maggie to live in the woods, always keeping her away from his followers. Many here had wanted Gordon to continue the exile. They said she scared their children, but it was usually the adults Gordon caught crossing themselves whenever Maggie came near.

Gordon took a step forward, not trusting the look in Maggie's eye. However, before he could intervene, he was stopped in his tracks by the bounding energy of a huge Irish wolfhound. Tad had obviously been out hunting. His huge paws were wet as he came up on his hind legs and placed them on Gordon's shoulder. "Down—" Gordon started to say, but was stopped by a big slobbering dog kiss.

The crowd roared their amusement while Tempest, his horse, pawed the ground and snorted disapproval. There was no love lost between Gordon's pets.

Gordon pushed Tad to the ground with a scratch behind his ears and ordered Tempest to behave with a low, "Here now." The horse stopped pawing but kept his ears pinned back.

However, Gordon's humor vanished when he heard Maggie's keening voice as cold as the wind over all the good-natured advice his clansmen were giving on dog training. They heard the sound, too, and stopped laughing.

Maggie stood in front of Constance, shaking her "baby" at her. "Send her away," she said. "Dispel her. Send her away." Maggie raised a fist as if to strike Constance.

Rae and Robbie stepped back in fear, but Gordon moved just in time to place himself between Maggie and Constance. He fended off the blow with his forearm, surprised by Maggie's strength.

Tad growled, ready to lunge, but Gordon ordered him back with a sharp, "Down." The wolfhound went to the ground.

"Have done, Maggie, what are you doing?" Gordon said.

At his sharp words, Maggie crouched in front of him, raising her arms in fear. The doll fell to the ground. "Don't hit me, Gordon. Don't hit me."

"I've never touched you, Maggie," Gordon said, defending himself.

"It's *her*," Maggie told him, pointing a finger at Constance. "She has a devil's heart." She spoke rapidly, the words tumbling out of her mouth. "I saw her coming in my dreams. There was water there. Everywhere. We were all afraid and yet she stood there without fear. She will use dark arts to destroy thee. She'll end it all, Gordon. *End it all.*"

Eyes widened at these words, and Gordon could have cursed. His clansmen were superstitious—after all, wasn't that why he wanted the sword?—and Maggie's fit did not bode well. Perhaps he should have tossed her out.

Constance stood still, as if carved from stone. Gordon didn't know what she thought. He spoke calmly. "You are full of malarkey, Maggie. Your mind is playing tricks."

Maggie jutted her chin forward, ready to refute him, but Gordon cut her off. "Enough. I'll not have you scaring the children."

At the mention of the last word, Maggie's anger fled. She physically changed before his eyes. Her body seemed to lose all energy as she shrunk down. What was left was a puzzled old woman who looked around as if just now realizing they had an audience. "Where's my Patty?" she asked in her rattling voice. "I've lost my Patty."

Gordon picked up the rag doll. "Here she is, Maggie, and she's been crying for you."

"*Och*, my Patty crying?" Maggie took the doll into her arms. She started rocking back and forth, sniveling and saying, "I scared you, didn't I, lovely one. I scared you." She began to weep, her body shaking with soft sobs.

Gordon straightened and looked around

the crowd until he caught sight of his sister. Fiona stood back, away from everyone. She was dressed in her habitual black, the Lachlan tartan around her shoulders. She had not come forward to greet him. She never did.

She'd joined their number two months ago. Gordon had hoped that being here with the clan would help Fiona. Instead, she stayed well away from everyone, her features tight and pinched . . . accusing.

Well, the time had come for him to give her something to do.

"Fiona, take Maggie to her hut. See that she has a cup of cider. You'll find the jug in my quarters."

"Cider?" Maggie said, her round face now a wreath of smiles. "What a lovely gift. Why, a nice cup of cider is exactly what I need. Patty would like one, too. May we have two cups?"

"Two cups would be good," Gordon answered. He looked to his sister, who had not moved. "Fiona?"

She pulled her shawl tighter around her body. She was thin. Too thin. At nine and twenty, he was six years older than Fiona. Her mother had been his stepmother, his father's second wife. That explained the rich mahogany of Fiona's hair and her wide brown eyes. He and she had lived very separate lives. They continued to do so in camp.

Just when Gordon thought she would publicly refuse him, she came forward. Offering her hand, she said, "Come, Maggie, we shall see you comfortable."

"And let me have cider," Maggie agreed with childlike anticipation.

"Yes, as much cider as you wish." There was little emotion in Fiona's voice.

Gordon watched them leave.

It was Emma who spoke. "She's not growing any better."

Did she speak of Maggie . . . or of his silent, stone-faced sister?

He decided to pretend it was Maggie because Fiona wasn't a topic he wanted to discuss.

"She has nowhere to go, Emma," Gordon said. "And she *is* one of us." He raised his voice as he spoke so that all could hear. "We are a clan, and that means we take care of our own. We stand together and then no one can stand against us."

Silence met his words. He could see from the expression in their eyes that they wanted to believe . . . and yet feared he might ask more than they were willing to give.

It was Thomas who answered. "Aye," he

agreed, his robust voice giving the others courage.

"You are right, Gordon," one said.

"Clansmen," echoed another.

"We take care of our own," Gordon reiterated. This time his words were seconded. This time they showed spirit.

Gordon turned to Emma Reivers. "I know Maggie isn't right in the head, but would you leave her behind?"

Wisely, Emma didn't answer that question.

Turning to Constance, Gordon said, "No harm will come to you from her, or anyone else, while you are under *my* protection."

"What of her prophecy?" Constance asked.

"Her prophecy?" he repeated, and then realizing what she meant, he laughed. "She speaks like that all the time. We're always going to be flooded, according to her. There's water in all of our futures."

Others laughed with him. Someone said, "Except for Brian. His well was dry."

The younger man waved off the jibe, laughing.

Only Constance frowned, her expression thoughtful. "You don't believe she has the gift of sight?"

"No," Gordon assured her. "What she has is

the madness of a woman who lost all her children to a fever. 'Tis said she was not too sensible before, and losing those wee ones did not help her. Her husband left her long ago. We are all she has left. The remains of her family."

"The Shawnee believe that the mad ones should be respected," Constance said. "Indians believe those prophecies come true."

Gordon shrugged. "We respect Maggie," he assured her. "We just don't *listen* to her when she's speaking gibberish, and that is all it is. Now go with the Reivers."

He nodded for Robbie to carry on before turning to Thomas and Brian. Thomas stood with one arm draped around Grace McEachin. Over to the side, Hannah Chisholm stood frowning. Thomas adored being fought over, and in a camp where women outnumbered men, he often had his wish—although he'd developed a strong fondness for Grace.

Gordon said, "After I've seen to my horse, I'll write the letter to Colster. Brian, rest up. Once I have it written, you shall be my messenger."

"Yes, Gordon," Brian answered.

Snapping his fingers for Tad to follow, Gordon led Tempest to the far side of the camp. They'd set up stables there, roping off paddocks for the grazing of fifty or so horses.

Gordon usually groomed his horse himself. Back at Nathraichean, Laird MacKenna had lived a lord's life. There had even been servants for the servants. At the time, Gordon had questioned the need for so many attendants, but he'd kept those questions to himself, until MacKenna betrayed them all. The laird had stolen what money the clan had and run off to Italy to save his hide from the English, leaving the rest of them to pay the price. Even innocents, like Fiona.

So, Gordon no longer trusted those who thought of power and money. He took care of his own horse, his own clothes, his own wants. In turn, these tasks gave him quiet moments alone to worry over the hungry mouths that needed to be fed . . . and the fear that his little army would be crushed by the English.

Gordon dropped Tempest's reins to the ground. The horse stood while he removed the saddle. Tad plopped down on the ground with a wide yawn. A flock of birds flapped into the sky, chased by another of the many dogs in the camp. Tad stood, but didn't chase.

"Go on," Gordon said, knowing the wolf-hound would enjoy the exercise.

Tad flashed a dog grin in his direction and took off after the others, sailing across the ground, his powerful legs easily catching up with them.

Tempest was happy to see him go and nudged Gordon as a way of showing his approval. He gave his horse a rare flake of hay. Tempest had carried two riders and earned the treat.

While he worked, Gordon started to frame in his mind the letter he would write to Colster. He was interrupted a few minutes later by the approach of two men, one as tall as the other was short. Tall Angus was a leather worker. Matthew was known for his incessant complaining.

"We need to talk to you, Gordon," Angus said. "Matthew is not paying me for repairing his shoes last week."

"Repairing them?" Matthew repeated. "Look here, Gordon. I'd do better work if my hands were all thumbs. I'll not pay for what the man hasn't earned."

These were petty grievances, but they could split the clan apart if not addressed. Gordon wanted to hand this task of listening to complaints to someone else, but so far none of his men showed either the talent or patience for it. The few times he had given the task away, it ended in disaster.

"Do the repair again, Angus," he said with

heavy sigh. "And pay him half before he starts," he told Matthew. "If not, then you both lose."

"Yes, but—" Matthew started.

"I don't want to hear it," Gordon said, cutting him off. "You came to me for my verdict and there it is. Be done. And, Angus, you know how Matthew is. Don't do anything for him if you don't want to hear him complain."

"Aye, Gordon," Angus agreed. He turned and left. He wasn't happy with the verdict. It meant more work for him.

"He's lousy at what he does," Matthew had to grumble.

"You hired him," Gordon answered.

Not liking the response, Matthew stomped away.

Gordon looked at Tempest, who had watched it all while munching his dinner. "They are both fools."

Tempest seemed to nod in agreement, and Gordon had to marvel that his closest allies, the ones who knew his mind halfway at all, the ones he trusted the most, were a dog and a horse. "What does that say about me?" he asked Tempest.

The animal's response was a soft nicker.

"You are right," Gordon answered. "At least I have some distance now from Constance Cameron. She's a handful . . . but you can't help but admire her."

Tempest snorted.

"Come down," Gordon said. "She has spirit. She's not afraid to speak her mind." He gestured with the curry comb he held. "I wish Fiona had that spirit. I wish she was stronger, like Constance."

Tempest glanced back at Gordon as if to say he knew better, and Gordon couldn't help chuckling. "You've caught me," he told the horse. "Another day spent with her on my lap and it wouldn't be you I'd be riding." He began rubbing Tempest down. "And that is why I needed to hand her off to someone else. Colster wouldn't like her rogered by some Scot bastard."

Although he wouldn't mind bedding her, he thought. Constance wasn't afraid to ask for what she wanted. She'd be the same in bed. Unbidden images of the sparkle of defiance in her eyes, the curve of her lips, and the swell of her breasts came to his mind.

"Oh yes, it is a good thing I passed her off," he confessed just as a cry went up in the camp.

"She's escaped! The English lass escaped!"

The alarm made Gordon turn. Old Rae was

hobbling toward him, and Gordon swore before asking, "How?"

The older man was out of breath. As soon as he could manage, he said, "My wife was fixing her a bite to eat, and when she turned her back on her, the lass pushed her down to the ground and then ran out the door before I could even believe what was happening."

"Did you untie her hands?" Gordon wanted to know, fearing the answer.

"Aye. She couldn't eat with her hands tied," Old Rae said. "And such a biddable lass, how did we know she would leave? She was as sweet as a cherry when we first took her in. Said she was frightened, and my heart ached for her."

"Your wife should bat you over the head," Gordon swore.

Thomas came running to join them, followed by others. "We've started the search for her," Thomas reported. "She can't go far."

"Don't count on it," Gordon said. "She's smarter than the lot of us. Organize the men. Fan out and start looking through every tent, every hut, every box and barrel in the place. And search the forest, too. We must find her."

The men hurried away to carry out his orders.

But Gordon didn't join the search.

No, he'd wait right there with the horses.

His earlier erotic thoughts of Constance vanished with the onset of his temper. He'd thought she'd given up that nonsense about running away to America. It was too dangerous a journey for a young woman alone.

However, if she wanted to make Edinburgh in three days, she needed a horse—and she was bold enough to try and steal one.

Gordon turned Tempest into the herd before moving toward the center of the grazing horses. He knelt among them. Tad came loping back to join him, obviously aware that something was amiss.

"Lay still," Gordon ordered. The wolfhound stretched out beside him, his head down. He'd remain that way until given the command to rise.

Shouting could be heard throughout the camp.

Gordon let them carry on. The more noise, the more confident Constance would be that she knew where everyone was.

A cramp started in his left foot. He was just about ready to stand and shake it out when the horses paused from their grazing.

A few lifted their heads. Others returned to eating but were watchful.

And then Gordon saw her. She'd stolen one of Emma's shawls and thrown it over her head to hide her hair. The tartan around her shoulders covered her fine dancing dress. *His* tartan, he noted. She'd not given it back earlier.

That she would attempt an escape didn't shock Gordon. What did surprise him was how she ducked under the rope paddock with the ease of a young boy, grabbed a hank of the mane on the nearest horse, and hoisted herself up onto the animal's back.

She was going to ride the horse without a saddle. All the way to Edinburgh.

He had to admire her courage, and was tempted to let her do it just because she'd be saddle-burned for weeks. Not to mention the fact that the horse she'd chosen so hastily was an aged mare they all called "the Bitch."

Actually, it was Constance's modesty that proved her undoing. She took a moment to rearrange her skirts so she wasn't showing as much shapely leg. Her attention was on the task at hand and the shouting in the camp. She never even heard him make a sound until he came up beside her and said, "Going somewhere?" in the mildest of voices.

She let out a yelp of surprise.

The sound startled the Bitch, who was ready

for a fight. The mare pinned her ears and bucked. Constance went flying right for Gordon. The two of them fell to the ground, but the Bitch wasn't done bucking.

Gordon tried to avoid the mare's hooves while protecting Constance with his body.

Tad rose with a snarl and began barking at the horse. The dog's attack gave the Bitch a target for her anger. She kicked out at him, but Tad moved to the left, drawing her away from Gordon and Constance.

Unfortunately, the bucking and Tad's barking had riled up the other horses, who started running. For a second it was chaos. Gordon anticipated being trampled at any moment. He jumped to his feet, half carrying, half dragging Constance to safety on the other side of the rope fence.

Everyone in the camp heard the noise and came running from all directions.

Fearing for his dog, Gordon leaned over Constance's body and commanded, "Tad, come back here."

The dog immediately came to his side just as Thomas and Brian arrived.

"What the devil?" Thomas said, and caught up short when he saw who Gordon had.

Constance was the worse for wear. Her skirts

were hiked up over her knees, she'd lost a shoe, and apparently her mouth was full of dirt because she made a face and spat it out.

Ignoring a pain in his side, a sign that the Bitch might have caught him with a hoof, Gordon stood and brought his captive to her feet by lifting her with one arm. "She was attempting to steal a horse."

"You could have been killed, Gordon," Thomas said, a comment quickly seconded by the growing number of people gathering around them.

"We need to calm the horses before they run through the fencing," Gordon said to Brian, who turned and barked an order at some boys to see to the matter.

Meanwhile, a grumble of anger rolled through the crowd. They weren't pleased with Constance.

"Emma hurt her wrist," Sarah Kimball self-righteously informed Gordon.

"You should have seen the way she acted," Old Rae said to the others, as if to justify losing their captive. "She's wicked. Maggie was right!"

"Let me have her," Thomas said, his eyes hard. "I'll school her in manners. We'll tie her up in the center of the camp, the same way the English treated the Widow Harrell. Do you remember what they did to that old lady, lads?"

"*No,*" Gordon said, drowning them all out before matters grew out-of-hand. "Colster doesn't want her abused. We'll treat her with respect."

"He'll never see a mark on her," Thomas promised, the intent of his threat clear.

Constance was still too disoriented from her wild escape to realize what was being said, and Gordon knew he had to act fast before his clansmen decided her punishment for themselves.

"Give me that lead line," he ordered Jamie Allen, an eleven-year-old lad, standing closest to the rope he wanted.

The boy handed it to him, and Gordon retied Constance's hands. He then tied the other end of the rope to his left wrist. He raised his wrist and hers for all to see. "There. Let's see if she can escape me."

"Are you going to keep her with you all the time?" Thomas asked.

"Aye, day and night," Gordon answered.

"And where will she sleep?" Emma Reivers wondered.

"With me," Gordon said.

Eight

Constance was still a bit dazed after the fall from the horse—but Gordon's words brought her to her senses. "I will not!" she informed him.

She was overruled as the Scots burst into cheers. "She'll learn her lesson now," Thomas called out. He emphasized his meaning with one of the crudest gestures Constance had ever seen.

Her temper swept aside any fear she might have felt. No one spoke of a Cameron woman in that manner. They were descended from earls, and if they weren't, she had learned a long time ago how to defend herself.

Gordon didn't respond to the cheers or any

of the comments. Instead, he turned and began walking off, expecting her to docilely trail in his wake.

Well, he was in for a surprise, she thought, digging in her heels. She only had one moccasin on but an oak tree would move before she would.

But he'd tied her hands differently this time. The bonds tightened as he walked, painfully squeezing her wrists, and she had no choice but to follow, her first steps a stumbling skip to keep her from being pulled flat on her face.

The Scots roared with approval.

Constance hated them for that. Of course, she'd already been angry at the lot of them before attempting another escape. Her pride had been stung by Gordon's callous passing her off to the Reivers as if she was of no consequence. It had felt like a betrayal, because she'd been cooperative. She'd even reconciled herself to the idea that she would miss the *Novus* sailing. Yet then he'd handed her over, dismissed her as if she meant *nothing* to him.

And it was that last that had made her decide to run. Of course, she didn't want to examine her motives too deeply. She wasn't certain if she'd decided to try and reach Edinburgh because she was a captive or because Gordon had rejected her.

But *now* she didn't want anything to do with him.

Her fingers were turning red. The binds didn't loosen just because she was forced to follow him. Then again, she thought, Gordon didn't care. He hadn't even glanced back.

He *expected* her to follow. Just as Charlotte and Miranda expected her to do as they instructed. No one ever listened to *her.*

The memory of the kiss rose unbidden in her mind.

He'd completely humiliated her with it, and if he thought to do such a thing again, he was wrong. She'd *not* go to his quarters with him. Let him be the one made out to be the fool.

Constance resisted him one more time, throwing all her weight into refusing to take one more step, and it worked. She stopped him in his tracks.

The pain shooting through her hands from the tightening rope was excruciating, but she held back. Better that the rope sever her hands than he be allowed to best her one more time.

Gordon turned. Realizing that she had made him do that gave her courage.

His eyes met hers. The Scots had gone quiet, as if holding their collective breath.

Constance didn't know if she could continue to hold out. Her hands had gone numb—

He took a step toward her, loosening the tension in the rope.

She'd won. The thrill of victory overrode any pain.

He had backed down first.

Gordon walked toward her, stopping when they were toe-to-toe. His fingers relaxed the tightness in the rope around her wrists. Constance could have cried out in triumph and relief.

However, her pleasure was short-lived, because without preamble, without completely untying her, he hoisted her up over his shoulder and carried her through the crowd.

The Scots went wild with laughter. They danced with glee as they followed Gordon through the camp. Children skipped in front of them and the adults acted as if they were on their way to a fair.

Constance couldn't look at them. She'd lost the will to fight. No matter what she did, how she resisted, he had superior strength, and he would use it.

She lowered her head, not wanting to see the jeering faces. "Send her back with a bairn" was the rudest and most oft-repeated suggestion.

Their coarseness reminded her of the trappers and frontiersman back home, reminded her of what she *hadn't* liked about the valley. Their father's drinking and often violent temper had made herself and her sisters outcasts and prey to rough characters. But it also taught her how to hold her head high in the face of public scorn.

Gordon carried her to a tent, one that was little different from the others in the camp, and perhaps in some way a bit poorer. His huge dog had followed at his heels, and now, tail wagging, pushed aside the leather flap that served as a door and went inside. Gordon flipped back the same flap and ducked inside.

In one last act of defiance, Constance grabbed at the tent's frame. It was a pitiful attempt and her fingers could not hold onto the canvas.

The crowd would have invited themselves inside except that before Gordon dropped the flap, he said to the dog, "Tad, guard."

Tad dropped before the door, the length of his body from paw to tail blocking the entrance. Someone tried to peep in. Tad growled and the person quickly backed away. Apparently the clan had a healthy respect for Gordon's dog.

The tent's low ceiling brushed the top of Gordon's head. Without ceremony, he set Constance down on her feet. She wavered a moment, regaining her balance, then raised her tied hands and attempted to strike him with all she was worth against the side of his head.

Gordon easily ducked her swing. The dog rose, barking, but not leaving his post.

"Quiet, Tad," Gordon said, catching Constance by the waist before she fell and dumping her into a rickety chair by the tent's center pole. The only other furnishings were a small table and a tack chest.

"Stay," he ordered, as if she was his dog.

Constance wanted to defy him. She wanted to rise to her feet and stomp him.

However, sitting felt good, and the pain in her hands was almost unbearable. But she would not ask for quarter. No, her limbs could fall off before she begged.

Gordon's rude voice said, "You shouldn't have let that damn rope become so tight." He knelt in front of her, to look at her wounds.

Constance frowned at him. "*I* shouldn't? How odd. I thought you were the one who tied me up, who wanted to humiliate me, who was on the other end of the lead rope, *yanking* on it."

The set of his mouth tightened. "You'd be

wise to learn when to keep quiet," he answered through clenched teeth.

He loosened the knot he'd tied. Blood flowed through her hands, making her gasp in pain. He turned to the tack chest a few feet away, but couldn't go that far from her without stretching the rope between them.

Constance drew in a sharp breath as her binds began to tighten.

Gordon paused, saw what was happening, and swearing under his breath, came back. He unbound her hands completely. "You won't be going anywhere. Not with Tad and me as guards." He went to the tack chest and pulled out bandages and a salve for her wrists. Returning, he dressed her wounds with efficient movements.

He then pulled out a bottle of amber liquid and poured some into a pewter tankard. "Here, drink this."

"What is it?" she asked, wrinkling her nose.

"Whiskey."

"Are you attempting to subdue me with spirits?" After witnessing her father's weakness for drink, she usually avoided strong spirits of any sort.

"Would it work?"

She shook her head.

He sighed. "I didn't think so. But it will ease the pain."

Constance drank.

The whiskey didn't taste as she imagined it would—but then it hit her stomach. Her whole being revolted, throwing her in to a coughing fit.

Gordon was completely unsympathetic. Still kneeling in front of her, he rested an arm on the table. "Next time, sip it."

She nodded. She couldn't speak. She pushed the tankard toward him.

He smiled, his expression grim. "Finally. You have nothing to say. 'Tis a blessed moment."

If looks were daggers, she would have cut the smile from his face.

This time he laughed with true amusement. Then he used the salve and bandages to doctor her wrists. The salve burned slightly, and as her eyes watered from the pain, she was glad that she'd had that bit of whiskey. As if to cool the salve's sting, Gordon blew softly on her wrist.

For a second her heart seemed to stop. She looked down at his blond head bent over her hands. His touch was gentle, caring . . . kind. These were not words she would have applied to a man before, especially a warrior. Then again, he was a warrior who noticed even trapped doves.

He glanced up as if noticing her shock. "I could say it is your own fault," he said. He made a rueful gesture as he reached for the bandages and began to carefully wrap her wrists, his gaze returning to his work. "The truth is, I lost my temper. I'm sorry."

If the earth had suddenly opened beneath her into a huge gaping hole, Constance could not have been more surprised.

Men didn't apologize.

Except *this* one had . . . and in her mind, he was more manly for it. He was crusader and king, humble and yet, if need be, ruthless. He could fit anywhere in the world and survive.

Walls around her heart that she'd never noticed before seemed to melt away. His touch did that. His simple kindness had challenged everything she'd thought about her world.

She watched him tie off the knot of her bandage, wondering if he was experiencing what she was . . . and knowing it was not so.

If ever there was a reason to escape, this was it. These tender, new feelings for him made her vulnerable, and she didn't like being vulnerable.

Gordon finished knotting off the second bandage and then rose. He poured himself a draught of whiskey into the tankard and downed it, without any sputtering. His gaze met hers. "'Tis good."

She shuddered her distaste. It was a way to hide the turmoil of her true feelings and to exert some semblance of control over herself.

He laughed and put the cork back in the bottle. "I'm going out. When I return, I'll see you fed. In the meantime, you will wait here."

"You're going to leave me?" She didn't want to be alone. Everything was too strange, too new. "I thought I was going everywhere with you."

"Obviously not." He placed the whiskey in the tack chest before reaching for a dark wood writing case and a small leather purse, which he tucked inside the case. He closed the tack chest.

As he headed toward the door, Tad rose, tail wagging as if in anticipation of going wherever his master was. She noticed Gordon hadn't bothered to retie her.

Did he think her beaten?

Never.

As if reading her mind, Gordon said, "You won't be leaving this tent, Constance. Not tonight. If all goes well, in two weeks' time you'll be sitting at Colster's table. So, stop playing as if this were a game or some drama for the stage. Be wise and stay here. I shall be back shortly. Tad, *guard*."

The wolfhound's tail stopped wagging. The dog's happy grin turned to what appeared a frown of disappointment as he swung his great shaggy head in her direction, and she knew whom he blamed.

"He can outrun any deer on this mountain. I've seen him take down a boar with his bare teeth. You'll be here when I return," Gordon assured her.

"How long will you be gone?" she asked, wondering if the dog ever acted on any of his grudges.

"Until I'm ready to return," Gordon responded, as if she were a distraction and little more—but then, at the door, he stopped.

He turned and walked back to the tack chest. He set aside his writing case, opened the lid and took out two pistols, a powder horn, a dirk, and a sword. He placed the dirk in his boot, tucked the pistols in his waistband, lifted the horn's cord around his neck, and attached the sword around his waist with a belt. "I don't want you tempted," he explained to her before picking up the case and leaving the tent.

Constance sat back. The tent's canvas was heavy and muffled most of the sounds outside. For a moment she gave in to defeat, but only for a moment . . . until she realized she had a new enemy—boredom.

There was nothing to do in the tent. After two minutes of sitting, she was ready to move. She didn't bother trying to slip out the door. She knew Gordon well enough to know he meant what he'd said, and if he claimed Tad could stop her, then it was true.

However, that didn't mean she couldn't while away the time satisfying her curiosity about Gordon. She opened the lid to the tack chest. Tad watched with undisguised curiosity, one ear cocked higher than the other.

Gordon's clothes were folded neatly. Constance ran a hand over them. He was not a vain man. They were plain and hard worn.

Beneath them she found a Bible with an inscription on the inside cover. The light in the tent was too poor to read the writing. She poked around the chest, found a tinder box, and lit the oil lamp hanging from the tent's center pole.

The boldly written inscription said:

*To my son,
in whom I am well pleased.
Remember justice without heart
mocks the very meaning of the word.
Your father.
September 8, 1797*

Amidst the Bible's pages she found a watercolor miniature of a woman with Gordon's sharp, intelligent green eyes. She turned the portrait over. Someone had written: *d. 1788.*

There was not much else in the tack chest other than some tools, the whiskey, a jug of cider, and miscellaneous leather pieces of tack. She wished he hadn't taken his weapons.

Constance replaced the Bible under his clothing. The huge dog had watched her every move. He didn't seem so mean. She'd always had a way with dogs. She could usually coax them into doing what she wanted them to do.

Closing the tack chest, she rose and cooed, "Nice Tad." She took a step toward the door.

Tad leaped to his feet and barked furiously.

Constance pulled back in surprise. The animal even bared his teeth. Fearing he would attack, she fell back into the chair.

As if having said his piece, Tad flopped down and with a sigh placed his head on his paws, peacefully returning to his post.

Constance sat still. There must be a way out of the tent, she thought, one that didn't involve having her head bitten off by either the dog or his master. And she was determined to discover what it was.

Dusk had settled over the camp. Gordon crossed to Thomas's tent and found the giant sitting outside before a small fire, a bottle in one hand and Grace McEachin on his knee.

"I don't think it wise of you to be free with your hands and your drinking when we have women and children around," Gordon said.

Thomas raised the bottle to his lips. His gaze held Gordon's in open defiance. The man was tired. Gordon understood. Still, he would do what was necessary to have the rules of the camp followed.

The bottle came down. Thomas hadn't taken a drink. Instead, his lips curved into a lazy smile as he shifted his weight, sliding Grace off his lap. "I was teasing you, Gordon. I know my place."

Gordon doubted that.

"Where's Miss English Princess?" Thomas

asked. "Or are you out hunting her now?" he said, nodding to the weapons Gordon carried.

"Tad's watching her. I removed these for safety. I'll place them in your tent."

"You believe that dog can do what we haven't been able to?"

"Aye," Gordon answered, giving a passing glance to the insolent young woman who now stood at Thomas's side. She was a former vicar's daughter who lived by her wits and her looks.

She was comely enough to do so. 'Twas rumored that more than one man had been tempted to stray because of her silvery blue eyes and black curling hair. Gordon didn't mind if she was Thomas's plaything. Single men needed their release. But he'd bluntly warned her off the married men.

"Fetch Brian," he said to Thomas. "I'm going to use your quarters to write the letter to Colster."

Thomas nodded for Grace to leave and then did as Gordon had ordered.

The giant's tent was as sparsely furnished as his own, although Thomas's table and chairs were of better quality and he did have a cot. Gordon preferred to sleep on the ground because that was how most of his men slept.

He set aside his weapons, removing the pistols from his waistband and the sword at his waist, lit a candle and opened his writing case, removing paper, ink, and quills. The tip of his quills were dull. A sound at the door made him look up.

Grace stood there, her arms crossed, a hip cocked back in resentment. "Must you interfere every time I'm with Thomas, Gordon?" she demanded.

He began sharpening the quills with a knife from his case. This wasn't a discussion he wanted. She'd not thank him for it.

"Answer me," she ordered. "Or am I not even good enough to talk to?"

Gordon set his penknife aside. "Why are you in the business you are in, Grace?" he asked, answering her question with his own. "You have beauty, brains, your health. Why whore? And why *here*?" he asked quietly.

She straightened. "Why are any of us here, Gordon?"

"I know why I am here, Grace. Do you?" He sat at the table. "Use your brains, lass. There is more to life than laying with men. You'll never receive any satisfaction from the likes of Thomas. He's a good fighter but he'll never be faithful."

He'd struck a nerve. "I don't want a faithful man." She'd uncrossed her arms, her hands curled into fists, which she hid in the folds of her skirt. "If there is such a thing. Look at your sister, Gordon. She played right and good and what does she have to show for it? What future does she have? At least *I* choose who I sleep with and am paid well for my efforts."

Gordon went still. There had been a time when his sister was the delight of the countryside. A laughing, beautiful, frivolous young woman with a line of suitors out the door.

But then, after the rebellion at Nathraichean was discovered, English soldiers went to Dougal MacLeod's house, where Fiona had been living since their father's murder. The English kept her in prison for a week at Fort William before tossing her out into the street like a stray when they were done.

Gordon had arrived in time to bring her to the clan . . . but laughter was gone from her.

Now, Fiona wore black, never smiled, and spoke only when necessary, even to him—or should he say, *especially* to him? She wouldn't even live with him, choosing instead to have her own tent where she kept herself separate from the others.

He leaned toward Grace. "Has she talked

to you? Has she said what happened at Fort William?"

Grace shook her head, her mouth twisting with cynicism. "She doesn't have to tell me anything. The truth is there in the way she holds herself. Can't you see it? Or are you, like everyone else, pretending ignorance?"

Before he could respond, Thomas returned, with Brian at his heels. The giant looked at his woman and Gordon, a frown forming between his eyes. "Grace, I'd not thought you'd still be here."

She shrugged. "I was leaving."

"Aye, go then," Thomas said.

The woman did. After she left, Thomas turned back to Gordon. "Was she wanting you?" he asked.

Gordon frowned, surprised by the question. "You know I have other matters on my mind."

"I want her just the way she is. Don't be giving her any of your lectures, Gordon. Don't interfere."

"I won't. I haven't." Gordon held up his hands to show he held no tricks.

"Yes, right," Thomas said, his doubt clear on his face. He turned and stomped out of the tent.

Gordon couldn't hide his frustration. "I wish that woman would leave," he said to Brian.

"She has him whipped," the younger man agreed.

"Does she know it?"

Brian rolled his eyes. "What woman doesn't?"

Gordon shook his head, clearing his mind of the matter. He had no time for Thomas's love life. "Let me write this letter," he said, turning his attention to the task at hand.

He knew what he wanted to say and did so in straightforward language. He and Colster knew each other. At one time the duke had been a member of the clan, until Colster betrayed them by taking the Sword of the MacKenna.

Gordon sanded and sealed the ransom note. "Deliver this but don't wait for an answer," he told Brian. "I wrote instructions on how he should send word to make the exchange, and I've given him one week from receipt of the letter to do so. You won't have time to linger, and don't trust anyone."

"Yes, Gordon."

"Now ride, and ride fast." He tossed the money purse to Brian. "I expect you to return in five days' time. That's hard riding. Take only the freshest horses. If you are not back, I shall worry."

A grin split Brian's face. "You needn't worry." He bowed and left.

Gordon was tired and ready for his bed. Outside, he saw Thomas, who had found Grace . . . or perhaps Grace had found him. As the second in command, Thomas wielded a good amount of power in the clan. Grace would keep her eye on that. They stood by the fire in furious conversation.

Nodding a good night, Gordon would have walked past, but Thomas stopped him. "What if the duke doesn't give you the sword?" he asked soberly.

"He'll give it to me," Gordon answered.

"But if he doesn't?" Thomas pressed.

"Then we won't return Constance Cameron," Gordon said.

Thomas's eyes narrowed thoughtfully, "And what will you do with her?" He shook his head. "You lack the ice in your veins to deal with such a matter."

"But you don't," Gordon answered.

"No, I don't," the giant said, satisfied.

"Then I shall hope Colster gives us the sword."

Before he could be pinned down further, Gordon moved on.

When he'd conceived the kidnapping plan, it

seemed simple. Now he knew kidnapping was a dirty game. And for a moment he was thankful that Constance wasn't some shy, fearful debutante. She would recover from this—and Colster *would* give him the sword. There was no alternative.

Darkness had fallen. Cooking fires dotted the camp as each family, each group, prepared their own meals.

A footfall sounded behind him. He turned, and was surprised when Fiona fell into step beside him.

"You aren't going to hurt the English girl, are you?"

Gordon stopped. His voice low so they wouldn't be overheard, he said, "Fiona, I'm tired and more than slightly irritated that you would ask such a question."

"Are you?" she repeated.

"What do you think the answer is?" he asked, looking straight into her eyes. Her gaze slid away from his, and it bloody well hurt. She was all the family he had left.

And, yes, Grace was right. He did have an idea about what happened to her at Fort William. He believed she'd been raped. After all, the soldiers had committed the crime against other women. Why should his sister be spared?

Perhaps the time had come to talk about it.

"Please, Fiona, I know what the English did. I know it wasn't good. But the rest of us are not like *them*. You must be strong."

Her face grew set in a frown. She stared at a point beyond his shoulder. "Strong?" She pulled her tartan closer around her. "I *am* strong. I'm still alive." Tension radiated from her body.

"I hate that they hurt you," he whispered. "I despise myself that I wasn't there to protect you. It's me they wanted, Fee, not you."

"I know," she agreed as if speaking to a simpleton. "I had nothing to do with this." She made a short sweep of her hand, indicating the camp, the followers, the rebellion. "You ruined my life, Gordon. They thought to draw you out, just as *you* wish to use the English lass to receive what you want." There was a beat of silence, and then she looked at him. "Let her go, Gordon. *Now*, before any harm comes to her."

"No harm will come to her. *I'm* not like them," he repeated, clipping each word.

"You *are*," she countered. "You are a man. You can't help yourself."

"Fiona," he protested, but she whirled away from him, hurrying back in the direction she'd come. The expression on her face had been as distrustful as Grace's.

If he ever discovered the name of the man who'd done this to her, Gordon vowed, he'd kill him.

As it was, his sister would have nothing to do with him now.

Continuing to his tent, Gordon discovered that someone had left his tack, the moccasin Constance had lost during her battle with the Bitch, and a pot of stew outside the front flap. That was usually how he ate. He knew that the women of the camp had done this for him.

He pushed aside the leather flap and carried the pot inside, expecting to step over Tad guarding the door.

The dog wasn't there.

Instead, over by the chair, Tad, his loyal and most trusted companion, lay on his back at Constance's feet, his tongue lolling in ecstasy as she rubbed his belly.

Nine

"Tad," Gordon snapped.

The dog flipped over as if stunned to be caught and scrambled to his feet. He cowered, certain he was in trouble.

And he was.

Gordon snapped his fingers, pointing to his side. Tad slinked over to him, but actually had the audacity to give Constance a look of regret.

"A minute more and I would have been gone," Constance said confidently. Her braid was over one shoulder and, dressed as she was in the dancing gown of the night before and her bare feet, she looked for all the world like a renegade debutante.

"He's a bloody traitor," Gordon grumbled. He put the stew on the table before bringing in his saddle and her moccasin. He tossed the shoe into her lap, realizing his lamp had been lit. "Was someone here?"

She shook her head. "Why . . . ?" and then answered her own question by following his gaze to the lantern. "You didn't expect me to sit in the dark, did you?"

He hadn't expected to be gone so long. But it was a sign of Constance's resourcefulness that she had made herself completely at home. "I'm glad I took my weapons with me."

Constance smiled her response, and Gordon knew he'd best be on his guard. "Are you going to tie me up again?" she wondered, reading his mind.

"I'll truss you up like a deer if you give me good cause," he assured her. To his surprise, she laughed, completely without fear. He knew she didn't doubt his words. It was just that she had courage. Whatever life gave her, she'd make the best of it.

He wished his sister had even a touch of Constance's spirit.

He pulled three china plates and two spoons from his tack chest. The plates were pieces of a set his father had owned. He ladled the stew into one and set it down for the dog, saying, "Here. Don't forget whose side you are on."

Tad dove into his food without remorse.

Gordon ladled two more plates and offered one to Constance. She took it, helping herself to a spoon and attacking her stew with enthusiasm. He had been just as hungry . . . except his appetite disappeared at the sight of the cleavage she displayed as she bent over her food.

Her ball gown had not been fashioned for travel. For most of the trip, she'd worn his tartan. Now, he couldn't help but notice the swell of breast over the lace at her bodice, the hollow at the base of her throat, the way she ran the tip of her tongue over her lips as she savored the stew.

Perhaps Fiona was right. Perhaps they shouldn't be alone—

"It's good," she said. "You should eat . . . " Her voice died off as she realized he was staring.

Gordon looked away, embarrassed to have been caught gaping like a schoolboy.

Thomas would have laughed.

He sat on the ground next to Tad and focused on his own plate, all too aware of the moments when her gaze had drifted toward him. He'd thought he was bone tired, but suddenly parts of him were wide-awake. He shifted, not wanting her to notice, silently cursing his male nature, *and* her female one.

They ate in silence. When he finished, he gave the plate to Tad to clean off. Constance made a horrified sound.

"Please don't tell me you clean all your plates that way?" she said.

Gordon frowned. "I wash them." He could have added, *Sometimes*, but thought it best to keep that to himself.

She curled her lip in disgust. "I suppose men don't worry about those things."

"We do."

The lift of her eyebrow said she didn't believe him.

A moment of silence stretched between them. From his position on the ground, he couldn't help but notice how trim her ankles were. He liked slender legs, and he already knew she was muscular and strong—

She cleared her throat. "I need a private moment."

It stood to reason. It had been a while. And the fresh night air would cool overheated thoughts. "Come along, then."

Darkness had completely fallen. The moon was full and golden. A good number of people had already gone to bed.

This was usually his favorite time of night. He walked her toward the latrines. "Here," he said at the door to one of the privies.

Constance held back. "This place doèsn't smell good."

That was an understatement. A party of men, all too old to fight, were responsible for the latrines and other areas of the camp. He'd noticed that they had been slack in their responsibilities. He didn't want to admit that to her. "Consider what it is and be happy we have one," he said. "Go on, Constance, see to your business."

The corners of her mouth turned down, the expression almost comical. Gingerly, she went inside. He stood guard.

The smell seemed more pronounced now that she had pointed it out to him, and he was relieved when she came running out, so that they could both find some fresh air.

"May I wash my hands?" she asked.

He led her to the loch's edge. They passed a few couples who nodded to Gordon but watched them with curiosity.

"We will be the talk of the camp," she whispered to him.

"I always am," he assured her. He stopped at an outcropping of rocks everyone used for washing. "There's soap right there."

"This is soap?" she said with distaste, holding up the gray, mushy mass. She tossed it to the ground and then washed her face and hands.

He did the same. "The women in the camp make it," he answered in his defense. "It's fine enough."

"They didn't let it cure long enough." She made an impatient sound as she rose to her feet. "Your latrines are disgusting and your soap too soft to be of use, and that is just the beginning of the problems here."

She was right, except he didn't want to hear this from her. Not now. He was too damn tired. He needed six hours sleep and then he'd solve all the problems of the world. "I suppose *you* know better?"

"I do," she said without flinching. "I've lived my life out-of-doors. I know what is important. These are everyday matters, but they must be attended to or you will find your people losing their will to go on."

Which was what had been happening.

Gordon scowled, angry at her for no other reason than because she was so capable. "Why couldn't you have been an empty-headed debutante?" He turned and started walking to the tent, knowing she would follow.

And she did.

161

"I'm going to have the latrines moved," he said. "We weren't going to stay here that long anyway."

"With this many people, it doesn't take long," she answered, her voice as stiff as his.

He didn't reply because he saw the stew pot on its side in the doorway of his tent. Tad was nowhere to be seen. He had been so focused on Constance, he'd not secured his quarters before he left. "Damn dog," he muttered.

He picked up the pot and set it upright by his door. Tad hadn't left a lick behind. There was nothing that would attract a wild animal. Whoever had gifted him with the stew would collect the pot in the morning.

Indicating for Constance to enter the tent first, he followed, dropping the flap over his door. He didn't waste time, but brought out the rolled quilted pallet and blanket he stored behind his tack chest. He made quick work of making his bed on the hard dirt floor.

Constance stacked the dishes—Tad had licked those clean as well—and picked up his tartan from the chair where she'd left it. She wrapped it around her shoulders. "Am I sleeping there?" she asked.

"We're both sleeping here," he answered, daring her to raise a complaint.

She bit her bottom lip but remained standing.

That was fine. She could stand all night. *He* was going to sleep, although he had planned on Tad keeping guard.

"You'll have to use the tartan for your cover," he told her as he sat in the chair and began pulling off his boots. He set them aside and stood, pulling his shirt from his breeches. "You don't need to worry that I'm going to ravish you," he said.

Two bright spots of color appeared on her cheeks, and he knew that had been on her mind.

Good. She *should* be uncomfortable around him. For that reason—and because she'd been right about the latrines and the state of his camp—he stood and started to take off his shirt.

"What are you doing?" she asked, her voice sounding strangled.

He paused, savoring the moment, and then pulled the shirt off over his head. She stood as far away as she could from him in the narrow confines of the tent, a distance of only a foot or two, his tartan protectively pulled against her. If he had not been standing in front of the door, he had no doubt that she would have run right out it.

Gordon smiled, feeling wolfish. It was about time she saw him as a man.

"I'm undressing for bed," he said.

Her eyes widened with alarm and she whirled around, giving him her back. Dear Lord, had he ever been that innocent?

"How far do you expect to go undressing?" she asked.

"This far," he said. He dropped the shirt on the chair close by her. She gave a little jump, as if the cloth was alive.

Pleased to finally have the upper hand, Gordon said, "Come, Constance, you've seen a man's chest before, and probably more, out in your wilderness. Why, I hear the Indians run around naked."

"They wear clothes," she assured him.

He stretched out on his side of the pallet. His bed took up most of the floor space. His leg was close to her moccasined foot. There would be enough room for her on the pallet but it would be close between them. "What's this? Bold, fearless Constance Cameron blushing? If I'd known I could subdue you by taking off my clothes, lass, I would have removed them sooner."

"I don't think the Duke of Colster would approve," she responded primly.

Gordon yawned. "Then we'll keep it our

secret. After all, I *want* the Sword of the Mac-Kenna, not to be run through *by* it. But don't worry, I'm too tired to think about anything but sleep. Although," he added quickly, "I'm a light sleeper. You won't be able to move without my knowing it." He didn't want to tie her up again. Not with her wrists as bad as they were.

"Wait," she said, her suspicions aroused. "You are teasing me, aren't you? You haven't taken off your clothes."

Constance whipped around so quickly to accuse him, her foot tripped on his leg.

She came crashing down on top of him just as he closed his eyes.

Gordon acted on reflex. He caught her and rolled over, his body settling on hers. They were leg-to-leg, hip-to-hip, chest-to-breasts . . . nose-to-nose.

Her eyes rounded.

He'd wager his were, too.

"You *are* naked," she whispered. Her hands rested on his shoulders. She didn't move them.

He could have corrected her impression, told her she was only half right—except right now all he could think about was how well they fit together. How warm and welcoming she was.

How hard *he* was.

Other men weren't alone. They lay beside

their wives and their sweethearts. They had someone to share the burdens of the day, salving them with the sweet release that could only be had in a lover's arms.

Gordon knew he had nothing to offer a woman. His sister had already paid a very dear price. He chose to be alone.

And yet, right now, all he wanted was another kiss. One kiss.

Was that so much to ask?

Ten

Constance didn't move. She was paralyzed by what she saw in Gordon's eyes. He wanted to kiss her.

She *wanted* that kiss.

For the first time in her life she understood the power of attraction.

His arousal, strong, present, demanding, didn't frighten her. Instead, it filled her with pride, and an aching need that she'd never experienced before.

Her legs seemed to open with a will of their own, knowing better than she did how to bring him closer. His weight felt good on her body, and she couldn't help but let her arms relax, her hands feeling the play of honed muscle beneath the warmth of his skin.

Gordon's lips hovered just above hers.

Constance swallowed, waiting.

He lifted her braid, wrapping it around his hand, binding him to her—and just when Constance couldn't take it any longer, he kissed her.

She parted her lips. He'd taught her that much in the first kiss . . . but she discovered there was a great deal more she had to learn.

Their mouths melded together. Her hips raised, as if this part of her, too, needed to be closer.

His tongue found hers, stroked, cajoled, caressed, and Constance was lost. Kissing this man was as natural as breathing. She liked the taste of him, the feel, the touch . . . the everything.

He moved his hips. Her very core tightened, yearning for something more. Her breasts grew full, as if reaching for him, needing him.

With a soft sigh, Constance opened herself fully to him.

The earlier kiss had been an assault on her senses. This one was much the same, except now she was assaulting him right back. And she wanted more than just a kiss. She wanted to climb into his skin, to completely surround herself with him.

She was no fool. She'd lived close to nature. She knew what happened between a man and a woman, but knowing and experiencing were two very different things—

Gordon broke off the kiss, throwing himself onto the pallet beside her. He breathed hard, as if he'd just run a long race.

A chill skittered across her skin. She turned to him, wanting his warmth and his touch. She was not ready to quit quite yet. As she leaned to kiss him, he stopped her by pulling the tartan tight around her shoulders, his hands holding her prisoner.

Constance smiled. His pupils were dark and wide, his eyes glassy with desire. She knew how he felt. Her senses were as stimulated, and she wasn't about to quit something that was proving so pleasurable.

However, he stopped her. "Good night," he said.

Then he rolled over onto his side, away from her.

"Good night?" Constance repeated dumbly. She frowned. She wasn't ready to sleep yet. In fact, sleep was the furthest thing from her mind. And she defied him to pretend he felt different.

"Stop wiggling," he said.

"I haven't moved."

"Good."

Constance frowned at his back. Her passions were beginning to cool, replaced by a profound embarrassment. "Was that another one of your tricks to humiliate me?"

When he ignored her, she reached over and gave his side a pinch.

"Ow," he said. He lifted his head to give her a cross look. "Go to sleep."

"I would have, before you did *that*."

His brows came together.

She tensed, preparing to defend herself against whatever charges he might make that she deserved such treatment. "I didn't ask you to kiss me," she muttered.

"I know." He sighed heavily, raking a hand through his hair before laying down on his back beside her. "I shouldn't have done it."

"Yes, you should," came out of her mouth before she could question the wisdom of such words.

His expression softened. He raised a hand as if to touch her hair but then let it drop. He whispered, "You know we can't play that game."

She nodded, disappointed.

Gordon's gaze dropped to her lips. His own

twisted ruefully. "I wish we could have met at another time, another place."

"Like where?" she wondered.

He considered a moment. "A party, in London. I would be a talented young advocate with a promising career in the courts ahead of me."

"What would I be?" she asked.

"What you are." This time when he raised his hand, he touched her hair. "A vibrant, challenging creature who knows how to set hearts on fire."

His words melted her last remaining defenses. "Not I," she said, secretly wanting him to repeat those words, to substantiate them with more. "My sisters are the ones who turn heads. Everyone notices them first."

"I don't believe that," he countered. "But I shouldn't have said what I did." He let go of her braid, a sadness in the seriousness of his expression. "I shouldn't have kissed you—"

"I wanted you to."

He acknowledged her words with a small nod. "'Tis wrong. You have no choice in the matter, Constance. We both know that. You are our hostage."

She drew her brows together. "You weren't forcing me. I kissed you back."

He rolled on his side to face her. His gaze

171

traveled over her face as if memorizing the details. She wanted to touch him, to place her palm against the side of his jaw and promise him that everything would be all right.

But she knew better.

"I understand," she whispered.

"I know." In the same serious vein, he added, "I have nothing to offer a woman, Constance. My life will probably end with a hangman's noose. But every once in a while, I yearn for a taste of what I can't have."

A coldness crept through her at his prophetic words. "Your rebellion might succeed. Freedom is a good thing. My country rebelled."

"Aye," he agreed.

But he knew differently, and so did she.

Constance folded her arm under her head. "Why?" she asked. "If you know you will fail, why do you continue?"

"Justice," he said, as if that one word explained all.

"Is it worth your life?"

"Yes."

She shook her head. "I don't understand the way people think here. Why stay if you are mistreated?"

"It's our home."

"This?" She cast a glance around the tent.

172

"Scotland is," he corrected. "And there have been many good men who have died for it."

"Yes," she conceded. "But how long does a fight continue? I come from a place where if a man doesn't like where he is, he moves on. He doesn't attempt to overthrow a government."

"A man can't move on forever."

"In America he can," Constance said boldly. "There is so much land there, he can keep moving forever."

Gordon shook his head. "You don't understand, lass. A man *has* to take a stand. If he doesn't, if he keeps running, then he isn't much of a man. Now, go to sleep. You have had a long day. We can argue tomorrow."

He closed his eyes.

Constance didn't. She lay awake, watching him. The lamp's soft light turned his skin the same golden color as his hair.

With the exception of Alex Haddon, her half-breed brother-in-law, she generally had not admired men. They held all the power and didn't hesitate to use it against others, especially women. She'd scoffed when Miss Casey had taught the "knightly ideal" in classes on history at Madame Lavaliere's. Men *always* thought of themselves.

But Gordon Lachlan *was* different.

Cathy Maxwell

She knew because moments earlier, when they were kissing, he could have done anything he wished . . . and yet, he'd put the needs of his people before his own desire. He'd known he could not return her as damaged goods.

Constance pulled his tartan up around her shoulders, snuggling into the wool-stuffed pallet, her gaze never leaving Gordon's sleeping face. She was safer with him than anyone else in this camp.

He *was* like Sir Galahad, the knight Miss Casey used to illustrate her position. He believed in ideals larger than himself.

She didn't want him to die.

She reached out to touch his golden hair, wanting to see if it was as silky as it appeared. She stopped just when the tips of her fingers could reach him.

Her feelings for him weren't wise.

But sometimes the heart challenged wisdom.

After all, hadn't her sister Charlotte married a man who was once her enemy? And Miranda had defied not only their father, but all society, to marry a half-breed.

In light of that . . . what was one Scottish rebel?

Constance pulled her hand back, suddenly all too aware of the risks.

Charlotte and Miranda were stronger than she. They were more intelligent and far more lovely. She was just the youngest and the least graceful. Everyone was always telling her she was too young to know her own mind. What if they were correct?

She formed a pillow of her arms, ensuring that her hands would not be tempted to touch him again. She had to keep her wits about her. She had to be wise.

That was her last thought as she drifted off to sleep.

Constance was attempting to paddle a canoe in swirling, angry waters. Mad Maggie sat in front of her, shouting that they were going to die and it would be her fault. She wanted her to be quiet but the crone kept rocking the boat back and forth until it was in danger of tipping completely—

The tightening of a hand on her shoulder woke Constance with a gasp. A woman about her age with hair the color of cinnamon leaned over her, the woman whom Gordon had ordered to take care of Mad Maggie. He'd called her Fiona.

"I didn't mean to startle you," Fiona said, rocking back on her heels.

Constance nodded that she was fine as she

pushed her hair back from her eyes. Her braid had fallen out in her sleep. She started to rise and realized she was alone on the pallet. Gordon was gone. Tad, once again, guarded the doorway, his ears alert as he watched Fiona's every move.

"Don't mind the dog," Fiona said. "He listens to me as well as Gordon. I can slip you by him—" Her words broke off with a soft sound of distress. She took hold of Constance's wrist. "He hurt you. He promised he wouldn't."

"He didn't do this on purpose," Constance said, defending Gordon. "It was what happened."

Fiona pressed her lips together as if trying to hold words, but she failed. "It was what happened *because* he brought you here," she said in a flash of temper. "Please, gather what things you have quickly. If I am to help you escape, we must hurry."

"Help me?"

"To escape," Fiona said impatiently, rising to her feet and shaking off her black skirts.

The last traces of sleepiness in Constance scattered. "You want me to leave? You're helping me?"

"*Yes,*" Fiona said. "My brother has gone too far. You'll bring the English down upon us. I don't want that. None of us wants that."

There was true fear in her voice, fear Constance ignored because she was too stunned by this new information. "Gordon is your brother?"

"My *half* brother," Fiona said, as if wishing to disclaim him. "We don't look much alike."

She was right. Her eyes were brown, her hair red to his blond . . . but Constance could also see a resemblance. It was there in the way she held her head, the sensual curve of her lip, and the aristocratic tone to her voice.

"Your brother has not harmed me," Constance said.

"But he could," Fiona warned. "You must go now. I've prepared a pack with food." She moved to a cloth bundle on the tack chest. "I told Gordon I would see to your needs today since he will be busy drilling the men. That gives you at least ten hours. I don't know about a horse, but it would be best to walk anyway—"

"You would betray your brother?" Constance interrupted.

Fiona drew herself away at the accusation. "I'm protecting *you*."

Something about the way she said those words set Constance on guard. There was a fragility to Fiona. She appeared strong and whole, but she wasn't. Someone, or something, had hurt this woman.

177

"Your brother is leader of this clan," Constance answered. "To betray him betrays all."

"You *can't* stay." Fiona snatched up the bundle.

"Yes, I can," Constance replied. "You need me to ransom the sword."

"We *don't* want the sword." Fiona moved toward her.

"Who is 'we'?" Constance asked, fearing the answer. What if Gordon's clan was turning against him? What if they had all grown afraid like his sister? If so, Constance thought, she had arrived just in time.

"*Everyone,*" Fiona declared, and then amended it to "Me." Her gaze fell. "He didn't . . . " She paused as if almost afraid to ask. " . . . *hurt* you, did he?"

It was then that Constance realized she wasn't asking about the bandages on her wrists.

Fiona glanced at her with an anxious expression. She feared the answer.

And Constance understood.

Fiona's fear for her was based on her own experience. She had been raped. Constance had met women who had been raped before. Some could manage, all were left with scars.

Gently, she attempted to reassure Fiona. "Your brother has not touched me in any way that is dishonorable—"

"He *kissed* you. I've heard the others talk about it. He slept with you here. *Alone.*"

"Gordon has been completely honorable."

"Look at your wrists," his sister ordered. "That was not honorable."

Constance held up bandaged hands. "This couldn't be avoided."

"Yes, it could have." Fiona held out the packet. "There's cheese and bread for a day or more. I gave you what money I have. It isn't much. Gordon has spent all we have on his rebellion. Now, go."

Constance raised her gaze from the packet to meet the other woman's eyes. "I can't," she said simply.

Being her brother's sister, Fiona frowned as if unable to believe Constance would disobey an order. "And why is that?"

"Because I'm going to join the rebellion," Constance said, not knowing until that moment that she would say it, that she had swung over to his Cause. But once she heard the words spoken, they sounded right. She was too late to reach Edinburgh harbor before the *Novus* sailed, and she didn't want to return to Madame Lavaliere's or be put on the marriage mart in London. "I'm going to stay and fight," she announced. "I'm joining the Scottish Cause."

Fiona dropped the hand holding the bundle in stunned surprise. However, her reaction was not one Constance could have anticipated. "Dear Lord," she said. "You've fallen in love with my brother."

Eleven

The accusation stung with a hint of truth.

Constance frowned at Fiona. "Where would you gain such—" Words failed her. "—such an idea?" she blurted out, anxious to make the denial.

Yes, she was taken with Gordon. How could any woman not be? He was all things strong and honorable. He could be considerate and protective, but there was an air of danger about him, too. He had a man's needs, yet he *chose* to rein in his passions—and thankfully so. Constance had discovered the night before that all her defenses vanished when he kissed her.

But that didn't equate with love. *Lust*, maybe—

The direction of her thoughts startled Constance. She'd never been one to go moon-eyed over a man.

"My reasons for joining your rebellion are simple," she assured Fiona.

The Scotswoman crossed her arms. "And they are?"

That she wanted to help Gordon achieve his dream of freedom. But she didn't say that . . . because that *did* sound as if she was falling in love with him.

"I'm an American," Constance said, grasping for ideas. "We thrive on rebellion."

Fiona snorted her opinion. "Let me warn you, Miss Constance, I already know your story. You and your sisters are infamous since the oldest married Lord Phillip Maddox, the most eligible bachelor in England. You came to this country to win our men with your looks."

"*I* didn't," Constance said. "Charlotte dragged me here. I want to go home. I was running away when your brother kidnapped me."

Fiona indicated the door with a sweep of her hand. Tad was now sitting up on his hind legs, his ears perked as if he took great interest in the conversation. "No one is stopping you from leaving now," Fiona said. "Come, we'll pretend I am guarding you." She picked up the lead rope from the table. "I'll walk you to the edge of the camp and then you can push me down and make your escape."

Constance pulled her arm away from the woman. "I won't go."

Fiona all but sneered with triumph. "Because he has won you over. Don't trust him."

"But he's your brother," Constance said. "You should support him."

"Do you support your sister in everything? Is that why you are running *away* from her?"

Turnabout was *not* fair play. "The relationship between Charlotte and me is different."

"Is it?" Fiona shook her head. "Why do you want to return to America?"

Constance crossed her arms around her waist. "It's my home."

Fiona nodded as if that had been the answer she'd expected. "It's what you knew. You had dreams there, didn't you? I had dreams once, too. I had a place in society. I was to go to London for a Season. I would have married and been happy."

"How can you be so certain?"

With a shrug Fiona said, "It was expected. I'd been groomed to be the wife of a fine gentleman. I *dreamed* of that day."

Constance caught herself before she made

a face. Charlotte had always gone on about what a lady should know and how she should behave. As the granddaughters of an earl, albeit a disreputable one, Charlotte had insisted that they learn the proper manners so that some day they could return to England and claim their birthright.

Well, here they were in England, Constance thought, and she hadn't met a single man she'd considering worthy enough to marry—*save for Gordon Lachlan*.

"What?" Fiona asked, suspicious. "You don't believe I'm telling the truth, that I was to be a great lady?"

"Great ladies are made in how they think," Constance said. Those words felt good to speak aloud. She'd had to hold her tongue too often with her sister and Headmistress Hillary. "If you want to be a great lady, then do great things."

"I can't," Fiona said, her eyes narrowing. "My *half* brother decided to take part in a rebellion. He made me an outcast."

"No, the men who murdered your father did that. Gordon wants justice."

Fiona threw down the lead rope and bundle she'd been carrying. "I know that. He was *my* father, too. *I was just as affected*."

"Then why aren't you as angry?"

"I *am* angry," Fiona countered. "My blood boils with anger. But there is nothing I can do about it. Father didn't think of the impact his stand against our *friends*, our *neighbors*, would have on Mother and me. He was like Gordon, always so concerned about fairness and justice— *for everyone else.* His wife, his daughter didn't matter."

"Your mother is here also?"

"No." Fiona crossed her arms, gathering the tartan close around her shoulders. "She died shortly after they murdered Father. It was grief that took her. Gordon placed me with Sir Dougal MacLeod's family. Sir Dougal had been a close friend of my parents. Lady Mac-Leod had offered to chaperone me during my London Season after the mourning period was over—not that I would have had any prospects. Gordon used my dowry for this rebellion. He's used everything we owned." A shadow crossed Fiona's face. "And then one day, after the rebels were discovered at Nathraichean, English soldiers took me away from Sir Dougal, who didn't dare put up a protest. He just handed me over."

"What did the soldiers want?" Constance asked.

"Gordon." Fiona took a step away from Constance. "You can think what you like about my feelings toward my brother, but I didn't give him up. They tried to make me tell them where he was. I wouldn't."

And she'd paid a terrible price for her loyalty. Constance's heart broke for the woman. "I'm sorry," she whispered.

"Don't be," Fiona said with a bitter laugh. "Just leave. Go, so that this will all end. We can't fight the English, and if Gordon persists, we will all die."

"You are already in danger," Constance countered. "And they will never let him go. He has a price on his head. He has no choice but to fight, and I'm a key to his claiming the Sword of the MacKenna. Is that why you want me to leave, so he can fail? Would you choose the opportunity to go to London and marry some man over your brother's life?"

"There is no marriage for me," Fiona said, her voice brittle. "I'm ruined. No decent man would have me. I'm not even fit to be a scullery maid. Gordon is wrong to carry this rebellion forward. People are hurt by it."

"People are hurt by the cruelty of others. And that is all the more reason to fight," Constance answered. She approached Fiona, stopping just short of taking the other woman by the shoulders and giving her a shake. "Gordon isn't fighting for his own vanity. He wants justice for the wrongs done your clansmen. If that's not worth fighting for, I don't know what is."

"You don't understand because *you* can leave at any time," Fiona said.

"I *do* understand," Constance said. "And I'm attempting to make you realize that you don't need to be ashamed—"

The leather flap on the tent was lifted.

Both Constance and Fiona expected to see Gordon enter. Instead, a slim woman with curling black hair and vivid blue eyes stuck her head in. Tad growled a warning. The woman looked at Fiona. "Call off the dog." Her Scot accent was as refined as Fiona's.

"No one asked you here, Grace," Fiona responded with even more coldness than she'd shown Constance.

Grace ignored her. "Are the two of you going to come to blows?" she asked in her soft lilting voice. "Because if you are, the other women and I gathered outside would like to see the fight. There's little entertainment in this camp."

Annoyed at the interruption, Constance asked, "Who are you?" And what right did she have to put her nose in other people's business?

"Grace McEachin, the camp whore," Fiona answered. "She believes she can do and say as she pleases because she has Thomas eating out of her hand. But not around me." She didn't wait for a response. "Come, Tad," she said, and with her shawl still pulled tightly around her shoulders, pushed past Grace, then stopped at the door. "You can come or go, whatever you please, Miss Constance Cameron. I tried to help. You have yourself to blame for your foolishness."

When Fiona left the tent, Tad followed right at her heels.

Grace released a long sigh. "Every time she adopts that manner, I feel like I've just left an audience with the queen."

"Perhaps she has good reason for being the way she is?" Constance suggested, wanting Grace to be charitable.

The whore would have none of it. "A woman must learn to toughen up to survive. You understand that, don't you? My impression is that you are a survivor."

"I'm not dishonest with myself," Constance replied, "if that is what you are asking."

Grace cocked her head as if reevaluating her. "So, are you going to leave?"

"How much did you hear?" Constance asked.

"Enough to know" was the cryptic answer.

"No, I'm not leaving," Constance said, and was pleased to wipe the smug assurance off the other woman's face.

"Why not?" Grace asked.

Constance bent down to pick up the bundle of food. She had to eat to maintain her strength for what lay ahead. "Because I've decided to join your fight," she said, untying the bundle. There was bread and a hardened piece of cheese in it. She took a bite of the bread.

"Join us?" Grace repeated, no less surprised than Fiona had been.

"Yes. Let's go out and meet the others." She started toward the door, but Grace didn't budge.

"Why would you want to join us?" Grace's gaze grew speculative. "It's the Lachlan, isn't it? He's caught your eye."

For the briefest second, Constance wanted to deny it . . . then changed her mind. "Aye, it *is* the Lachlan. A more noble man I have never met. And a more disreputable group of followers I have never seen." She crossed to stand toe-to-toe with Grace. "Do you think because you are a willing woman, it gives you airs over the likes of Fiona?"

Grace pulled back. Apparently no one had ever challenged her before.

"It doesn't," Constance said, answering herself. "You are just as afraid as she is. All of you are. You don't believe in this fight. Not truly. And so you're biding your time, not putting a great deal of effort into the Cause or the men who will fight it. Well, I'm not so namby-pamby." She moved toward the tent flap.

"What does that mean?" Grace demanded.

Constance paused. "Lacking in character. Being afraid because fear is comfortable. Are the others outside? Are they listening?" She didn't wait for a response but flipped open the flap.

Sure enough, it appeared as if every woman in the camp was gathered around Gordon's tent, unabashedly eavesdropping. Constance came to face them.

They actually took a step back. Some of them held babies in their arms. Others had small children clinging to their skirts. They returned her stare with undisguised hostility.

Well, that was fine with her. The only ones *not* paying attention seemed to be Mad Maggie, who stood off the side rocking her "Patty," and Fiona, who was nowhere to be seen.

Grace came out of the tent behind her. Constance didn't wait for an introduction, but decided to charge right in with her opinions.

Charlotte would be proud. No one had ever accused a Cameron of being shy.

"You heard what was said in there?" she asked.

No one said yea or nay. They didn't need to. Constance understood frontier politics among women. They always knew more than they gave away, and no one wanted to be the first to speak out, although she was certain they all had opinions.

"You know I've decided to join your cause." The words filled her with pride.

In response, not one of the women batted so much as an eyelash. No congratulations. No welcome to the clan. Instead, they stood in grim, condemning silence.

She realized that this might be more difficult than she had imagined. The Scots could be stubborn. But she refused to be deterred.

"You heard me accuse Grace of not being supportive of your cause. Well, I believe that of all of you."

Now she received a reaction. A collective gasp of outrage rose from the crowd at her audacity.

"So you *do* have some pride," Constance plunged on. "Well, you couldn't tell as much if you looked around this camp." She boldly strolled forward, and they backed away to clear a path. "See with your own eyes what is happening. Livestock roaming freely, children with dirty faces, no order, no cleanliness. Everyone is involved in their own little lives without anyone working together. Except for making soap," she remembered with a snap of her fingers. "And I believe that is shared because whoever made it created such a sticky mess, she didn't want it around her home."

Chins shot up, eyes glittered with outrage. "You don't know one thing about us," a woman with squiggly orange hair said.

"Or about what we've lost," an older woman agreed—and Constance realized that in her boldness, she'd surrounded herself with angry Scotswomen.

For a second she had the very reasonable urge to run. The circle of women looked no less menacing than a Shawnee war party.

Except they weren't, she reminded herself. She had nothing to fear. They needed her, and so she raised her voice, daring to say, "Perhaps I don't know what you've lost, but I know what you *are* going to lose. Your husband's lives, your children's birthright, your pride as a nation."

"We've already lost that," Grace answered.

Constance turned to her. "No, you haven't. Not as long as you have fight left in you." She noticed that several heads nodded at her words. Emboldened, she continued, "If it wasn't for women, there would be no civilization. Men know nothing about the home and the hearth. We are the ones who care, who force them to make laws and build homes. We are the ones who know how to make soap, and make *them* use it."

It wasn't the best rallying cry, but it hit its mark.

"That's right," she heard several murmur to each other.

Then a woman from the back of the crowd said, "Malcolm McDowell and his family left last night."

Apparently, this news was distressing to most of the women. Frowns formed and lines of concern marred foreheads.

Constance turned to Grace. "What is this? Why are these people important?"

"Lucy McDowell was a good friend to many of them. Her husband was a strong supporter of Gordon's cause."

"*Gordon's* cause?" Constance repeated, indignation rising. "I thought it was the Cause of everyone here?" Now Constance understood why Gordon wanted the sword. He was battling for the very life of his rebellion. And if it failed, *he* would be the one to pay the price.

Constance's blood boiled. Why, Gordon couldn't even count upon the support of his sister, his own flesh and blood.

Well, he had one ally. *Herself.*

"So what did these people do?" Constance demanded. "Sneak away in the middle of the night? Do they run like cowards? Because if they do, it is a shame. And where did they go?"

"Probably to London or wherever they can find work," the orange-headed woman said.

This information horrified Constance. "London? Where their children can starve on the streets? Have you been there?" She didn't wait for an answer. "I have, and a dirtier, nastier city you could never hope to see. The streets are teeming with people looking for work, including women and children who would do anything for a slice of bread. And the air—" She shuddered. "One can barely breathe. There are parks, but they aren't for you. They are for people with money and privilege. You are better living here, where your children have clear complexions and clearer eyes. Why, I once saw a child no more than a babe sucking on a gin bottle."

That description widened more than a few eyes. Mothers gathered their children closer.

"We are at a moment in history when leg-

ends are made," Constance declared in a ring-
ing voice. She noticed Fiona had come to stand
a bit away from the group. *Good. She needed to
hear this.* "If you give up now, what is left to
you?" she asked them. "Nothing. Not even
your self-respect. You are here for a reason.
Your men can't fight without you. I come from
a country where a woman knows how to load
a gun. If there are Indians at the door, we all
fight. And that is what you have here—Indians
at the door. You can either throw your apron
over your head and hide, or stand alongside
your men and fight."

She let her words soak in, hoping she was
persuasive enough. Taking the leadership role
was new to her. Always before, she'd answered
to her sisters. Few people had ever listened to
her.

The women looked at each other. There was
a whisper here and there. Constance feared she
hadn't swayed them.

And then Grace asked, "What would we need
to do?"

"We start by cleaning," Constance said. "And
I'd recommend a common cooking fire. A few
women could cook for all, leaving the rest of us
free to see to other matters."

Grace's brow furrowed with concern, and

then she said, "I like the idea of a common cooking fire. I'll organize it. What else needs to be done?"

"The latrine area needs fresh dirt. It's not nice work, but necessary."

Silence met this task.

Heaving a weary sigh, Constance said, "I'll see to it. At home, as the youngest, my sisters always expected me to do it anyway."

Grace turned to the orange-haired woman. "What about you, Sarah Kimball? Are you with us? And how can you help?"

"I will help with the fires. I'll send my sons out to gather kindling for the whole camp. I'm not so interested in the latrines."

Her words were met with a smattering of laughter.

Grace sighed. "Then I shall help with the latrines." She looked to a pale blond woman with a baby in her arms. "Linnea, will you cook? You are the best cook in the clan."

Linnea shifted her baby in her arms before admitting, "Cook what? My family has no meat and very little but oats and barley."

"Why did you not say something?" the woman closest to Linnea asked.

Linnea didn't answer. She didn't have to. They all understood pride.

"Everyone will bring what they have to you," Constance said. "We will all share, and you will cook for the clan." Her words were quickly seconded with offers of food and other aid from everyone.

The tension eased from Linnea's shoulders. "Very well, yes, I will cook."

"I have meat," Grace said, mentioning an item that few of the others had claimed.

The clanswomen turned tight-lipped. No one spoke. Constance realized it was up to her to answer. "Thank you—" she began.

"I don't know that we should include her," Sarah challenged.

Emma Reivers, the wife of the couple Gordon had put in charge of Constance the day before, stood beside her, nodding agreement. Others shifted uncomfortably.

"She's a tart, plain and simple," Sarah said. "Good folks don't associate with her. She gives our daughters bad ideas of how a woman should act. There are many of us who question the Lachlan's judgment in allowing Thomas to keep her."

Constance understood what Sarah was saying. Whenever there were men and women together, this was always an issue. The clanswomen were content to let Grace do what they didn't have the courage to do—such as confront Fiona—but that didn't mean they wanted to break bread with her.

Grace lifted her head in defiance, but a bright spot of color rose on each cheek.

Constance stepped between them. "You don't have time to pick at each other. You are in a dangerous situation. Why else would Gordon want the Sword of the MacKenna? However, Grace is one of you. And I will say, I know how hard it is to survive as a woman alone. I don't know that I would turn to a man for protection, but I won't hold it against any woman who is forced to place herself in those circumstances. *We*"— she used the word deliberately—"can't afford outcasts. We are all we have, until we convince others to join our cause."

Dead quiet met her announcement.

And then Sarah said to Grace, "Bring your meat to Linnea."

That was it. Afterward, three of the women volunteered to help sort the food supply and others came up with ideas about what they could contribute. Constance stood in the middle of the chatter, bemused that her words had actually inspired them.

Grace looked to her. "What of you? You can't be digging in dirt in those clothes."

Constance looked down at the muslin dress that was hopelessly the worse for wear, and felt strangely buoyed by it. She would miss the sailing of the *Novus*, but in its stead she'd found a new adventure. "Do you have something I could borrow?"

For the first time, a hint of a smile came to Grace's lips. "I might."

"Good," Constance said. "Let's set to work."

Within the hour the camp thrived on activity.

Gordon couldn't remember a time when he'd been so frustrated. As he suspected, the men hadn't been drilling while he was gone, and they were listless today, ever since word went out that Malcolm McDowell had deserted. Malcolm had been involved in the Cause long before even he had, and now he was gone, sneaking away like a thief in the night.

The men were losing heart, and Gordon feared that not even the Sword of the MacKenna could raise morale. He'd had to break up three fights today because tempers were short and nerves stretched thin.

The irony wasn't lost on him. These men could be so headstrong when battling among themselves, but act completely cowed by the English. There had to be a way to switch their attitude around.

His only recourse was to work them doubly hard, but tired men didn't fight—

"Do you smell that?" Thomas asked, interrupting Gordon's thoughts.

"What?" Gordon asked, just before he caught a whiff of freshly baked bread.

"It's been a long time since I've smelled anything that good," Robbie said.

"And there's meat cooking too," Thomas agreed. "Smells like heaven. I wonder whose fire it is?"

At that moment, Anna and Madge, Willie MacKenna's daughters, came around the bend in the road from the camp carrying a bucket filled with cold, clear water to drink. The men were surprised. The women had never done this before. Usually the men had to fetch their own.

"Is that bread we smell?" Robbie asked.

"Aye," Anna answered. "Supper is almost ready and we've come to invite you to join us."

"Us?" Robbie wondered.

"Yes, all the women have joined together to cook one meal for everyone this night," Anna answered. "And a fine meal it is. Roast hares and bread and those turnips Father brought last week."

Thomas didn't wait for an order but started walking the quarter mile back to camp. The others quickly followed on his heels, Gordon among them.

The smell in the air was uncommonly delicious. He couldn't remember when he'd had a meal that wasn't some stew boiled to blandness.

They were met at the edge of the camp by two of the wives, Jane MacKenna and Rosie Dumbarton, who informed them there would be no eating until they had washed. The men did as ordered, some albeit grudgingly. Those were the ones who merely dipped their hands in water, while others willingly sought out the mush of soap.

Walking up to the camp from the loch, Gordon found many of the tents and makeshift dwellings relocated. And the livestock had all been headed to the far side of the camp.

Everyone, including Mad Maggie, was gathered around three huge fires that had been situated together in the middle of the camp. Black kettles bubbled with supper. Meat was being turned on a spit by several lads, while loaves of bread cooled on some wooden planks.

For a second Gordon was overwhelmed with thankfulness at seeing, finally, a show of organization. This was wise. It was as it should be.

However, his pleasure turned sour when he caught sight of Constance testing the contents of one pot with a wooden spoon. She had changed into a serviceable brown dress, an apron tied around her waist. After announcing the stew good, she happily spouted orders that his clansmen hurried to obey with far more enthusiasm than they had shown for anything he'd said in weeks—and an unreasonable anger settled upon his shoulders.

Twelve

Silence fell upon the camp as Gordon made his way toward the campfire, although those close to the food continued to help themselves.

Only Constance seemed unaware of his approach. She was too busy taking Peter Mac-Kenna and Jamie Allen, two eleven-year-old lads, to task. The boys were constant trouble-makers. The other women, including their mothers, had given up disciplining them, often expecting Gordon to see to the chore.

But not Constance.

"I told you exactly where I wanted those ashes, and you'll not eat until you put them there," she said.

"But that means we'll have to scoop them *all* up," Jamie answered.

"Yes, you will," Constance replied without sympathy. "You should have put them in the bucket I told you to use in the beginning. Then, you'd be eating by now."

Jamie opened his mouth to protest, then caught sight of Gordon. Angry defiance evaporated from his face and he bowed his head as contrite as a choirboy. "We'll do it."

Shocked by Jamie's easy agreement, Peter glanced up and saw Gordon, too. His head lowered. "We will, miss."

"Thank you," Constance said with great satisfaction. "And hurry. There might not be any supper left if you dally."

Both boys groaned at the unfairness, but Gordon nodded for them to go on and they knew they didn't have a choice. They went scurrying off.

"There," Constance said to Emma Reivers, who stood with her hands wrapped in her apron, a worried eye on Gordon. "That went well. See? I told you all those two needed was a strict talking to and they'd behave." Pleased, she turned—and came face-to-face with Gordon. Or actually, face-to-chest.

He stood with his hands on his hips, expecting her to react. He anticipated some sort of her usual rebelliousness.

What he hadn't expected was a radiant smile.

For a second he lost all sense of place and purpose. It was as if the sun had come out from behind the clouds.

Her eyes shone with excitement. "What do you think of the improvements, Gordon? I believe we've made an excellent day of it. Wait until I tell you what we are going to be doing tomorrow. But first, let's be certain our new system of serving everyone works." She didn't pause for his response, but took advantage of his astonishment and organized the meal.

All he could do, all he *had* to do, was stand back and watch.

Her spirits were indefatigable. She herded, cajoled, and ordered everyone to do her bidding. If any of them, especially the women, thought it strange they were taking orders from their captive, they gave no indication of it.

The women had been a thorn in his side even well before the defeat of Nathraichean. Their inability to work together had created untold friction among the men.

Now, it was as if everyone was the best of friends. Even the children were happier and better behaved. Gordon gave up counting the number of times in the space of half an hour when he heard the words, "Constance, what do you think . . . ? Constance, should we . . . ?"

He was witnessing nothing short of a miracle, and he wasn't a man who believed in miracles. His guard went up.

Constance approached, carrying two plates of food. She'd twisted her braid into a knot at the nape of her neck and recently bathed. He could smell the soap and a crisp, clean fragrance that was all her own.

She held out the plates to him. He didn't move. Instead, he asked, "What game do you play, lass?"

She didn't pretend to misunderstand his question. "You are the one who brought me here."

"But for a purpose. You're the captive, Constance."

"I want to join your cause."

Gordon could have roared his frustration . . . except he didn't know where he'd direct it. Was he more angry that his clansman, and Constance, didn't take her position as hostage seriously? Or that she seemed better able to lead than even himself? That she understood this type of life and what had to be done?

Or was he angry because seeing her this way

brought out a longing in his soul the likes of which he'd never felt before? The yearning for a helpmate, a companion . . . a wife.

He tempered his tone. "You aren't one of us, lass. The day will come when you *will* leave."

A line of concern formed between her brows. She glanced down at the plates. The food smelled delicious. "For right now, I am here," she replied seriously. "And I've found that 'right now' is really the only time that matters. Here," she said, again offering both plates. "You need to go find your sister."

Alarmed, he asked, "Why, is something the matter?"

"You know there is."

He did. He didn't evade Constance's unspoken concern. "We're not close," he explained. "She isn't happy here."

"You are all she has," Constance said, refusing to accept the excuse. "If you don't help her, who will?"

"She blames me for all that has happened. She doesn't want to listen to a word I say." Life had changed for both of them, and if Fiona didn't accept those changes, how could he force her?

He'd used this excuse before. Everyone in the clan had accepted it.

Not Constance. She pushed the plates toward him so he had to take them. "Go eat with your sister. No one else can help her. You owe her an hour." She didn't wait for further argument, but turned and went to join the others.

For a second Gordon stood with the plates in his hands, feeling awkward.

He'd been dismissed. Nor did he have any idea where Fiona was; and even if he could find her, he preferred avoiding her stony silence.

Constance was new here. She didn't know what she was asking.

Then again, perhaps she did.

And because he wasn't a coward, because Constance had left him no choice, he went in search of Fiona . . . if for no other reason than to prove to Constance he was right.

In truth, he did know how to find Fiona. At the edge of the camp he gave a low whistle and listened a moment. In seconds he heard Tad's bark. Gordon knew that Fiona had befriended the beast. Keeping that friendship between his sister and the dog was usually his reason for leaving Tad in camp during the day.

Tad barked again, and Gordon followed the sound. He found Fiona and the dog at a place the clan called the Cliffs. It was an outcropping of rock overlooking the loch. The children liked jumping into the water here when the weather was warmer. Fiona had her arms around Tad's neck, hiding from him behind some bushes.

He stopped, a plate in each hand.

The days were shorter now and the dusky light gave them both some protection—and yet, he could tell she'd been crying. She'd cried all the time when she first joined the clan. He had hoped she would grow better.

"I brought supper—" he started.

"I'm not hungry."

Fiona rose as if embarrassed to be caught hiding and gazed across the loch at some point only she could see. Tad settled down with a happy sigh. He had his two favorite people in the world here, and his tail wagged in anticipation that one of those plates was for him.

Annoyance rose in Gordon's throat like bile. "How am I expected to talk to someone who refuses to grant me even the most common courtesies?" he asked, speaking his frustration aloud. "I'm your brother, Fiona. We are the only family either of us has left."

Fiona didn't move an eyelash. "You don't need to talk to me at all."

Usually, this was where he stomped off. This time, because he knew Constance would be waiting, he stayed. "That's what we *have* been doing, Fee. Not talking. Has it made anything better?"

"*Nothing* will make anything better!" Fiona snapped, her eyes angry and hard. "This isn't where I want to be. I once had *everything*. It's all gone, Gordon. Because of *you*, it's all gone."

He'd heard this accusation before. "Not everything is gone, Fee. We still have ourselves. We have our family name."

"Our family name is linked to a rebellion that is doomed to failure," she informed him without hesitation. "The doors that were once open to us are closed. Worse, we have no money. Oh, wait, there is the price on your head. What is the bounty now, Gordon? Fifty pounds?"

"About that," he answered tightly.

"Fifty pounds wouldn't have paid for one of my dresses when father was alive."

"I tried to see you safe," he insisted. "The money I gave Sir Dougal should have covered a closet full of dresses and a dowry fit for a princess. I gave you all that I had, Fee."

"Except what you needed to plan your 'war,'" she answered.

"I'm not the one who stole the money, Fiona. I believed Laird McKenna was a good man."

Her gaze, full of recriminations, slid away from his. No matter what, he knew she would blame him, and perhaps she should. He stood, holding two plates of cold food, a pitiful offering to replace what she'd lost.

Constance was right. He and Fiona had avoided this conversation for too long. He knew what was wrong. He knew he had to press. He set the plates of food down on one of the rocks.

"I'm sorry, Fee." The words hurt to say. "I failed you. 'Twas not my intention."

Tension lined her face. She stood at the edge of the Cliffs, looking as if the wind playing with her hair and skirts could blow her away like a milkweed. He remembered when he would come home from school on holiday and she'd be waiting, a chubby toddler expecting him to give her piggyback rides and taking her for walks to the stables to feed her pony . . . just the two of them. And then he'd gone on and she, too, had grown up and found other pursuits, until here they were—strangers.

"I didn't believe you were in danger or that the English would go so far," he admitted quietly. "I thought you were safe. Sir Dougal—"

The shell around Fiona broke. She whirled on him. "Tad has more courage and honesty than Sir Dougal. That man *handed* me over to the English. Gave them the money, anything to save his own family from harm."

"I'll make it up to you, Fee. I'll do what I must. I just don't want you this way any longer."

"What way is that, Gordon?" she asked as if she didn't know.

"You are punishing yourself . . . and it's not your fault. It never was."

"I know it wasn't. *It was yours*. You should have taken care of me." She came stomping toward him with every intention of pushing past, or running away, or any of her usual tricks.

Only this time Gordon wouldn't let her. He stepped into her path. She pulled up short, her eyes widening not in surprise but in fear.

Gordon hated the fear. Fiona pivoted, ready to flee. He caught her arm. "Please, don't run. Not any longer."

"Let me go," she said, her voice coming from deep within her. It was the voice of her anger, her loss, *his* betrayal.

"I can't," he said. "I won't. Fiona, what the soldiers did was wrong, but you can't let them beat you."

Her body stiffened in alarm. "You don't know anything—"

"I know they raped you."

She pulled back, her eyes wild. "How did *you* find out?"

"I knew, Fee," he admitted, ready to face all. "They made certain I would know."

For a second she seemed paralyzed, and then she started to crumple as if overcome with shame. Gordon caught her in his arms before she fell.

"I'm not fit for anything any longer," she whispered desperately. "I was to marry, to have a Season in London, a home and a place in society . . ."

"They were wrong, Fee, not you. You were the innocent. I would never have left if I'd thought such a heinous crime would be committed."

For a second he thought he'd reached her, but then she pulled back. "Well, it doesn't matter, does it?" she said, her voice tight with hostility. "Because you did leave, Gordon. You went off to *play* at war. *I* had to live it."

She was right. She had paid a terrible price.

"If I could go back, Fee—"

"Don't say it." She met his eye. "You wouldn't have done one thing differently. I'm just another reason for all of this. You've set your course and *you see no other way.*"

He opened his mouth, ready to apologize again, then stopped. "You are correct, Fee. There is no other way. I didn't ask to lead a rebellion, but someone has to stand for justice.

Honor is more important to me than life itself. Without it, the actions we go through day-to-day mean little. But I didn't shatter your childhood dreams. Perhaps if you had been born five years earlier or five years later, you could have gone to London, married a rich man, and ruled the world. But it would be a very narrow world, Fiona, and a *selfish* one. Trust me, someplace else there would be a Scottish lass being abused by a band of English buggers and no one would give a care. But you'd have your shoes, and your dresses, and your silver."

She flinched at his words as if he had physically struck her.

He took a step back. "We are different, you and I. I don't know how. We have the same sire, but you want to follow the English, while I can't rest as long as there are soldiers in this country with the power to murder, to rape, to steal, and *no one say nay*."

Gordon spread his hands, offering no solutions. "And as for you, this is where we are. I can't erase the past. I hate them for what they did to you. I do love you, Fee. But I can't change what is. The price would be my honor, and you are right—I can't give it up."

He dropped his hands, his heart heavy. "I'm sorry," he whispered, and turned to leave.

He had not taken more than a few steps when he heard her whisper his name. He turned, uncertain.

She stood, so alone, and as defenseless as a sparrow.

They were all each other had. Whether he was right or wrong, he knew he couldn't allow her pain, her anger, to stand between them any longer.

"Fee, come to me," he pleaded. He took a step toward her, and that was all it took. She flew into his arms, sobs racking her body.

"God, Fee, I would that no harm had ever come to you. But you can't let them beat you. You can't let them rob you of your spirit."

She cried so hard, it took her a moment to catch her breath. "I don't know what to do," she said into his shoulder, wet with her tears. "I have no future. I'm ruined. There's no one who will want me."

"Yes, there is," he said quickly. "There is going to be a wonderful man for you. He's going to be noble and love you more than life itself."

She pulled back to look up at him. "And what do I have to offer him?"

"Your heart, Fee."

Fiona shook her head. "I was scared, Gordon, so frightened—"

215

"If I could find the man who did this to you, I'd have his head on a pike," he vowed.

"I don't know who it was. It was dark and the next morning—" She broke down again.

Gordon held her tight, letting her release all the sorrow, all the tension, all the regrets of the past months. "We shall see this through, Fee," he promised. "Together, as a family. I will make it right."

She pushed away to look up at him. "Do you know what I've been thinking this day?"

He shook his head.

"I've been thinking how I wish I was like Constance." In answer to his obvious surprise, she said, "She's a bit of a bully."

Gordon had to smile, and was rewarded when his sister smiled with him. She wiped her wet cheek with the heel of her hand. "But she is brave and not afraid to say what she thinks or to defend herself. What if I'd tried to fight when the soldiers took me, Gordon? What if I had escaped?"

"You might have been hurt worse," he said quietly. "We aren't like the English. We don't brutalize our hostages."

"But we could be," she answered. "Those soldiers acted on their own, Gordon. Can you control your men any better? I think not."

He wanted to believe she was wrong, but then thought of Thomas. "I can and I *will*," he promised. He hugged her close. "Fee, don't let this defeat you. If you do, they've won. Perhaps our fortunes have changed. I can't promise you a Season in London or the hopes of marrying some duke. But perhaps it's time for new dreams. It's a new world we live in. We must learn how to adjust."

She contemplated the wisdom of his words. But when she spoke, it was not to say what he had expected. "You are right, Gordon. Our lives have changed, but if I am to accept the new, why can't you? Why are you fighting a battle to keep the *old* ways?"

He released his hold. She'd caught him. He shook his head. "The rebellion is different," he assured her.

"I'm not certain it is," she said softly. "Perhaps we *all* need to learn a new life."

He wanted to argue . . . *couldn't* argue. If she didn't understand—

A slurping noise interrupted their conversation. Both turned to see Tad greedily cleaning off their plates. He was standing on his hind legs, his front paws on the rock. His tail wagged until he noticed them. Then he had the grace to lower his head and slink off.

The moment broke the tension.

Both of them burst into laughter in a way neither had since a much happier time. It felt good. It reinforced this tenuous, still fragile connection between them.

Gordon took the plates. Tad had left a bit of the hare on one of them. "Here," he said, offering it to the dog. Tad appeared chastened but stuck his tongue out anyway to take the last licks.

The stars were out now, and there was little fog yet across the loch. Gordon knew what Constance would think about a dog-licked plate, so he took one and tossed it out over the water as if skipping a rock. Turning to his sister, he said, "Do you want this one?"

Her lips curved into one of her rare smiles. She came over to take the plate and managed to throw it farther than he had, a point of great pride.

He took her arm. "We need to head back."

They'd walked halfway to the camp, Tad trotting behind them, when Fiona slowed her step.

"There is something you should know," she said. "I went to your tent this morning to release Constance. I tried to help her escape."

And Constance hadn't taken advantage of the opportunity? "Why would you do that?"

"I feared for her."

She'd been frightened of him. "Do you still?" It hurt to think Fee could throw him in with that bastard who had hurt her.

Fiona rolled her eyes. "No, she knows how to take care of herself. I watched her today and I was so jealous. It is as if she never lets anything stand in her way, even dumping fresh dirt in a latrine. And you should have seen the women, Gordon. They *wanted* to please her. Not one of them could do enough, and this after weeks of lazy idleness. Constance is strong and full of faith and life. She made me realize what I was doing to myself."

"Did she say this to you?"

"She doesn't have to. It comes from every pore of her body. She truly does feel she can accomplish anything, and right now, Gordon, she has decided to help us. She's joined your rebellion. I think you should know. After what I saw today, tomorrow she'll be drilling your men."

"I don't know whether to be alarmed or thankful." He put his arm around his sister's shoulders, uncertain what Constance's new direction would mean. "At least, for now," he murmured, "I needn't worry about her running away."

"You may be wishing she would," Fiona answered, and they both laughed.

And suddenly he didn't care what Constance had or hadn't done or what new plan was brewing in that head of hers. She'd given him back his sister, the only family he had left, his only living bond with his father.

They'd reached the camp. Fiona turned in the direction of her tent. "Good night, Gordon," she said, almost shyly giving him a sisterly peck on the cheek. "Thank you for coming after me tonight."

"Fee, you're strong. You haven't let them break you."

"Oh they did, Gordon. But I'm thinking differently now. Perhaps you are right. Perhaps it is better to fight." She left for her bed.

Gordon waited until he could see she was safe before walking toward his own tent. It was only then that he wondered where Constance was.

He looked around the camp. Some of his clansmen sat around the cook fires, talking with a camaraderie he'd not heard among them for quite some time. The guard was posted. He could see one of them from where he stood. All was in order and there was a sense of unity, of purpose. It was what had been missing, what had driven him to search out the Sword of the MacKenna—

The silence was broken by a shout from Thomas's tent.

Gordon started in that direction but was almost bowled over by Grace carrying a blanket that appeared to be filled with her belongings. Thomas took a step outside his tent. "I've treated you well enough," he insisted.

"Aye," Grace agreed, sidestepping Gordon, "*for a whore*. But I'm thinking I want to try something different."

"Who is he?" Thomas demanded.

"There is no other man," she said. "I've a mind to sleep by myself for a while."

"And who will take care of you?"

"Not you," she informed him saucily. "Excuse me, Gordon. Do you believe Fiona will take me in?"

"I imagine she would," Gordon said, bemused.

"There," Grace said to Thomas. "I'll be sleeping with Maggie and Fiona, and you can take care of yourself." She flounced away.

Thomas started to yell something after her but then thought differently. "She's a bitch," he practically growled to Gordon. "More trouble than she was worth. She'll be back in a day." He went back into his quarters. Gordon heard him kicking something and then yelping in pain, probably having stubbed his toe.

And then he realized that it didn't matter where Constance was. Her presence had filled every corner of this camp. He also knew as certainly as he knew there was a moon in the sky that she wouldn't leave. Not now. She was in charge.

Suddenly tired, he went to his tent. Tad had escorted Fiona home and now met him there, going into the tent first, his tail wagging. Gordon followed, but pulled up short inside the doorway.

Constance slept on the pallet wrapped in the quilt. She'd left the lamp lit for him, its golden glow highlighting the curves of her body. She had removed the brown dress she was wearing earlier and appeared to wear nothing more than her petticoats now. Her dancing gown with its frivolous lace had been washed and was hanging to dry over the chair. Her hair was in a loose braid and she looked young, innocent, and exhausted. He knew about the latter because there had been many a night when he'd slept as soundly and for the same reason.

In another time and place, he thought, he would have met this woman in a ballroom without any other thought than begging an introduction. They would have flirted, perhaps courted, and life would have been so very, very different.

Or perhaps their paths would have crossed in life without one noticing the other.

He let the leather flap fall. She didn't stir.

Constance had not forgotten him. She'd folded his blanket next to hers, and he didn't know what to make of it—

Her eyes opened.

She smiled up at him sleepily, as relaxed as a wife. "Did you speak to Fiona?"

"Yes."

Her lashes slowly lowered. "I knew you would make it right," she whispered, and Gordon felt an irrational surge of anger. Did she not realize what she did to a man? How seductive she was curled up on his bed?

Or did she think he lacked the primal instincts of any other man? Because that certainly wasn't true . . . especially right now.

Right now he was tired of being alone. He wanted to lie beside a woman . . . even one he was honor bound not to touch.

If Constance had been wise, she would have searched out quarters with one of the families in the clan or shared a tent with single women like Fiona. But she hadn't. She'd placed herself here, on his pallet. If that wasn't an invitation, what was?

And yet, as he took off his boots, as he stretched

out on the pallet, his back to her, Gordon knew he'd not take advantage. He could not afford to give in to human weakness, though he knew he was powerless to leave her.

In front of the door, Tad grinned wolfishly at him.

"Keep your thoughts to yourself," he warned the dog.

Tad lowered his head, closed his eyes—and then opened one just as Constance, with a soft sigh, rolled over and snuggled into Gordon's back.

The warmth of her body felt good. Her curves melded against him.

For a minute he dared not breathe. Tension ripped through him. He'd never been so damn hard. At that moment he'd like nothing better than to roll her on her back and bury himself to the hilt.

But his soul hungered for something more. Something he dared not name.

There was no place in his life for a woman. It was the choice he'd made. If something happened to him, he would not be able to protect her . . . just as he'd failed his sister.

Still, that didn't mean he couldn't curve his body to shelter hers. He was even bold enough to rest his arm over her waist, needing to hold her close, although he knew better than to go further.

Constance didn't move.

"What have you done to us?" he whispered. And then added silently, *to me?*

Her answer was to sleep with the contentment borne of trust . . . something he'd all but forgotten.

Thirteen

"So, are you my brother's mistress now?"

Constance was so shocked by Fiona's question, she almost stumbled over her own feet as she carried a bundle of dry brambles and twigs toward the fire they were preparing.

She, Fiona, and Grace were doing laundry and had set up their enterprise by the edge of the loch so they wouldn't have to carry water very far for the different tasks. Besides the water they were preparing to heat, Grace was filling a tub of cold water for rinsing.

Constance was surprised Fiona had volunteered to help. Although, to be fair, she knew that Fiona had been doing more than her share of the work around camp since that first day. However, aware that Gordon's sister watched her closely, Constance was thankful that Grace had volunteered, too.

It was Grace who answered Fiona's too direct and too personal question. "You'd best be careful what you ask," she advised. "You may not want the answer."

"I *want* the answer," Fiona said. She poured another bucket of water in the kettle prepared for the fire and asked Constance again, "Are you his mistress?"

"No," Constance replied. "And I don't know why you even asked such a question." She avoided Fiona's eyes by pretending to search for the tinder box in her apron pocket.

"Because you've been sleeping in his tent these past two nights when you didn't need to. He no longer has you tied to him or treats you like a prisoner. And now you are preparing to do *his* laundry," Fiona answered.

Constance finally pulled out the tinder box. "I'm doing *laundry*," she emphasized. In fact, she'd made a point of gathering a number of people's wash to avoid just such an impression. "I'm a captive here. Why wouldn't I be doing these things? If I was an Indian captive, I'd work from sunup to sundown."

"Or you could be doing these things for the same reason you follow him with your eyes whenever he's close," Fiona suggested quietly. "Don't think we are blind. We see how you anticipate whatever it is he needs. How you wait for him in the evening."

"I'm usually asleep before he comes into the tent," Constance said in her defense. "And he is usually gone before I wake." It was true she hadn't moved from Gordon's tent. She didn't want to . . . and she didn't want to examine her motives too closely. It just seemed right that she be there.

Constance pulled out flint and cloth from the tinder box and tried to strike a flame. It failed because her hands shook.

Fiona knelt beside her. "I like you," she said. "You've been good for all of us. But I don't want you to forget *why* you are here." She took the tinder box, flint, and cloth from Constance. "My brother's life is dedicated to only one thing, and that is his cause." She struck a spark and caught the cloth on fire. Leaning forward, she held it to the kindling. "I don't believe he's thought this whole endeavor with you through. He didn't anticipate you being the woman you are." The kindling caught fire and she blew on the flame to encourage it.

Constance glanced up at Grace, uncertain if she should trust this new side to Fiona. Grace shrugged. She didn't know, either.

Fiona rose and offered the tinder box back to Constance, who had no choice but to come to her feet to accept it. But Fiona didn't release her hold on the palm-sized tin immediately. Instead, she met Constance's eyes and said, "I'm asking again, for a *third* time, are you my brother's mistress?"

"He has not touched me."

"But you are wishing he would?"

Constance was horrified by the guilty heat that stole up her face. "We've said less than three words to each other."

"See?" Grace said to Fiona. "You have no worries."

Fiona shook her head, her gaze never leaving Constance. "I'd wager you know his scent better than your own. You probably know when he's been to his tent while you aren't there. You can *feel* his presence."

Constance didn't answer, but knew Fiona was right.

"What nonsense are you speaking?" Grace interjected, as if she was the voice of common sense. She placed herself by Constance's side. "We're blessed to have her here," she said. "I, for one, appreciate her."

"I appreciate her, too," Fiona said, surprising Constance. "She's left her mark on all of us, including my brother. You'll pardon me, Grace, if I deem it important to see to his welfare and ask the questions aloud everyone gossips over behind his back." To Constance, she explained, "I know how it is to have all their bickering tongues wagging about you, and how dangerous."

Of course, people would be talking, Constance realized. Of course, they would assume she was Gordon's woman. It added titillation to ordinary lives.

What caught her off guard was that *she'd* ignored the whispers—purposefully. What had mattered was being close to Gordon. The rest was immaterial.

Something of what she felt must have shown on her face. "You're in love with him," Fiona said.

"I *admire* him," Constance quickly corrected.

"And what is that, if not love?" his sister countered.

Grace rolled her eyes. "This is foolish." She threw a twig she'd been holding in her hand on the fire, stepping between them as she did so. "People don't fall in love in a matter of days. And Constance has too much sense for such poetic humdrum."

"What would *you* know about love?" Fiona asked .

"I've been in love before," Grace answered. She looked at the shocked faces that greeted this news. "What? I'm four and twenty. One would expect me to have been in love at least once if not more. Haven't *you* ever been in love?" she asked Fiona.

"Never," Fiona said. "But given that you are a wh—" She broke off, hesitating only a moment before plowing on. "Doesn't your choice of profession betray the whole notion of love?"

"I'm no longer in that 'profession,'" Grace primly informed her. "Sometimes life takes us in directions we don't understand. That we never would have anticipated." She shrugged. "I ended up here . . . and, perhaps, this is where I was meant to be." She looked to Constance. "You've pricked my conscience."

"How could I do that?" Constance asked, startled by Grace's candor.

"By taking your life into your own hands," Grace said. "At first, when I heard they'd caught you attempting to run away to *America*, of all places—you, a woman alone—I thought you strange. Unnatural. A woman doesn't just go off and do what she feels like. But over the past several days, watching you work as hard as any man and stand up for yourself, I've come to realize that each of us makes our own fortune. I was making mine on my back, and not doing very well at it. I have nothing to show from Thomas except relief that I don't have to smell his breath in the morning anymore. I want to be something more than a whore." She directed this last to Fiona.

"I never said you were a whore," Fiona countered, and then added honestly, "Not lately."

"Thank you, Grace," Constance said, deeply touched by the other's appraisal. "I fear my sisters would not admire my independence—"

"Who were you in love with?" Fiona interrupted, her interest not leaving Grace. "Is that why you chose the devil? Unrequited love?"

Grace frowned at the "devil" description. "Do you not fear the same fate?" she countered.

Fiona immediately took a step back. "I don't know that I need or even want marriage." She picked up a bundle of clothing lying nearby and dropped it into the pot of warming water. Taking up a wooden paddle from the ground, she pushed the clothes under the water.

Grace wasn't about to be lenient. "A woman like you—one born, bred, and molded to be a wife—is helpless for anything else," she challenged Fiona.

"I *have* to be worth something more," Fiona answered fiercely. She began stabbing the clothes. "I refuse to believe I'm ruined. *I* did nothing wrong."

Grace's response was to begin clapping her hands.

"What are you doing?" Fiona said irritably.

"Congratulating you," Grace answered. "There may be hope for you yet. You've shown more spirit today than you have all the days before Constance arrived."

Fiona's brows came together. "There are times I don't like you."

"Or I you," Grace countered.

"Then there are other times when I believe we could be friends," Fiona said.

For once, Grace was apparently too stunned to answer.

"In truth, I admire both of you," Fiona continued, turning her attention back to churning the laundry with her paddle, as if not wanting to meet their eyes. "I'm trying to be as brave as you are, and I'm not certain I want to see you go, Constance. My brother may very well be a fool if he releases you." She caught some clothes on her paddle. "Here, are these done?"

Constance recovered from her shock enough to murmur something about letting the water heat more and putting in a bit of soap. Not that she didn't appreciate the change of topic. Fiona was far more perceptive than she had given her credit for, and was right—she was falling in love with Gordon.

No other word could describe the way her heart raced and her mind went on alert anytime there was the possibility of catching even a glimpse of him. Sometimes, when he slept beside her, she'd lie awake watching him breathe, wishing . . .

She reached for the paddle, taking it away from Fiona, needing something to do with her hands.

Grace spoke. "I think Gordon Lachlan is the finest man I've ever met."

Constance agreed . . . although she sensed Grace had a purpose to her comment.

"Wasn't it amazing," Grace continued, "how he alone heard Jamie Allen and Peter McKenna's calls last evening?" The young troublemakers had scaled down the Cliffs and discovered a cave, but found they couldn't climb back up. "No one else, not even their own parents, noticed they were gone."

"My brother has always been that way," Fiona said, adding a hunk of the soap Constance had made to the laundry water. "He sees taking care of everyone as his personal responsibility. As hard as he is on his men, he's harder on himself."

That was one of the things Constance admired about him. Gordon was the sort of man she'd learned to respect in America. Resourceful. Fair-minded. Industrious. She'd not seen many of their sort here.

But she wasn't about to even hint at the depth of her feelings before these women. To do so would make her feel awkward and foolish, especially since nothing could come of it.

Fiona and Grace waited as if they expected her to say something, and Constance had a panicked moment when she feared that perhaps her feelings weren't as hidden as she'd believed. She lived on pride now, trying to hide her deepening feelings for Gordon.

"He will turn me over for the sword," she murmured. She looked at the other women. "I'm here for a purpose. I must remember that."

"Isn't it peculiar," Fiona said, as if not speaking to anyone in particular, "how the strongest people are often the most vulnerable when it comes to love?"

Love.

Fiona had said the word . . . and Constance knew they had guessed her secret.

"Aye, a pity really," Grace answered.

Constance stared at the water she stirred, both humbled and frightened that they knew. She glanced up to see them both watching her. It made her want to run.

She set the paddle aside. "Do you know what has come of Brian and the ransom note?"

Fiona frowned as if disappointed. "Gordon expects Brian back shortly."

"So," Constance said quietly, "my days here are numbered." A knot tightened in her stomach.

"They don't have to be," Grace said. "*You* can change *his* mind."

Constance shot a look at Fiona. Gordon's sister shrugged, as if to say it was out of her hands.

"I don't believe I can—" Constance started.

"Of course you can," Grace said. "You are the bravest woman we know. Lay your soul bare. Let him know."

"And what of the sword?" Constance asked. "What of the Cause?"

Grace and Fiona exchanged glances but said nothing.

It was the silence that bothered Constance the most. "I'm not a fool," she said. "I've heard the rumblings that most of the clan would rather stay here and not fight the English. But you can't," she pointed out. "Gordon is right. Sooner or later the soldiers will come. You either build an army or flee. He'll never run."

Fiona picked up the paddle. She studied the wood a moment before saying, "It's just that I thought you cared for him."

Constance could have shouted that she did, but she also loved him and knew there was only one course for Gordon, one path.

Besides, they were wrong. She wasn't brave. She'd never reveal the depth of her feelings for Gordon. What if he didn't share them? It would crush her.

The subject was dropped. The other two women talked of the weather or gossiped over some bit of camp nonsense as Constance busied herself with the laundry, Fiona and Grace's words heavy on her mind.

A part of her *wanted* to lay her soul bare to Gordon. But her pride wouldn't let her. After all, she was a Cameron. She'd learned the hard way how to hold her head high.

Still, she *was* anxious to see Gordon, and in the back of her mind, Grace's words were taking hold.

Unfortunately, he did not make an appearance at supper. Constance overheard Fiona ask after him. One of the men said that he'd struck off on horseback an hour ago. Not even Thomas knew where he was going or to what purpose.

That left Constance alone. Again.

She wondered if he'd left because he received some word from the duke. The thought spoiled her appetite. Later, she paced the confines of the tent. The hour came when she usually went to bed. Instead, she waited, folding and refolding the clothes. Tad watched her as if he, too, worried.

At last Constance couldn't take it any longer. "Why am I such a fool?" she asked Tad aloud.

The dog wagged his tail, an agreeable grin on his face.

"He can't love me. He doesn't have anything to give, not with this rebellion brewing."

Tad's response was to come over and nudge one hand with his wet nose.

Constance pushed her hair back with her hand, giving the dog's head a pat with the other. "It's not meant to be," she whispered. "It never was. Grace and Fiona don't understand, but I do." She wanted to cry.

Suddenly, the close confines of the tent, of being surrounded by what he owned, threatened to overwhelm her. A Cameron didn't cry over what couldn't be changed.

Grabbing the Lachlan tartan she used as a shawl, Constance went outside. The damp night air felt good against her overheated skin. She skirted the edges of the camp, wanting to be alone. Tad trotted at her heels.

She walked in the opposite direction of the Cliffs, where she might run into someone she knew. She skirted past the stables and took the route along the shoreline.

There was a ring around the moon, a sign that the weather would change. Already clouds were drifting across the sky.

She should have brought the lantern with her, she thought. She'd left it burning in the tent. But she was just as happy to move without being seen. Tall firs lined the shore, giving her a sense of being enveloped by nature and the night. Tad left to chase game, his usual routine.

She had to concentrate on where she was going to keep from tripping—and yet, she could not rid her mind of Gordon.

Constance stopped at the edge of a small cove. So this was what it was like to love someone? They consumed your thoughts, your well-being. Such strong emotion could not be healthy. She'd been happier before he came into her life.

She decided that a swim was what she

needed. She'd grown up on the edges of the Ohio River. Cold water would clear her mind, and the brazenness of the act would exert her independence.

Before common sense could intrude, Constance tore off her clothes to her petticoats. Tossing moccasins and skirts aside, she ran into the loch, moving fast, knowing from experience that the best way to fend off the first icy shock was speed.

It worked. She was three steps in, the water barely up to her knees, and the last thing on her mind was Gordon Lachlan. One quick dip under and she'd be so frozen she wouldn't be able to think of anything but a warm fire.

She turned to rush back to shore when, belatedly, she realized she wasn't alone.

A tall shadow of a man stood some ten feet away from her.

She ducked down in the water for cover, even as he made a sound of surprise. *It was Gordon.*

He had no trouble recognizing her, either. "Constance? What you are doing here?"

"Bathing?" she suggested, panic making her stupid. Or perhaps it was the cold. The shivers set in. Dear mercy, the water tightened her skin to numbness. "What are you doing?"

"I'd gone for a walk. I went to the tent, saw

you were up, and thought to give you a bit more privacy."

No amount of cold water could keep the thought from her mind that what he'd actually meant was that he was wasting time until she was asleep again.

"Come here," he said, sounding worried. "That water is too cold to stand in."

He was right.

"I'll c-come in," she said, even her words starting to shiver. "Y-You g-go."

"I'll not leave you alone. Not naked."

"I n-n-not an n-naked," she answered nervously. "P-Petticoats."

"Fine. Come in." When she still didn't make a move, he picked up her dress. "Here, I'll close my eyes. Trust me."

She decided she would. That was the kind of man he was. Meanwhile, parts of her body were growing numb from the water temperature.

"A-All r-right. C-Close your eyes."

"They are closed."

She stood to run the short distance to shore. At first her legs refused to move. The loch bottom was soft and muddy and she no longer had feeling in her toes. But at the same time, her face was burning hot with embarrassment.

Reaching the bank, she snatched her dress

from his hands and charged into the deeper shadows of the trees. Standing behind one trunk, she quickly threw on her dress, not bothering to dry herself.

She could hear him move. She glanced around the tree, her body still shaking from cold.

He waited, his body a silhouette against the moonlit water. He'd picked up the tartan and was holding it for her.

Constance drew back to her side of the tree and flipped her wet braid over her shoulder. Her beloved moccasins were still on the shore, but she wasn't going to waste time searching for them. Instead, she would sneak away now and reach the tent before he did. She longed to be wrapped up in her quilt and feigning sleep. That way she wouldn't have to explain why she'd run all but naked into the loch.

Unfortunately, Tad chose that moment to return. He showed up at Constance's side, and then hearing Gordon, happily bounded over to him.

She was caught.

Drawing a fortifying breath, she came out behind the tree.

"Here, sit down," Gordon said, not waiting for an answer but gently pushing her to sit on a rock. He threw his tartan over her shoulders and then helped put first one moccasin and then the other on, taking a moment to brush fir needles and dirt from her skin.

His shoulders appeared very broad as he bent before her over the task. He wore his shirt open at the neck. "So," he said. "Why were you in the loch?"

A thousand plausible stories came to her mind. She surprised herself with the truth. "I've missed you. Missed *seeing* you." There was no coldness in her body now. She was too aware of him.

He raised his head to meet her gaze, his eyes silver in the moon's light. "We've seen each other."

"I mean to speak."

His lips lifted into a smile. "Or to argue."

"That, too."

"So because you missed me, you jumped into frigid water?"

What else could she say? Her actions spoke for themselves. Silently, she pleaded with him to understand.

He leaned forward, his brows gathered in concern. "Constance, I understand. I've been taking nightly swims in the loch, too. I was on my way down here for my own dip, and for the same reason. I think of you constantly. It seems

I must swim for miles before I can lay beside you at night, and even then I receive little rest. I can't tell you the hours I watch you sleep. But we shouldn't tempt fate. You have one path and I have another. I'm trying to do what is honorable—"

She cut him off with a kiss. She just leaned forward and pressed her mouth against his.

For a long second she held it, her blood pounding in her ears.

Gordon had gone still. He didn't move . . . and she didn't know how to take it further. She was foolish and awkward and there was no hope for them.

Feeling defeated, Constance broke the kiss—and at that moment, a hairbreadth from the moment she leaned away, his hands came down on her arms. He pulled her back to him, and this time it was *his* mouth that came over hers.

Fourteen

Yes, Constance wanted to cry out. This was what she'd hoped for. Her very soul opened to him.

Gordon stood, bringing her up with him. His arms slid around her waist. She grabbed hold of his shirt, not wanting to give him the opportunity to escape. Not now, not ever.

His kiss was hungry, almost angry. It was as if he had denied himself for too long. He held nothing back, and she was his oh-so-willing accomplice.

"Constance, we shouldn't—" he began, but she shut him up with another kiss.

No more arguments. She knew what she

wanted. From the moment she'd met this man, he had reshaped her life. *He* was what was important. He was what she valued.

The ferocity of his kiss robbed her of breath. Her knees no longer held her weight. She leaned into him for support, and when he swung her up in his arms, she offered no complaint.

Gordon moved back into the sheltering darkness of the pines. He laid her on the soft, thick bed of needles, stretching his long body along hers, his tartan a blanket beneath them. Constance didn't care what he did as long as he kept kissing her.

A wet nose sniffed close to them. Tad. Gordon lifted his head. "Go hunt," he ordered the dog, who quickly obeyed.

Gordon returned to her. "Now where were we?" He found his place by kissing her neck.

His fingers tugged at the lacings of her brown dress, deftly loosening what she had so hastily tightened. The bodice opened.

Gordon's lips followed the line of her jaw, lingering at a sensitive point where her head and neck met. Her body seemed to open to him with a will of its own.

Her breasts were full and tight, as if anxious for his touch. He brushed the nipples with his thumb and she wanted to sing with joy.

This was what she'd yearned for. This man.

She offered resistance when he settled his weight upon her. At some point he'd unfastened his breeches. He was aroused, his body hard and firm. Pride filled her that she did this to him. He wanted *her.*

"You are so beautiful," Gordon whispered against her ear.

"So are you," she answered.

He laughed, the sound joyful and mirroring her own heart. His mouth covered hers. No, it plundered hers. He'd pushed her dress up. Her petticoats were damp but she didn't feel the cold. His heat kept her warm.

Gordon's hand touched her intimately.

Muscles deep within her clenched and Constance gasped at the pleasure. She'd wrapped her arms around him, grabbing fistfuls of his shirt, not ever wanting to let him go.

She was not naive. She understood what happened between a man and a woman. As his hardness pushed its way inside her, she braced for the pain. There was a momentary tightness, as sharp as a needle's prick.

He held himself back, waiting for her to grow accustomed to the size and shape of him.

"I've hurt you," he said, his voice tense, as if it took all his power to hold back. "It becomes better," he promised, and lifting her hips with his hand, began moving inside her.

He was right.

Constance buried her face in his golden hair. His movements were slow at first, as if he was still being careful. She didn't want him to do that. She wanted him to take her, to make her completely his.

She dug her heels in, curving her body to meet his, and Gordon let go. His thrusts went deeper with an increasing pace. His lips were by her ear and he kept repeating her name as if she alone drove him.

Constance vowed she'd never, never, *ever* let him stop. They were going to spend the rest of their days just like this—

Suddenly, she felt as if she'd been struck by a bolt of lightning. For a glorious moment all her senses were centered on him. Her blood sang— and she couldn't move, couldn't think.

Her legs wrapped around his, bringing him as deep as she could, and still it wasn't enough.

He thrust, once, twice, and then completion.

She could feel the life force leaving him. It filled her, a molten bonding of two souls.

Ever so slowly, the tension left his body. His weight felt good on her. She hugged her arms around his neck, cradling his head close. Smiling. She stroked his hair, drinking in the warm masculine scent of him mingled with the fragrance of pine needles.

"That wasn't just a coupling," she whispered. "It was a miracle. A complete and wondrous miracle."

He lifted his head to look down at her. "We will pay for it—" he started.

Constance kissed the end of his nose to keep him quiet. "Whatever the price, it's worth it."

A fierce pride filled his face. "Aye, it's worth it," he agreed, and made love to her again.

Constance's legs could barely hold her by the time he'd finished loving her. So Gordon carried her back to the tent, where Tad waited, his tail wagging.

Gordon helped Constance undress, hanging her wet petticoats on the chair. She put on her dancing gown as a night dress and helped him pull off his boots . . . which led to his breeches . . . and his shirt . . . then her dancing gown— and they were making love again.

It seemed they couldn't leave each other alone. And each experience was better than the last.

Drifting asleep in his arms, their naked bodies entwined, Constance murmured, "I don't know how we can ever stop doing this."

He laughed, the sound throaty and masculine. "I don't want to stop," he assured her, and she sighed her agreement.

But just before she drifted to sleep, she whispered the words of her heart, "I love you."

Was it her imagination, or did he hesitate and then quietly answer, "I love you, too?"

Gordon held the sleeping Constance in his arms. He told himself he should consider the problems this night's work had created.

He couldn't.

It was all too precious to him right now. Tomorrow, he'd worry.

Tonight, he just wanted to hold her, to pretend they had no fears.

What had she said earlier—about their making love being like a miracle?

It was. The anger that had driven him for so long, that had been renewed by Laird MacKenna's betrayal, that led him to kidnap her was evaporating. Slowly, steadily, Constance Cameron was changing him. Her courage, her willingness to make the best of her circumstances, to embrace love, chipped away at the hardness surrounding his heart.

He didn't want to die the author of a rebellion.

He longed for peace in his life, for a wife and children.

That was the reason he'd avoided Constance. He'd feared exactly what had happened this evening.

But now he didn't regret it.

Gordon pressed a kiss against her temple. "I love you," he said again, the words stronger than before. They were dangerous words. They could bind her to him, and he'd not do that. He had to protect her. Love demanded no less.

The next morning, Constance woke to Gordon making love to her. He'd entered her with her sleepy consent and once again took her to the very peak of pleasure.

Lying together afterward, Constance caught the scent of the cook fires. Everyone would be up and about by this hour—and wondering where they were.

She pulled the tartan up to her nose and slid down next to him. Laughing, he drew her back up. "You're afraid to face them," he accused.

Constance nodded. "I don't know what they'll think."

"They believe we already are lovers," Gordon told her.

251

"Not everyone. Fiona asked yesterday." She told him of the conversation she'd had with his sister. "Now I shall have to confess differently."

Gordon kissed her shoulder. "Let's not say anything. It's none of their affair."

For a second she was tempted to ask the questions crowding her mind, then decided against it. What was between them was too new for close examination. It needed time to settle. She believed all would work out as it should. He loved her. She loved him.

Was anything else important?

They dressed quickly. Constance's petticoats had dried. They smelled of the night air and the crystal clear lake.

Before leaving the tent, Constance shyly held back. Gordon reached for her hand. He lifted the flap to allow her to go first.

Most of the clan appeared to be gathered around the cook fires. At the first sight of Constance and Gordon, conversations died down. Heads turned. Necks craned.

Constance had taken great care with her hair, but for the first time she wondered if she looked as lovingly used as she felt. Her body ached in places she'd not known it could ache before. Could they tell by looking at her?

Tad came trotting over to greet them, as eager

to please as always. He'd been at Fiona's side. Gordon scratched the dog's head, taking the opportunity to place his possessive arm around Constance's waist. "Courage," he whispered, and she realized he was as self-conscious as she herself.

And then someone started clapping, and another person joined in, and then another and another until the clearing rang with applause.

Even Fiona clapped. She came to her brother's side, gave him a kiss on the cheek, and offered Constance a hug.

"'Tis a good thing," Emma Reivers said. She wiped her hands on her apron. "'Tis time you handfasted a woman, Gordon. A strong, strapping man like you has needs, and as you can see, we all like Constance. She's a good one. You don't want her to escape. Many a lad here would take her in a wink."

At the word "escape," several people burst out laughing. One who didn't was Thomas. From the corner of her eye, Constance saw him standing apart from the others in much the same way Fiona once had.

He caught her glance and turned away with a scowl.

She didn't care. Right now she didn't think she'd ever been happier. These people included her as one of their own. She felt more a part of them than she'd felt anywhere, including her life in the Ohio Valley.

"Handfast?" she asked Gordon.

"It's the old ways," he explained. "If there is no man of the church available, a couple can pledge their troth in front of the clan and then their hands would be tied together. They had one year to either marry or part."

"And we have the rope for you," Old Rae Reivers shouted, holding up a lead rope like the one Gordon had used to tie them together days ago. Everyone laughed.

But Gordon didn't take it further.

He kept her by his side. He touched her shoulder, her waist, her cheek. He deferred to her in conversation and, when their eyes met, smiled with such affection her heart made a funny skip.

She remembered him whispering "I love you" the night before. She *knew* he'd said it, although in the light of day her practical nature warned her to be cautious, but she wanted to heed it.

And in the end the truth was that she didn't want to be cautious. She was in love. Her heart sang with it. She would not let doubt rob her of this happiness.

If any of the other women noticed that Gordon

had not picked up the idea of handfasting, they were kind enough to not say anything.

Besides, work waited. Gordon went off to drill his men; Constance continued with the challenges of seeing to the needs of so many people.

By the time dinner was over, she was exhausted. Nor did she see Gordon. Her last glimpse of him had been almost an hour earlier. She'd caught sight of him with Jamie, Peter, and some of the other children.

Doubts teased Constance as she walked back to the tent. Perhaps nothing had changed between her and Gordon? Perhaps he was reconsidering what had happened last night?

She'd thought he had been as pleased with the clan's approval as she, but what if he hadn't been?

Constance stopped in mid-step. Gordon's tent was no more than ten feet ahead. Tad wasn't waiting, and she didn't know if the dog's absence was a sign that Gordon wasn't there. Was she brave enough to go forward? Because if he wasn't in there, if he wasn't waiting for her, she feared her spirit would shatter.

How much better would it be to turn away? To not test this fragile love she'd just discovered. Certainly the Reivers would take her in, or Fiona.

In the end it was pride that made her enter the tent—and what she discovered inside sent her heart soaring.

Gordon was there, waiting for *her*.

He sat in the chair, leaning forward, resting his arms on his legs. His gaze was on the tent flap, and at her entrance the smile on his face erased all her doubts. She ran to his arms.

Pulling her down in his lap, he asked, "Are you surprised?"

"Yes," she admitted.

"I had my hands full planning this behind your back," he said.

Constance frowned. "Planning what?"

"The bath," he said, as if it were obvious.

She glanced around and only then noticed the washtub full of steaming water.

"I thought it would please you," he said. "You said you liked to bathe. This way, you won't be jumping in the loch for your bath."

Constance was so touched by his thoughtfulness, she could barely speak. "I didn't take a dip last night to bathe," she answered.

His teeth flashed in a heart-rending smile. "I believe we are both tired of ever stepping foot in frigid water again."

She laughed and heartily agreed by kissing him.

He picked up a bar of soap. "There isn't

enough room for us to take a bath together. What do you say that you use the tub first and I'll do the scrubbing?"

It was an excellent idea.

Of course, this "bath" took hours.

Constance hadn't ever thought of laughter in connection with lovemaking, but Gordon taught her differently. He teased her and tickled her and loved her.

Then, when they were both "scrubbed" clean and relaxed, he made love to her on the pallet. Afterward, he pulled his tartan over their satisfied bodies and held her close.

She smiled drowsily. "I never want to leave this tent."

His hold on her tightened.

She opened her eyes. "What is it?" she asked, sensing his tension.

He reached for her hand, lacing his fingers with hers. He kissed her where her thumb met her wrist, his teeth skimming the skin.

She waited, refusing to let him ignore her.

"Don't want to think of the future," he said. "Right now, you give me peace, and that is enough."

Peace. Constance rolled on her side toward him. Placing her hand along his jaw, she asked, "Could there not be another way?"

"Not for me," he answered. "Too much has gone on."

"You could leave Scotland," she suggested.

"You know I can't," he said. "I won't leave them the way MacKenna did."

Of course not. And yet, she couldn't help but say wistfully, "I wish we could take everyone here to the Ohio Valley. A man can be what he is there. He makes his own rules."

"It would still be running away," Gordon answered.

He nuzzled her neck. He was hard and ready, again. She shook her head. "Gordon, there must be a way."

His gaze met hers. He reached out and ran a finger over her lower lip. "I won't desert them, Constance."

"Would you desert *me*, then?"

His hand fell away.

She reached for it, placing his palm over her heart. "I had no right to ask."

"You had every right, lass," he whispered. "But I'm afraid of the answer."

"Love me," she begged.

"Ah, Constance, I do."

She buried her face in his neck, breathing in the scent of him, never wanting to let him go.

He pulled her up to sit on top of him—and Constance pushed her fears away.

Tomorrow would take care of itself. Right now her only desire, her only purpose, was to love this man.

Tad's barking woke them.

Then they heard Thomas outside the tent, "Gordon, wake up. Brian has returned."

Constance rubbed the sleep out of her eyes. They couldn't have been sleeping more than a few hours.

Gordon had come immediately awake and was already dressing. "Stay here," he ordered, pressing a kiss to her forehead.

She wasn't about to do any such thing, not when the messenger who held her fate in his hands had returned. She scrambled into her clothes, yanked on her moccasins, and, throwing the tartan over her shoulders, went outside.

The sun was just rising. Someone had built up the cooking fires. The men were gathered there. Constance went over and had to work her way to the center of the group. Thomas held a lantern to provide more light while Gordon leaned over an exhausted Brian. As she drew closer, she saw that Brian's shirt was covered with blood.

Fifteen

The bleeding was coming from the side of Brian's head. Constance was almost afraid to move closer. "I'll fetch bandages," she said.

"Fiona and Grace have already gone for them," Gordon said, recognizing her presence although he didn't look at her.

"I've bad news, Gordon," Brian said, his voice frighteningly quiet. "The Duke of Colster and his men have been tracking me. They caught up with me just an hour ago."

"Did Colster do this to you?" Gordon asked. "Did they cut your ear?"

"One of them did, the one tracking me. He had long black hair and wore a metal collar around his neck. I saw him at Colster's house in London several days ago. He jumped out of the woods at me, said he had followed me the whole way. He called Constance his sister by marriage."

"Alex?" Constance said, surprised.

Everyone turned to look at her. She crossed her arms, sensing that her position in the camp had changed. "Alex Haddon is married to my sister Miranda. He's half Shawnee. His father was an English officer. He owns sailing ships. He and Miranda left London months ago on a trading voyage. They must have returned."

"Would he have done such a heathen thing as to cut Brian's ear?" Sarah Kimball asked. She and most of the other women had come to join them. Their expressions were angry and worried. Several held their children close.

"Slicing the ear would be a Shawnee warning," Constance said. "He would do it to create fear and make you wonder what could happen next. And, yes, Alex is a good tracker. He could follow Brian for days without him being aware of it."

"I delivered your letter, Gordon," Brian said. "I did as you ordered. I didn't wait for an answer but handed it to the servant and left immediately. I never saw a sign of anyone following me." He nodded toward the paper Gordon now held. "He told me my ear was only a small part of what we'd have to pay if she'd been harmed."

"Is he bringing an army?" Thomas demanded. Fiona and Grace pushed their way back through the crowd with the bandages. They knelt beside Brian, who was sitting, and began tending his wound.

Constance couldn't prevent herself from saying, "I've seen ears like this. He'll heal. The bleeding is bad but he'll be fine."

Fiona nodded, her eyes wide. Her hands trembled as she cleaned away the blood.

Again Constance could feel the shift of opinion moving away from her.

"I don't know how many men he has," Brian answered Thomas. "There was only him."

"The duke is not bringing an army," Gordon said. Everyone turned to him. He held up the letter. "This is from Colster. He says for me to meet him on the hallowed ground of the ruins at St. Columcille's. I know the place. It is an hour's ride south of here."

"Does he want you there alone?" Thomas asked. "I don't advise it."

His voice reflecting mild surprise, Gordon said, "He actually encourages me to bring as many as I wish. He says he hopes to see a good number of his clansmen there. He wants to discuss a matter with us."

"*His* clansmen?" Constance asked, puzzled.

"The duke was one of us at one time," Gordon said. "Then Laird MacKenna attempted to destroy him and his brother Lord Phillip. When Colster lived as one of our clansmen, we knew him by the name Tavis the Blacksmith."

Several people nodded.

Gordon held up the letter so all could see its bold, slashing writing. "He's bringing the Sword of the MacKenna."

Constance feared her knees would give out beneath her. If the duke brought the sword, then an exchange must be made. She looked to Gordon, but he would not meet her eyes.

"It could be a trick," Thomas warned.

"I know Tavis," Gordon said. "It is no trick. Nor do I believe he knows about the attack on Brian. It's not his way."

"What is *his* way?" a man in the crowd asked.

"He's a fair man," Gordon said. He sounded preoccupied, and Constance wondered if he thought about her, about what might happen to her . . . to them?

"A fair man?" Thomas challenged. "Look at what has happened to Brian. There is nothing to discuss." He pulled his dirk from its scabbard and waved the knife in the air. "The time has come for us to fight for our homes."

His words were quickly seconded.

Gordon took charge. "We'll be riding in the hour. Thomas, handpick the men. I want at least fifty. The rest of you will be on guard. Protect the women and children." He looked to Fiona. "See that Tad is tied up and doesn't follow."

"Yes, Gordon," she said.

At last Gordon looked at Constance, his expression giving nothing away. "You will be riding with us."

She nodded dumbly, her mind crowded with questions that she dared not ask in front of the others.

"I want to ride with you," Brian said.

Gordon nodded agreement and started in the direction of his tent. Constance fell into step behind him, Tad at her heels. She waited until they were inside to speak.

"Will you turn me over?" She waited his answer, her heart on edge.

He'd opened the tack chest and pulled out a clean shirt. "I don't know."

"What does that mean?" she demanded, a sense of hysteria rising in her throat.

Gordon was to her side in a blink. He took her by the arms, lifting her and pressing a hard, possessive kiss on her lips. There was pain in this kiss . . . and fear.

She responded by putting her arms around his neck. His hold on her loosened as he brought her close. The kiss softened. They opened to each other.

He held her against his chest. "It will work out," he said. "It will be as it should."

Her response was to hug him tighter. She refused to let him go. She didn't want to leave the tent. She didn't know if she could bear to live past this moment.

But they must. They had no choice.

So when Gordon stepped away, she let him go.

He changed, putting on a jacket of dark green that matched his eyes. She resisted the urge to smooth a hand over his shoulders.

As for herself, she put on a dark blue day dress Fiona had loaned her. It had become one of Constance's favorite dresses because it set off to advantage the Lachlan tartan. She'd wear that plaid today, and wear it proudly, no matter what happened.

Gordon placed his low-crowned hat on his head. His gaze skimmed to his tartan, draped over her shoulders. "'Tis a bold statement, lass."

She nodded, not trusting herself to speak.

As if agreeing no words were needed, he lifted the flap, to let her leave first.

Outside, the camp was a hive of activity. Gordon took her arm and started to walk toward the stables when Mad Maggie unfolded herself from beside the next tent where she'd been sitting with her Patty. This was a cleaner, more cared for version of the woman who had attacked Constance that first day, but she could still be as agitated.

"It's happening," Maggie said, her voice rising. "It's the water. It will come."

"Maggie, go find Fiona," Gordon said.

"I can't. I have to warn you," she said directly to Gordon with an intensity that alarmed Constance. "The water will close over you. It will carry you away."

"Hey now," Emma Reivers said, hurrying up. "I've been looking for you, Maggie. I've been wondering where you were. Come along, and bring Patty, too."

"I had to warn Gordon," Maggie said.

"Yes, and you have," Emma soothed. "However, Gordon has work to do now."

"I know. He must fetch the sword."

"Yes," Emma agreed, and taking Maggie by the arms, started to steer her away. She paused in front of Gordon and said in a low voice, "Did you know, we lost a daughter who would have been just about Maggie's age?"

"I didn't know that," Gordon said.

Emma looked at Constance. Tears welled in her eyes. "After she died, my husband and I shut off our hearts. However, since we've had the care of Maggie, she's opened us up a bit. Maggie will never be right in the head, but we were needing someone to look after. Thank you."

She didn't wait for Constance's reply, but hurried off, Maggie reluctantly going with her. "It will be all right, Gordon," Maggie called over her shoulder. "Patty says you will be all right. Just watch the water."

Constance touched Gordon's arm. "Do you believe she has a gift of prophecy?"

Gordon shook his head. "I've known her for years, and she has been talking about water all that time. It's nonsense, Constance. Leave it be."

"I want to believe all will be fine," she said soberly.

"It will be," he answered, taking her arm by the elbow and directing her onward.

Thomas and the men were already saddled and ready to go. Fiona was there, too. She came forward to meet them before they joined the others. She gave Constance a long, hard hug and then said to her brother, "Please, I pray that you haven't been fighting for so long that you've forgotten there is another way to live."

"I haven't forgotten, Fee," Gordon said. "I'm fighting to reclaim it."

Her doubt was clear in her eyes. "Please bring Constance home to us," she begged.

The hardness left Gordon's face. "Yes."

Constance wanted to believe he could.

Someone had saddled Gordon's horse. There was no question but that Constance would ride, once again, with Gordon.

Settling back against his chest, she whispered, "We have come a long way." He squeezed her tight and then nodded for his men to follow him. Tad howled at being left behind, but Fiona had tied a rope around his neck and he had no choice other than to stay.

It was a grim band of warriors that rode down from Ben Dunmore. Thomas rode at Gordon's side, the others in double file behind them.

Constance didn't speak. Instead, she rested her hand on his arm circling her waist, their touch a vital link.

The horses were fresh. They covered ground swiftly. After an hour of riding, they rounded a bend in the road and came upon the abandoned abbey of St. Columcille's.

A party of some twenty men and horses waited for them on a stretch of cleared land beside the ruins. A coach waited to the side, and as the Scots drew closer, a woman opened the door and came out.

Charlotte.

Constance caught her breath at the sight of her sister. Feelings that she thought she'd buried away filled her throat. Yes, Charlotte could be overbearing, but the Cameron sisters loved each other.

Her sister was fashionably dressed in an emerald green and yellow traveling ensemble in the military fashion currently in vogue. A cap of the same emerald sporting cascading yellow feathers sat at an angle on her head.

"That's my sister, Charlotte," Constance whispered to Gordon, who reined his horse to a halt some fifty yards from the English just as another woman climbed down from the coach. She wore a marine blue velvet coat and was hugely pregnant.

"It's Miranda," Constance said, breathing the words. "Gordon, she's with child. No wonder she and Alex returned to England."

Before she realized it or could stop them, tears spilled from her eyes.

"What is it?" Gordon asked. "You never cry."

"I know," Constance agreed, the tears still coming no matter how hard she tried to stop them. She pressed her hand against her cheeks. "I just am overwhelmed to see them. And Miranda is going to have a baby." She smiled through the tears. "That is such a blessing. She and Alex have been through so much."

"What do you want us to do, Gordon?" Thomas's businesslike voice cut in.

"The one in the blue jacket is the one who cut me," Brian said.

The Scots all turned to take the measure of the man. Alex Haddon stood proudly beside Charlotte's husband, Lord Phillip. In tall boots and breeches, he wore his long hair loose, a Shawnee sign to his enemies that he was not afraid of them.

Lord Phillip appeared equally angry. Constance could not like him. He'd tried to destroy her family over Miranda jilting him for Alex . . . and yet, they stood side by side, a unified family.

She had only met the Duke of Colster once, briefly, a few months ago. He'd changed since then. Before, he'd been rough around the edges. He now appeared the very model of an English gentleman, and the similarities between him and his twin Lord Phillip were more pronounced.

They'd all come to fetch her, she realized. Even Miranda, who probably shouldn't be traveling.

What would they think if they knew she'd brought all of this on herself by first planning to run away? And she hadn't even left a note . . . and yet here *they* were for her.

Gordon sensed the change in Constance—and it tore at his heart.

Her sisters stood holding each other as if needing the extra support to stand. Constance should be with them, he thought. They were family.

Colster signaled for one of his men to come forward. The man carried a broadsword in an ornate scabbard, its hilt decorated with bloodred rubies. A ripple of excitement went through the Scots. Colster knew what he was doing. He pulled the Sword of the MacKenna from the scabbard, the sound of metal against metal filling the air. He held the weapon up so the morning's thin light caught the blade, turning it to silver.

Gordon noticed Lord Phillip stiffen and knew he was not in favor of this transfer. Lord Phillip understood, as did Colster, what this sword meant to the Scots.

Colster walked to the halfway point and stuck the sword into the ground.

The time for decision was at hand.

Constance tensed. Gordon wished he knew what she was thinking. He prayed for guidance, for wisdom.

"Wait for me," he ordered his men. He dismounted and began leading Constance on Tempest toward the duke.

As he walked, Constance whispered, "I love you."

Gordon halted, suddenly unable to go on. He stood as if rooted to the ground. Every fiber of his being wanted to turn to her, and yet, too many watched.

The actions he took and decisions he made over the next few minutes would determine her future. And they would seal his fate.

He drew a deep breath, his own eyes burning. He dared not turn to her. If he did, he knew he would break.

Without moving, he confessed, "I love you, too, with a passion and depth that has changed my whole being. I want to do what is right, but I no longer know what that is."

"What does your heart tell you?" Her quiet

voice was like the whisper of his own conscience.

He tightened his hold on the reins. "It wants to be free of this quest for justice. But the best I can hope for is compromise. I can't bring my father back . . . and even if those who lost homes had their possessions returned to them, they are scarred."

"People rebuild," she answered.

"But can they forgive? Is it wrong that I love you so much that I long for a life free of this, that I want a home we build together? What of justice? Am I not called to protect those who can't protect themselves?"

"Sometimes, Gordon, there is no right answer. My father could never even look at a Shawnee without remembering what happened to my mother."

"And what sort of man was he?" Gordon asked, knowing the answer.

"Angry. Sad . . . " She paused. "Lonely. There could never be peace for him, and he didn't care that he had three daughters who loved him."

"I don't want to be that angry man." And yet, it was too late to turn back.

"Then what are we to do?" she whispered.

"What we must," he answered, the words hard to speak.

273

"Please God save us," she said.

Yes, God save them.

Gordon dropped the reins to the ground, a signal for Tempest to stand. He walked up to meet Colster.

"Lachlan," the duke said in greeting.

"Your Grace." Gordon couldn't keep the irony from his voice. If Colster heard it, he gave no reaction. He truly had become ducal.

His expression stony, Colster said, "I've brought the sword, but I have one condition before I agree to give it to you."

Gordon's guard went up. "You are in no position to ask for conditions." *Perhaps he could keep Constance with him.*

"I am," Colster contradicted him. "I wish to talk to your men. They have a right to hear what I have to say." The duke had raised his voice so it carried to all corners of the field.

Shaking his head, Gordon said, "Come now, Tavis. What trick do you play?"

"No trick," Colster answered. "An opportunity to speak in exchange for the sword. My brother doesn't want you to have it. He tells me that handing it over to you could be considered treasonous since we know you will use it against the Crown. I'm asking for a few moments. Nothing more. I have an offer to make, something each of your men will want to know."

"And what is the offer?"

Colster gave him a grim smile. "You'll hear it when I talk to my clansmen."

"You are not a part of us any longer," Gordon said.

The duke's gaze narrowed. "Would you stop me?" he challenged, and began walking toward the Scots. He stopped when he reached Constance's side.

Gordon stood by the sword, almost afraid to leave it. This weapon had become his holy grail, and he knew he must be alert to some sort of trickery.

Thomas and the others had placed their hands on the hilt of their pistols and swords.

Lord Phillip, Alex Haddon, and Colster's men moved to do the same. They didn't appear any more pleased with Colster's actions than Gordon was. Constance's sisters watched with worried silence.

The duke raised his voice, addressing the Scots and saying, "You believe the Sword of the MacKenna will take you to victory. You're wrong. There is no victory in civil war, and that's what you'd be doing. I know a good number of you men. I lived amongst you. I've heard your stories. I can't give back your homes, but I can offer something else. I have land in England. I have enough to deed to each of my clansmen— those who followed Laird MacKenna in his ill-advised rebellion—a parcel. You can use this land to rebuild your lives, to let your children grow healthy and strong."

The duke pointed to the sword in the ground. "There is the Sword of the MacKenna. Those who wish to pledge their allegiance to it may do so. Those who want something more for their children, come to me. My man is waiting at the Stag, an inn in Fort William. Use my name and he'll see to your needs. As for Miss Constance Cameron . . . " He turned to Gordon. "I want her back. You have the sword. I receive the girl. Those were your terms. She's not a part of this."

Gordon was too stunned by Colster's offer to reply immediately. He was offering peace, a gift so generous and rare, it forced Gordon to reevaluate everything he thought he'd wanted.

His father had been a man of peace, and Gordon realized he'd taken that memory and subverted it through his pursuit of rebellion. In a blinding moment of insight, he realized how deeply his love for Constance had changed him.

But before he could speak, Thomas shouted,

"We support the Lachlan. 'Tis not land we want, but justice."

"Justice!" Brian echoed, and the others took up the call, the word louder and stronger each time it was repeated.

Justice. The word he had used over and over to spur them on, Gordon thought.

Colster was not pleased. "They'll think on it," he said to Gordon. "It's a good offer. An honest one. You have your sword, Gordon, and it appears that unless *someone*"—he emphasized the word, letting Gordon know he meant him—"convinces them otherwise, the Highlands will be set on fire."

"If you are so certain of war, why are you giving us the sword?"

"Because I believe *you* will do the right thing," Colster answered. "It has to be laid to rest sooner or later. That sword is an evil thing. Use it for good, Gordon. Create a new legend with it." He walked to Constance. "Are you ready to go, lass?" he asked.

She looked to Gordon, panic in her eyes, and Colster took a step back in surprise. "You've fallen in love." He made an exasperated sound. "Lachlan, have you no sense? Haddon and my brother want to rip your throat out over your kidnapping her. If they think you have touched her—"

"*I touched him,*" Constance said proudly. "I love him. And I don't care who knows."

Colster glanced at the Scots and the English. "Keep your voice down," he warned, "or you will see the three of us murdered." On either side of the field, people strained to see and hear what was happening between the three of them.

Constance's face tightened in defiance but she didn't argue.

The duke looked to Gordon. "And what of you? Are you in love, too?"

"Yes," Gordon answered, the word coming straight from his heart.

Colster swore. He pulled Gordon away so he could speak without Constance overhearing. "And now what?" he asked bitterly. "What do you have to offer her, man? Even if you rein this rebellion in, you are heading for the gallows. The girls at that school for young women came from families all over England. They wrote home about Constance's kidnapping. My brother has enough influence to keep this story out of the papers but it is whispered everywhere. Constance will not find it easy in London. Her sisters are beside themselves with worry over how to protect her. Meanwhile, the government has declared you an outlaw and increased the price on your head a hundred-fold. You are a hunted man, Gordon." He made an exasperated sound. "And you say you love her? How much, then? Do you love her enough to let her go?"

Gordon looked at Constance sitting on Tempest. She was so valuable to him.

She shook her head as if she had an inkling of what he was thinking. "What did the duke say?" she demanded, not caring whether her voice was overheard. "What has he told you?"

And it was then Gordon knew Colster was right.

Because she loved him, Constance would follow him to the end . . . and it would destroy her.

He loved her too much to let her make such a sacrifice.

On the Scots' side of the field, Thomas had urged them to start calling for the sword. They shouted, "MacKenna," a demand for the symbol of not only their clan's pride, but also their heritage. A man didn't walk away from that, not even for love.

Gordon knew his way was clear. There was only one choice he could make.

"Take the girl," he said, and placing his hand on the sword hilt, pulled it from the ground.

The Scots cheered.

Sixteen

Take the girl.

Constance wasn't certain she'd heard Gordon correctly. He couldn't be talking about her.

It wasn't until the duke swept her down from Tempest's back that she realized she hadn't been mistaken.

Gordon gathered Tempest's reins and, without so much as a sideways glance at her, mounted and rode off, holding the Sword of the MacKenna high above his head. The Scots cheered.

Constance wanted to go after them, to grab him and demand an explanation.

Instead, she rounded on the duke, pushing

him away so he was forced to set her on her feet. "What did you say to him?"

Charlotte came running to her side. "Constance, are you all right?" she cried as she threw her arms around Constance's shoulders.

But Constance didn't have time to talk to her sister. She had to stop Gordon before he left her. She pushed away to see the Scots riding away, shouting their battle cry. Gordon was already gone.

He'd left her.

A cold numbness stole through her. She couldn't move. Couldn't think.

"What has he done to you?" Charlotte worried.

"Come." It was Miranda, on her other side. Constance hadn't even realized she'd approached.

But she *wasn't* going to leave. Not yet. She dug in her heels, turning to the duke. *"What did you say to him?"* she demanded.

To his credit, Colster didn't flinch. "I asked him to think of you, of what was best for you."

Constance's first thought was to scream *No, this couldn't be good for me.* "In what sense?" she wondered. "My heart belongs to him." Couldn't he see?

Lord Phillip, who had also joined them,

swore colorfully before starting for his horse. "I'm riding after Lachlan, and when I get my hands on him—"

The duke grabbed him. "No. Phillip, you'll make it worse."

"How could it be worse? You gave him that damn sword."

"Because he is a good man," Colster said. He looked at the small knot of them gathered in the middle of the field. "I believe Lachlan will do what is right. Let the Scots think on my offer. They will see the wisdom of it."

Lord Phillip shook his head. "I hope you're correct, because you have just placed this whole family in jeopardy."

"Phillip," Charlotte warned, placing a loving hand on his arm, a wifely wish for him to keep the peace. He covered her hand with his.

"I want him to be prudent," Lord Phillip said.

"He has been," Charlotte answered.

Lord Phillip shook his head but held his tongue.

"We need to take Constance home," Alex said. He had joined them, to stand by Miranda. "And my wife needs to sit."

Constance looked to her middle sister. "Yes, you must take care of yourself."

"I was too worried about you to stay behind," Miranda said. "Alex has been furious with me for insisting I come."

"You didn't need to," Constance answered. "I wanted to stay with the clan." And yet, she felt the pull here, as well. She crossed her arms, realized she still wore the Lachlan tartan, and hugged it even closer. "I love him. I love him so very much."

"And he cares for you," the duke said. "He left you here for your own protection."

Constance brushed a stray strand of hair back from her face. She saw the worry in her sisters' eyes. She felt odd, as if she didn't belong here. Didn't belong anywhere.

"I've changed," she informed her sisters quietly. "I'll not return to Madame Lavaliere's."

"No," Charlotte agreed, shaking her head. In fact, everyone appeared to have grasped that Constance and Gordon had been lovers. Explanations had not been necessary.

Where would she go now? Constance wondered. Her dream of sailing on the *Novus* seemed a distant memory. And through the sadness came a bolt of pure anger. Gordon hadn't had faith in her. In *them*.

He'd walked off. She never would have. And now, what was left for her save pride?

"I believe it's time we left," she said, self-conscious at how closely everyone watched her, even Alex and the outriders they had brought with them. She didn't wait for help but started toward the coach. A footman helped her inside.

This was a plush coach, the likes of which Constance had never seen before. The exterior was painted a dark green, the Colster coat of arms on the door. The seats were a buttery soft leather trimmed in velvet. There was a pillow and a blanket. She helped herself to them as she settled in the corner of the compartment. A terrible coldness was creeping into her bones.

Miranda and Charlotte climbed in. Charlotte said, "You might want to let Miranda use the pillow. She's in a delicate condition—" when Miranda interrupted.

"Sleep, my dear sister," she said to Constance. "Don't worry about us. Nurse your heart."

Tears burned Constance's eyes as she closed them. Miranda could be counted on to understand. Charlotte was too pragmatic. She always fretted over what they should do next. She did so now with her usual indefatigable energy.

"We shall have to see her married, and quickly," Constance overheard her whisper to Miranda. "Mr. Fryson said that most of the girls knew she had disappeared from the school. Rumors will start. However, if there is a babe from that Scotsman, she's more than ruined."

Miranda hushed her. "There's time to worry about that later. I'm just happy we have her back without bloodshed."

Constance thought of Brian and his poor ear. She could tell Miranda what Alex had done. She was certain it wouldn't surprise her. Alex could be ruthless . . . So could Gordon. Look at what he'd done to her.

In the end, before she escaped into sleep, Constance decided that of the two, Gordon was the more hardened.

"We have the Sword of the MacKenna!" Thomas burst out triumphantly, nodding to the sword Gordon had looped through a piece of leather on his saddle. "I didn't think you would succeed," he said. They were halfway back to camp and Thomas couldn't hide his pleasure.

He grinned at the other men riding with them. "Wait until this news is spread throughout the Highlands," he crowed. "The man with the sword could become King of Scotland. There are those who would pay the price on your head and more for that sword."

Gordon kept his own counsel. Thomas

bragged enough for both of them. Some of the men agreed with him, but a good number more were as silent as Gordon.

Instead, his thoughts were on Constance.

Colster had been right. He had nothing to offer her, nothing save his heart. Or what was left of it now that he'd given her up.

Over the past months, years, he'd forced himself to believe that they could fight the English. He'd nursed every injustice—the clearing of the lands, his father's death, Fiona's rape—using them to keep his belief in the Cause alive.

Gutted by Constance's loss, he faced stark reality. There was no way all the Highlanders together could fight the English. The clans were too weak, although that wasn't the only reason. No, the times had changed. His countrymen had grown more English.

Always before, he'd taken pride in his rebel status. He was not afraid of death . . . or so he'd thought.

Constance had made him want for other things. To yearn for a family, for peace. He could see himself practicing law . . . coming home to a wife and child. These were visions his anger had barred him from seeing before.

But was it too late to have those things?

"What is eating at your mind, Gordon?"

Thomas asked, trotting alongside him. He didn't wait for an answer but said, "If it's the woman, forget her. There are plenty enough women in the world. And more than a few anxious to climb into your bed."

"It's not like that, Thomas."

"She hasn't turned you soft, has she?"

Guilt pricked Gordon's conscience. "I chose the sword, didn't I?"

Thomas hummed his doubts. "What were you and Colster discussing when you had your heads together back there? You appeared close as mates."

"He didn't want to give me the sword," Gordon said, fobbing the question off.

The giant frowned. "There is something wrong here. She's changed you."

Gordon made a half laugh, but he didn't deny it. "Does it matter?"

Thomas's gaze narrowed. "You wouldn't be thinking of turning on us, would you now?" he suggested.

The charge shocked Gordon. "You know better." Had he not just proved himself? But then an errant thought caught him off guard. Why would Thomas leap to such a conclusion? Gordon knew enough about men that they rarely accused someone of thoughts they hadn't had.

"What an odd idea, Thomas."

A dull red flush crept up Thomas's neck. "What do you mean?"

"I would not doubt you," Gordon said with a shrug.

"'Twas not loyalty I was questioning," Thomas averred. He snorted his disgust. "And you've spoiled my good mood. I'm *proud* we have the sword." His tone implied Gordon wasn't.

Gordon could feel the men around them look at him askance. "Go to the devil, Thomas," he answered, and kicked Tempest into a gallop, using speed and the wind in his face to clear his head of regret.

Immediately, everyone else followed his pace, and it was practically a mad run until horses and riders were exhausted.

Thomas didn't make any more jibes at Gordon, and they managed to reach camp in some sort of harmony with each other.

Those who had stayed behind were gathered to greet the men as they rode in. Gordon immediately noticed Fiona and Grace standing together. They both searched the party with their eyes, and he knew they were hoping to see Constance.

His sister's gaze met his. He saw her disappointment. Grace burst into tears when she realized the truth. When Grace went running off, Fiona went after her.

Not even Tad greeted him, but lay with his head down.

Gordon dismounted. The sword weighed heavy at his side, especially with the added disapproval of his clan. He headed to the stables, the better to let everyone adjust to the idea of Constance's absence and have their say among each other.

He had no doubt that they would discuss Colster's offer. He'd just finished turning Tempest out when a group of the older men approached him. Old Rae spoke for them. "We hear Tavis has offered land."

"Aye, he has," Gordon said carefully.

"Where is it?"

Gordon shrugged. "I imagine in England. His father sold any Scottish land years ago." That was a well-known fact about the Maddox holdings. "But best beware. He's not Tavis any longer. You'd have to call him 'Your Grace.'"

Rae considered this a moment. "I could. He was a good man."

"A good blacksmith, too," another said, referring to the profession Tavis had before he became a duke. Heads nodded agreement.

Rae said, "It's a good offer?"

Gordon wouldn't lie. "A parcel of land and a roof over your head. I know no more than that, but certainly it is more than you have now."

"I've never run from a fight in my life," Old Reivers said, curling his hands into fists. "I'm not a coward."

"No one says you are," Gordon answered.

The older man's eyes were grave as he said, "Then there will be a good number of us leaving. Emma and I will take in Mad Maggie. We've become accustomed to her wild ways."

Gordon struggled with the right answer. He told himself it was all right. It was fighting men he needed.

Robbie came running up to Gordon's side before he could speak. His step slowed as he saw the older men. "You'd best come to camp," he said in a low voice to Gordon. "There is a good number of our clan leaving. They want to take Tavis's offer. Thomas says you need to come talk to them."

Gordon picked up the Sword of the Mac-Kenna and went marching into camp to see the truth of Robbie's words.

Everything appeared as it usually did this time of day. Most were gathered around the cook fires, although no one would meet his eye.

For a second Gordon stood transfixed. This was the way the camp had been before Constance. Resentment, selfishness, a lack of confidence and belief in their own dignity as a people. His captive had rallied his clansmen better than any sword ever could.

The realization hit like a blow from the Almighty.

Gordon looked down at the sword in his hand . . . and wondered what he had done.

The sword had no power. It was their bond as a clan that had kept them going, that made them stand together. Yes, there would be hotheads drawn to his leadership because of the sword, but did he really want an army of Thomases?

"I want you to listen to me," he shouted, calling his clan together. He hopped up on a chopping block, balancing himself on the log so all could see him. "Come closer," he ordered.

They came, their faces solemn.

"You've heard about the Duke of Colster's offer. I'll not lie to you, it's a good one. He's in a position to help, and he will." He held up the sword so the afternoon light caught rubies on the hilt. "This is cold metal. Nothing more. With it, we've been successful in battle, but that is because *we* have heart, not this sword. If you wish to leave, you have my blessing. Those of you who wish to fight, I'm here." He spread his arms to show he had no tricks. "I have no choice," he admitted. "'Tis my head the price is on. Not yours."

Fiona, with Grace by her side, had come to stand at the edge of the crowd. There had been a time when Fiona would never have lowered herself to associate with the likes of Grace. Nor would Grace, with her resentments, have given a minute of time to Fiona. That, too, Constance had helped.

He should never have let her go.

"So there you have it," he said. "An opportunity. Wise men take opportunities."

"I have a question," Willie MacKenna asked, but before he could speak, a sentry came running.

"English troops," he shouted. *"They are almost upon us."*

As if giving truth to his words, there came the crashing sounds of men attacking the camp. A party of some twenty armed redcoats came charging out of the forest.

"Run," Gordon ordered his people as he pulled the Sword of the MacKenna from its scabbard, ready to protect his clan.

But instead of scattering, they closed ranks around him. His clansmen picked up whatever was close at hand to defend themselves. Tad was barking. Some of the women shepherded the children to the safety of the trees, while others joined their men, picking up buckets and cooking utensils and using them as weapons.

And above all the confusion, standing out and away, separated from everyone else, Gordon saw Thomas. The giant waved to the English, pointing in Gordon's direction. "There he is. There's Gordon Lachlan, just as I promised you."

Thomas had betrayed them. His earlier notion, Gordon realized, hadn't been a flight of fancy, but a sense of the truth.

The officer turned, the sunlight bouncing off his metal helmet. For a moment his eyes met those of Gordon, who recognized him as his rival for Constance's attention that night at Madame Lavaliere's.

The man pulled out a pistol and took aim. He would have fired except that, with a vicious snarl, Tad attacked his shooting arm. The wolfhound sank teeth into the man's sleeve. The officer screamed, dropping the pistol, at the same time that Grace grabbed Gordon's arm, saying, "Come, you must escape."

"Where's Fiona?"

"Fighting."

There was a sharp yelp of pain. Gordon looked to see Tad fall away. One of the soldiers had stabbed him with a bayonet. The wounded dog struggled to his feet. Gordon took a step toward him and then sensed what must be done. "It's me they want. They'll leave after I make them follow me."

"Gordon—" she started, but he didn't stay to hear protests.

"See to Tad," he ordered, moving in the direction of the horses.

Thomas saw him and shouted an alarm. *"He's going to escape."* The English were too involved to heed him. The clan outnumbered the soldiers by over five to one when women armed with cooking forks were counted. The soldiers were literally battling for their lives.

Seeing as much, Thomas, holding his pistol, started after Gordon. When they were apart from the others, Gordon turned, waiting until the traitor was close enough.

"Why?" he demanded of this man who had claimed to support the Cause.

"For the bounty," Thomas said. "And because you interfered with my woman. Grace was mine. Someone had to pay for my losing her. You knew I left the clan after Grace walked out on me. Or didn't you? Well, it stands to reason you wouldn't notice. From the moment Miss Constance Cameron came into the camp, she's all you could think about."

Thomas nodded back toward the fighting. "I ran into those officers. They were the ones who had been at Madame Lavaliere's that night. They'd been looking for us, especially when they heard how high the bounty had grown on your head. As king's men, any reward they receive would have to be shared with their superiors. So we struck a deal. There's a share for each of us for turning you in. I told them to wait for the sword. There are men willing to pay a fortune for it. MacKenna down in Italy is one of them. I left a prearranged sign for them when we rode down the mountain. 'Tis one of the reasons I had to make certain we returned in good time. The best news is, the bounty will be earned whether you are alive or dead." He raised the pistol and took aim at Gordon's chest.

Gordon felt his temper snap. He swung the Sword of the MacKenna around his head as Thomas cocked the pistol. The huge broadsword made a graceful arc. Its heft felt good in his hands as he released the weapon and sent it sailing. The sharp blade hit Thomas full in the chest, running him through just as he fired.

The shot went wide.

For a second the giant was cognizant enough to look down at the sword sticking through him. "I'd not thought you would do that."

"I'd not thought you would betray your clan." Gordon walked over and pulled the sword from the man's body.

Thomas fell to his knees. "I'd not thought you would do this," he repeated, and fell forward.

Gordon turned and shouted to the soldiers. "Here, I'm over here!" He waved the Sword of the MacKenna at them.

They were receiving the worst of the battle and appeared almost relieved when Gordon gave them a reason to chase after him. They came running.

To give his clansmen a chance to escape, Gordon put distance between himself and them, bypassing the horses and running toward the Cliffs' rocky, flat table over the cold water. Swimming was his best chance of escape . . . that is, if he didn't break his neck in the fall.

Raising the Sword of the MacKenna over his head, he dove over the edge. His last thought as he hit the water was of Constance, and he cursed the sword that had cost him so much.

Seventeen

London

"Constance, may I come in?" Miranda asked from the other side of the bedroom door.

In response, Constance turned over in her bed, pulling her pillow over her head and pretending she didn't hear her sister.

She'd been in London over a week and had yet to leave this room. But if someone had asked what color the drapes or walls were, she wouldn't have been able to tell them.

For almost a fortnight she'd laid awake on her pillow, unable to sleep. Nor had she been hungry for food and drink. Her stomach couldn't seem to keep anything down, especially in the morning.

She knew her sisters worried. Both Charlotte and Miranda had petitioned her relentlessly to eat and drink more. Miranda was always kindly encouraging, while Charlotte's temper often found the best of her. She would plead, cajole, and then order.

Except, ordering didn't work with Constance any longer.

The sister they had known had changed. She blamed them for playing a hand in turning Gordon away from her. Every part of her being wanted to reject the memory of him leaving. She couldn't escape that terrible moment. It sucked her dry, stole her will to live, and destroyed the courage that had once been so much a part of her.

Even the duke's wife, Francesca, had joined their entreaties.

None of them understood. They thought she would recover. Recover into what? The life they chose for her? That was what she'd attempted to escape from in the beginning.

Miranda knocked once more on the door and then did not wait for an invitation to enter. They never did. Not even the maids, of which there were an overabundance. After the simplicity of life with the clan, the duke's London mansion came across as overly lavish. Constance missed the fresh Scottish air and going to bed tired and happy after a good day's work.

She stared at the far wall, refusing to acknowledge Miranda in any way . . . then remembered there was something she wanted to say to her sister. It had haunted her through the wee hours of the night before and she could not find peace until she said, "Alex shouldn't have cut Brian's ear."

There was a beat of surprised silence, and then a distinctly *male* voice said, "Brian? Brian McAllister?"

Constance shot bolt upright, moving so fast her head went dizzy. She turned and was shocked to see the Duke of Colster standing by her bed instead of her sister. "Where is Miranda?" She pulled the covers up to her shoulders to modestly hide her night dress.

"She's outside," he said, reaching for an upholstered chair and pulling it up to the bed. Without waiting for an invitation, he sat down. "We'll need to light the lamp soon. It's almost dark."

"I don't want it lit," she informed him. "I like the dark."

"Your sisters are concerned," His Grace said. The burr in his voice reminded her of Gordon's own soft accent. "They've patiently come to see you almost every hour for the past several days. I thought I would try my hand at talking sense into you. But first, what happened to Brian's ear?"

"Alex cut it," Constance said, not trusting him.

The duke made a commiserating sound. "Miranda warned me that Alex can go to what we would consider excess. It's the Shawnee side of him. He told me he'd put the willies into you all, but didn't say what he'd done. But we Scots can be an equally bloodthirsty lot. Brian likes the ladies. He'll have to let his hair grow so they won't notice a piece of him missing."

"It was terrible," she said, sounding even to her own ears a touch self-righteous.

"Kidnapping is terrible, too. Alex was just protecting his own." The duke paused a beat and then said, "I have word of Gordon Lachlan. Are you interested?"

All thoughts of modesty fled Constance's mind. "Yes," she said, leaning forward. "Tell me. What do you know? Has he contacted you?" *Is he looking for me?* She prayed he was. He had to be—and then she realized how terrible she must look. Her hair was unkempt and there had to be deep circles under her eyes.

The duke's gaze dropped to the untouched supper tray on her bedside table. "I will answer you but first you must eat."

"It's bad news," she whispered.

"No, not completely." He took a glass of lemonade off the tray. "Try this."

Constance didn't like being pandered to, but she was also pragmatic. The easiest way to gain the information she wanted was to do as he asked.

She took a sip. The lemonade was sweet and tasted surprisingly good. She drained the glass, realizing at the same time that the walls of the room were painted a soft, dusky rose. The bedding was rose, too. Rose and cream. The carpet was a pale green over dark wood floors.

Handing the glass back to him, she demanded, "What word have you had of Gordon?"

He held up a finger, reminding her of the bargain they'd made. He took the covers off a bowl of rich, dark broth. "Oxtail. Simple but tasty." He offered the bowl to her and picked up a spoon.

"I'm not a child."

"I didn't say you were," he answered, flipping the handle of the spoon around to her.

A part of Constance rebelled at this treatment. However, the lemonade had sparked her senses. She was hungry. She'd done no more than nibble at her meals. Still, he deserved some defiance. She ignored the spoon he offered and drank right from the bowl.

Colster sat back in his chair. "I imagine Lachlan had his hands full with you."

She picked up a napkin off the tray and daintily wiped the corners of her mouth. The broth had been good and she could feel her body respond to nourishment. There was an ache in her legs as if they longed to be stretched.

"Would you like more?" he asked.

"I would like to know about Gordon," she answered.

He offered her a roll from the tray.

Constance stuffed the roll in her mouth, glaring at him the whole time she chewed. After making a point of swallowing, she waved her hand, indicating it was his turn.

The duke didn't disappoint. "I didn't want to leave you. I asked him to think of you," he said. "And he did."

"I knew that was his reason," she said tightly. "He was wrong."

"No, he wasn't," Colster disagreed, shaking his head. "I know a rebel's life sounds romantic, especially to a young woman such as yourself."

"I may be young, but I'm not naive."

"Did I say you were?" He poured some tea into a cup on the tray and offered it to her. This time she didn't bother to argue but took the cup and saucer.

"I know my own mind," she said. "I love him. I will *always* love him . . . no matter what Charlotte or Miranda or the rest of the world thinks."

"Then he *was* a lucky man," the duke answered.

"*Was*? What have you heard?" she demanded, her chest tightening in panic. She put her legs over the edge of the bed and set the cup and saucer on the tray.

"The camp where the clan was staying was attacked."

Her heart stopped. "By whom? Did you betray him—"

"You go too far when you accuse me," he said, cutting her off quickly. "I am a man of my word. And don't think to accuse my brother. He was not pleased with my decision to give up the sword, but we are twins. He is as loyal to me as I am to him."

"Then whom?"

"From the reports I've received from the clansmen who have come to me, it was a man named Thomas Ovens."

"*Thomas*? He was Gordon's right hand."

"Gordon wouldn't be the first man to be betrayed by a friend."

Constance could barely think. A thousand questions bombarded her, but only one was important. "Is Gordon dead?" she forced herself to ask. Breathing was becoming more difficult.

"No one knows," he answered, and she thought she would collapse. No wonder he'd insisted she eat something before delivering this news.

She doubled over, folding her arms against her waist, attempting to hold herself together. "What happened? And what of the others? Please, Your Grace, please tell me the clan is safe."

"From what I understand, most escaped. We are still piecing together the story from those who have come to me for shelter. The belief is that Thomas turned Gordon in for the ransom money. Clansmen say a party of English soldiers attacked, but after Thomas was killed, they ran."

"Who killed him?" she asked, already knowing the answer.

"Gordon."

Constance nodded. "'Tis justice."

The duke didn't argue. He said, "We were surprised we heard of the attack from the Scots first. My brother has excellent military resources and they knew nothing of the event. In fact, we told them about it first. Of course, military channels move slowly and it may take some time before we know the complete story.

Whitehall has ordered a few officers to London for information."

Constance couldn't give a care. "It was the bounty they wanted," she said with certainty. "The one that was raised because Gordon kidnapped me."

"The Scots say he sacrificed himself for them," the duke said. "He led them to a cliff overlooking the loch where the camp was."

"Yes, the Cliffs. They were a popular meeting place."

"And then he jumped into the water. No one saw him surface, nor has anyone received contact from him since the attack."

"But he swims," Constance said, her heart taking hope. "He can swim like a fish."

The duke leaned forward, resting his arm on his knees. "Constance, the water was very cold. Lachlan was fully clothed. He took the sword with him. A man would have to be an incredibly strong swimmer to beat those odds."

"What of his sister?" Fiona would know what happened to her brother.

"No one has seen her since the day of the attack, either. Some of the Scots were killed that day. A handful, but we don't know how many. They scattered into the surrounding forest and not everyone is accounted for. It's possible that *both* Lachlans died. The feeling is that certainly someone in the clan would have heard from one or the other."

The room started to go black and Constance realized she was about to faint.

The duke reached for her, taking her arm and giving it a squeeze. "Be strong," he whispered.

"How?" she asked, her throat closing.

"In the only way women have been strong for centuries. You were a warrior's woman. You must think of what he would want you to do."

"I can think of nothing other than how much this hurts." Her mind was finally realizing the terrible reality of his loss. "If he was alive, he would have come for me," she said. "I know he would have. Your Grace, I don't think I can go on. It's as if my soul is being ripped in two."

The duke kneeled on the floor in front of her. "Constance," he said sternly, forcing her to listen to him, "I know this conversation is not easy. The question would be better coming from your sisters, and yet, they fear upsetting you. They think it best I do so. Then they can console you."

"What question do they want to ask that they fear how I would react?"

"Have you thought that you could be with child? Gordon's child?"

His words were a dousing of cold water. She shook her head. "I couldn't be."

"It's too soon to tell," he replied. "But your sisters say there are signs. There is the possibility, is there not?"

A child? She'd not considered such a thing. But now . . . ?

It could be possible. She'd been so busy at the camp, and then with Gordon, she hadn't thought about the dates. She wasn't even certain what the dates were anymore. Time had ceased to have meaning.

She placed her hand on her belly. "How soon does one know?"

"Miranda said that she felt a change in her attitude almost immediately."

Constance searched herself. "I have no idea." She shook her head. "I've been sad." It felt strange to speak openly to this man, and yet there was a kindness about him. An empathy. "You knew Gordon. You liked him."

"I admired him very much," the duke answered without hesitation. "I want you to think on this—Gordon was the last of his line. That child you could be carrying would be important to him. You have a responsibility to care for that wee one. To see him safe."

Constance forced herself to sit upright. She

combed her fingers through her hair, realizing how she'd let herself go. Nor could she imagine herself with child. She didn't know what she was expected to feel . . . or even if she could trust this concern on the duke's part.

A certainty came over her. A *knowing* as completely mad as one of Maggie's fits. "He's still alive," she said, wanting it to be true.

Still kneeling, Colster shrugged before gently saying, "Even if he is, Constance, he is a wanted man in England. You've been shut away from all of this, but right now his name is in every paper. It was the kidnapping that made him infamous. He's called too much attention to himself to be safe on these shores."

"I don't suppose I'm infamous, too?" There was bitterness in her voice.

"There are those who know," the duke said. "Phillip has done what he can to keep your name out of the papers in any form." When she frowned at Phillip's name, he said, "I know you don't trust him, but Phillip isn't a bad sort. He may have let his temper have the best of him over your sisters, but Charlotte has him completely wrapped around her finger. My brother loves your sister very much. He would not do anything to harm you."

His brow creased with concern as he said,

"However, if Gordon were alive, if he were to come for you, he'd risk hanging. The government would have no choice."

"What about the others? The rest of the clan? Are they not as guilty?"

"Gordon was the instigator. The rebellion at Nathraichean would have ended months ago save for him. If he did escape," he said, meeting Constance's gaze, "he'd best not be in the country."

But he would be alive. And for her, that was enough.

"I only knew him almost two weeks," she murmured. She frowned. "I know what Charlotte is going to say. She'll think me odd for having fallen so completely, so utterly, in love."

His Grace laughed. "She has no room to talk, lass. She's in love with my brother." He turned serious. "I love my wife very much, and yes, it came upon me in less time than a week. One day I was alone, and the next my world was filled with her. Heart and mind."

"Yes," Constance agreed, understanding exactly what he meant. "I didn't even like Gordon when I first met him."

"Ah, well, that's true of everyone who meets Gordon." She knew he was teasing, understood then that he'd known this man well. That's why Gordon had listened when the duke spoke to him in private that fateful day at the ruins.

"I wish I'd returned with him," she whispered.

He sobered immediately. "We're glad you didn't. Who knows what your fate would be . . . or the fate of that bairn you might be carrying? Gordon didn't want anything but the very best for you. I saw the look on his face when he made his choice. He loved you, lass."

Her eyes burned at tears she blinked back. She'd spent enough time on sorrow. Now, she had to be brave. "What should I do?" she asked.

He took her hand. "Something that will be very hard," he answered. "The family has talked, and for all his faults, my brother's suggestions make sense. Even my wife agrees."

"Suggestions of what sort?"

The humor left his eyes. In its place was compassion. He knew she wasn't going to like what he was about to say. She curled the fingers of her free hand in the bed sheets. "Go ahead. Tell me," she said, surprised at how calm her voice sounded.

"They are going to suggest a marriage."

She noticed his use of *they*. "You disagree?"

"No, I agree, even if there is not a child. You don't understand how devastating rumors can be. I hear whispers in my trail wherever I go. It's not easy for my wife, but our love is strong and we have each other."

"Whereas I have no one," she surmised. "And you would want me to marry for what reason? To squelch rumors. It seems a shallow course."

"Marriages have been made for much less. And I would want a man who can protect you and your child."

Constance shook her head. "Who would have me? Who would want another man's child?"

"You are looking at this the wrong way," the duke said. "You should consider that any man would be lucky to have you."

"And the child?"

"Yes, him too. Only, time is of the essence, Constance. The man must think the child is his own. You can never let him know the truth."

His suggestion shocked her. "But that is a lie."

"No, it's survival. It's the only way that child will stand a chance at living a good life."

"What of the child? Is he never to know his true father's name?"

"In time, perhaps. If and when you deem it right."

Constance raised her hands, pressing the heels to her temples as if to shut out such a decision.

The duke stood. "I've said enough." He walked to the door. "Think on it, Constance. It's your decision to make. I'll support you whichever way you choose. However," he said, "I want Lachlan's son raised well. The blood of Scottish aristocracy will flow in his veins."

"But my child won't know if I don't tell him. He'll never know his true father's name. It will be lost to him," she said softly.

"Yes," His Grace agreed. "However, no door will be closed to him. He'll not be a bastard . . . unless that is what you want for him. And someday we may be able to tell him. When that time comes, we'll be certain he knows what a fine, noble man his father was."

He turned the door handle. "I'll have another tray sent up with more broth and perhaps something of more substance. You've been dealt a blow, lass, but if you truly cared for Lachlan, you'll do what you must to see his bairn safe. Think on it. In your heart you will know what to do." He left.

The room suddenly seemed very cold and empty. Constance reached for the tartan she'd kept close at hand and put it around her shoulders. *A baby.* A bairn, she amended.

For a second she was filled with joy.

And then overwhelmed by doubts. A part of her wanted to believe she'd imagined their whole conversation.

He'd suggested an arranged marriage.

She didn't have the courage.

Getting out of bed, Constance walked across the room to the window. It overlooked a garden in the back of the house. She rested her head against cold, hard glass, staring out at the twilight. Gordon couldn't be dead. She was certain she would know if he was.

Or was it that she missed him so much, she wanted to believe he lived? If there was any hope at all, shouldn't she embrace it? Or was she denying cold, hard reality?

Her answer was to break down in tears. Sobs wracked her body until she doubled over.

She didn't try and fight them. She didn't fight tears anymore. Gordon had taught her how to cry.

The door to the bedroom flew open and in seconds both Charlotte and Miranda threw their arms around her.

This time Constance didn't push them away.

This time she held them close, at last, letting them share her grief.

Eighteen

In surprisingly short order, Phillip found someone for Constance to marry.

"He's a *duke*," Charlotte informed Constance,
barely able to suppress her excitement. She'd
just returned from being out with her husband
and hadn't even bothered to remove her hat
and gloves before finding Constance in the
Morning Room. She, Miranda, and Francesca,
the Duchess of Colster, had just finished having
luncheon.

It'd been a week since Justin—which was
how she thought of the duke now—had his talk
with her. Her sisters' suspicions were bearing
weight. She'd still not had her monthly fluxes,

although there was still time . . . or so she kept telling herself. The possibility that she might be carrying Gordon's child had forced her to find the will to live again.

That didn't mean she was eager to marry. She was still in deep mourning.

Charlotte threw herself into the chair next to Constance's and gave her shoulders a happy squeeze. "Is this not wonderful? We came to England with the intention of one of us marrying a duke and now *you* are going to do so."

Constance couldn't muster the same enthusiasm. "Marrying a duke was your dream, not mine."

"Is it too soon to marry?" Francesca wondered.

A frown line formed between Charlotte's brows. "If she'd been a married woman, there would be a mourning period, but right now we are in a bit of a rush."

"I understand that," Francesca said. She looked pointedly at Constance, who pretended not to notice while she put jam on her roll. "But is it too soon for her?"

Constance gave Francesca a small smile, appreciating her concern. "The baby must be protected." That sentiment was all that kept her going right now. "In the wilderness, women often marry quickly just as a matter of survival."

"What's wrong with this duke?" Miranda asked, her skepticism clear as she brought the topic back to the matter at hand.

"Wrong?" Charlotte repeated as if unable to believe they weren't as excited as she was.

"Yes," Miranda said. "He's a *duke*. A duke can marry anyone. No one has to arrange marriages for dukes."

"As a matter of fact," Francesca said, "it's done all the time. Depending on the magnitude of the title and the amount of estate involved, well, they usually are the ones who *must* have arranged marriages. My father wanted to arrange mine. But then," she added with a secret smile, "I married a duke."

"See?" Charlotte said triumphantly. "This is a *good* thing."

"I mean no offense to you, Constance," Miranda said, "or to you, Charlotte, but why would this duke want to marry my sister?"

"The money," Charlotte said, as if it were obvious. She began pulling off her gloves, nodding to a footman for a cup of tea as she made ready to join them. "With the amount our husbands have settled on her, Constance is quite the catch. If we were to present her for a Season, the men would be lined up out the door."

Of course, they weren't going to give her a

Season, Constance thought. There wasn't time to waste. Then again, she didn't want one. She'd *never* wanted one. Toying with the spoon on the tablecloth in front of her, she studied the play of sunlight from the window off the silver. It reminded her of that fateful morning when Gordon had held the Sword of the MacKenna high in the air.

"Who is the duke?" Francesca asked.

"Holburn," Charlotte said. "Do you know—"

Her voice broke off as Francesca dropped the teacup she'd been lifting to her lips. Tea spilled all over the tablecloth—but Francesca ignored it. "She *mustn't* marry Holburn."

"Why not?" Charlotte asked, reaching over to blot up the tea with her napkin. A footman hurried to help, but Francesca dismissed him with a wave of her hand. "That's all we need, Peter. Please, give us a moment alone." She waited until the servant had withdrawn before leaning across the table so she wouldn't have to raise her voice above a whisper. "Dominic Lynsted, the Duke of Holburn, is dissolute. He's a drunkard, a gambler, a duelist—" Words appeared to fail her. She shook her head. "*No* family wants their daughter to marry him, although I'd never heard he was looking for marriage. He's not the sort."

317

Charlotte's brow furrowed in concern. "Phillip wouldn't offer my sister to such a man."

"Yes, I would," her husband said from the doorway. He walked into the room, followed by Justin. "I didn't have a chance to finish the complete story about the offer before my loving wife hurried to tell you all."

Phillip sat at the table. Justin stood to his right. He didn't appear pleased, but let his twin say his piece.

"Holburn's mother came to me with the offer. Said she'd heard I'd made a discreet inquiry. Francesca is right. Holburn is the worst sort of being. He drinks to excess, is blazing through the family fortunes with his gambling, and is known for all the worst vices. His uncles fear he shall ruin the family, but any attempts to rein him in have failed. The man is nine and twenty and as wild as any callow youth."

"And I should marry him because . . . " Constance wondered.

"Because his mother wants an heir and won't raise a question," Phillip answered. "Considering the number of duels Holburn has fought over other men's wives, it appears sooner or later he will be shot. The man is notorious. He can't keep his pants on. He's had amazing luck to date but someday it will run out. If he dies without an heir, his mother will be given an allowance and, knowing Holburn's uncles, a very strict one at best."

"I've met Daisy Lynsted, the dowager duchess of Holburn," Francesca said. "She's a silly, indulgent woman with a streak of avarice. The gossips have speculated for some time now which one of them, Holburn or his mother, will ruin the family financially."

Phillip turned to Constance before saying quietly, "Francesca's description is an apt one. She won't be the most pleasant of relatives. However, she claims she has convinced Holburn to marry."

"He doesn't sound like a man who could be easily led," Constance said.

"True," Phillip agreed.

"And what will Constance be saddled with?" Miranda asked. "The man sounds terrible."

Phillip shrugged. "Holburn is likable in his way."

"Not to a woman," Francesca countered.

"On the contrary, many women adore him," Phillip answered.

"Not decent ones" was Francesca's terse reply.

"In his defense," Phillip said, "he does show up in the House of Lords from time to time. Usually to avoid his mistresses or to sleep off whatever excesses he's practiced the night before," he conceded to Francesca, "but I've heard him speak on occasion. He has a good head."

Constance wrinkled her nose. She looked to Justin. "What do you think of this offer?" She wished Alex was here, but he was down in the shipyards and wouldn't be home until later.

The duke shifted his weight. "It's difficult to say. I don't know the man. The best you can hope for is to be a young widow."

"But a titled one," Phillip reminded her. "That title comes with great privilege."

"The first being protection for your child," Charlotte said.

Constance nodded. In the distance she could hear the servants moving about, making preparations for dinner and their own lives.

Her sisters had their own lives, too. They loved their husbands and were well loved in return. She longed for what they had—

No, that wasn't true. *She wanted Gordon back.* She could not imagine herself with any other man.

"I don't feel right," she murmured, "passing Gordon's child off on another."

Miranda gave her hand a sympathetic squeeze. Even Phillip appeared understanding.

"It's done more often than you can imagine," he said.

"Then what difference does it make whom I marry?" Constance answered, trying to be brave. "Maybe as a duchess, London won't frighten me so much."

"Frighten you?" Charlotte asked, as if unable to comprehend such an idea.

"Yes, frighten," Constance said. "It's full of rules and manners and intrigue. There's more gossip here than in the valley. But also, the city itself is confusing. It's too loud, too ugly, too smelly."

"It's not like home, is it?" Miranda agreed.

"No," Constance agreed softly.

Tears welled in Charlotte's eyes. "I'm sorry," she whispered. "It's my fault we are all here. I pushed us into it. I truly thought it best."

Alarmed, Constance moved to put her arms around her oldest sister. "You never cry," she said. "You are always the strong one for us. Please, I'm not sorry we came. I was meant to meet Gordon. How could I have done that in the valley?"

"Right now, I'm not too pleased with him," Charlotte confessed. "He's left you with a terrible dilemma."

"No," Constance quickly answered. "I want

this baby. And I want him to grow up with every advantage. He'll need it. Perhaps someday he will take up the Cause and succeed for his father."

And she would have a name for her child. She'd not let Gordon's son be called a bastard.

"I'm not averse to meeting Holburn," she said quietly.

Charlotte let out an audible sigh of relief. Miranda covered Constance's hand with her own. "Are you certain?" she asked. "Please, we'll all stand beside you, whatever you wish."

"You are my little sister," Charlotte said. "We've always been there for each other." She took Constance's other hand. For a moment, with Miranda on her right and Charlotte on her left, Constance could place herself back on that fateful night when the three of them had hidden from the Shawnee. She'd been no more than three, with a sister on each side, holding her hand, asking that she trust them.

She must trust them now.

"When do I meet His Grace?" she asked Phillip.

"Tomorrow night," he answered. "His mother suggested she arrange for him to be present at Lady Viner's ball. We'll have the introductions then. After that, a very short courtship and a speedy marriage arranged by special license."

"Are we to tell everyone it was love at first sight?" Constance asked.

"They won't believe you love Holburn," Francesca predicted.

Phillip sat back in his chair. "Come now," he scoffed. "Be fair. Holburn is a handsome man. He's set many hearts on fire."

"Only the hearts of women who admire rakes," Francesca retorted.

"Which is actually a good portion of the female population," Phillip pointed out.

"I don't care," Constance said, coming to a decision. "If this is what must be done, so be it." With those words, she excused herself and, rising from the table, left the room.

She surprised herself. She didn't feel happy or sad. Her practical nature had taken over and she refused to wallow in self-pity. That was how one survived the unthinkable.

She spent the rest of the day sitting out in the Garden Room, knitting to keep both her hands and her mind busy.

Alex came to fetch her for dinner.

"You've heard about the offer?" she asked him.

He nodded.

She studied the loops and weaves of her knitting before asking thoughtfully, "Alex, do you have a moment?"

"I do." He sat on the settee beside her.

"There was a madwoman among the Scots," Constance said. "She kept talking about water coming and overtaking Gordon." She ran a light finger over a line of her stitching before saying, "I know the Shawnee believe such people have gifts . . . but she could just be spouting nonsense, couldn't she?"

"She could," Alex said. "However, some people do have visions."

"Yes, but what if she was just a confused poor soul?"

Alex took the knitting from her. "Constance, why do you ask?"

"Because I don't 'feel' anything," she dared to confess. "When the duke first told me about the soldiers attacking Gordon, I *knew* he wasn't dead. *I knew*. But now, I keep trying to sense where he is, if he is alive, if he is dead, and I feel nothing. The bond between us was very strong, Alex. I would know if something happened to him . . . wouldn't I?"

Alex's dark eyes considered her a moment. "Did he love you?"

"Yes."

"Then he would have come for you if he was alive. It's been almost three weeks, Constance. I would let you wait forever, but you know you carry his child."

"I do," she admitted. "Justin and Phillip wouldn't *hide* him from me, would they?"

Alex sat back. "No. They are both honest men."

"I want to believe he is alive, Alex. Even if he doesn't come for me, I want him alive."

"What was this vision the madwoman had?" Alex asked.

"That Gordon was covered in water and that water took him away."

"And you don't believe that is a vision of him drowning?" He didn't wait for an answer but said, "If he is alive, he may not be in England. He could not stay."

Constance drew a deep breath and released it. "That's what I wanted to know," she murmured. "Before I take Holburn's offer, I have to be certain."

"Of course," Alex agreed.

She stood. "I don't feel well. Please ask the others to excuse me." She didn't wait for his response but went up to her room. There, she lay awake a long time, curled into a ball, her arms and legs protecting her belly and the fragile life she carried. Whatever the future held, she would honor Gordon's son.

Constance came down to the Breakfast Room the next morning to find Phillip furious on her behalf. Francesca and Charlotte were with him and equally as concerned.

"Look at the papers," he said. "The dowager duchess of Holburn has all but posted an announcement that you are betrothed to her son." He handed the *Morning Post* to Constance, who read an item in a column that chronicled the routs and balls around Town.

The very wealthy Miss C, youngest of three beauties from America, is soon to make an announcement concerning a certain Duke H. We are expecting to see both parties at Lady V's Roses at Twilight fete this evening.

"Roses at Twilight?" Constance muttered. "It sounds like a play, not a ball."

"Everyone does themes," Francesca answered. "I assure you, the room will be floor-to-ceiling roses if I know Lady Viner. She is as ridiculous in her planning as my stepmother."

Constance handed the paper back to Phillip.

"What does it matter? We are arranging the marriage as it is." She helped herself to the tea.

Phillip set the paper aside. "You haven't met the man," he told Constance. "I am not an ogre. I don't want to bully you into anything. I know you already think me a bit of one already. I'm not your enemy. Not any longer."

Constance turned at the sideboard. "I think I know that." She frowned. "But I don't know if I trust you."

"Trust me. I love your sister very much. I would never harm you. After all, I let my brother take that treasonous sword north."

"You did," Constance agreed. She sat at the table beside him. "And I do appreciate everything you are doing on my behalf."

"Wait until this evening. Once you meet Holburn, you may not be so appreciative."

She laughed . . . but noticed that neither Francesca or Phillip did. Sobered, she sipped a cup of tea, her gaze falling on the newspaper, where her name seemed to jump out at her.

Francesca was right. Lady Viner had filled every room in her house with roses. The air reeked of them, even outside, where Constance stood with Charlotte, Francesca, and their husbands, waiting in the line of guests entering the house.

A gentleman ahead of her began sneezing furiously. Apparently, he had a dislike of roses. He wanted to leave but his wife would hear nothing of it.

Constance felt ill at ease. She heard her name whispered often and knew that behind those fluttering fans women were gossiping.

Miranda couldn't attend because of her delicate condition, and Constance wished she could use the same excuse.

She knew she looked her best. She was wearing a gauzy, pastel blue muslin with a bodice of silver and lace. Her hair had been styled up on her head with pearl pins holding her curls in place. She'd wanted to appear regal and aloof, the way a possible duchess should be.

Inside, Lord and Lady Viner acted overjoyed to greet them. Charlotte whispered in Constance's ear, "We've made her ball. There will be a mention in every paper tomorrow."

Constance nodded. She dared not speak. Her stomach was a tight knot of anxiety. What had seemed relatively simple to agree to yesterday was revealing horrifying consequences. She felt as if every eye in the room was on her.

The duke's mother, the Dowager Duchess of Holburn, practically pounced on them the second they were done with the receiving line.

She seemed unaware of all the speculation. Perhaps when one was a duchess one became accustomed to all the attention. Francesca seemed at peace with it.

The dowager was a petite woman, as wide as she was tall, who wore ostrich feathers in her hair as if to add to her height. It didn't work.

Her fingers were covered with rings, and jewels were in her hair and pinned to her dress. She was a bright, lovely ornament who was very pleased with Constance. "So lovely, so lovely," she kept saying. "Just perfect. I was so afraid you were peddling a giraffe or a gorilla," she informed Phillip.

"A giraffe?" Constance repeated.

"Oh, you know, one of those women who is so unusually tall everyone has to crane their necks to look at them," the duchess said. "And a gorilla is ugly. Ugly, ugly, ugly. Big shoulders. You are a bit tall but not uncomfortably so. Then again, Holburn is huge, so you might suit."

Constance murmured a dubious "Thank you." Her initial reaction to the duchess was that she was more rude than silly.

"Will we have the opportunity to meet your son?" Charlotte asked to fill the uncomfortable silence.

"He will be here this evening," the duchess assured them, smiling brightly, and Constance sensed she didn't have a clue where her son was. In fact, Constance was beginning to wonder if there was any substance at all behind the dowager's bright blue eyes—and then she met Holburn's uncles. They swooped down upon the duchess like hawks after fresh prey.

There were two of them, Lord Brant and Lord Maven, and they dressed like Puritans. Their black was a stark contrast to the duchess's colorful style and to Constance's demure gown as well.

"So," Lord Brant said, drawing out the word in a sonorous tone after the introductions, "I understand we are to wish you happy." He didn't appear happy.

Constance smiled. "Thank you."

"Yes, Holburn is so ecstatic," his mother said. "Absolutely overjoyed. Wait until he sees you this evening and tells you himself."

"I have seen him this evening," Lord Brant said.

This was a surprise to the duchess. "You have?" she asked.

"Yes," Lord Maven agreed. "He's in the card room, his usual place. Did you know he's placed a wager on the books at White's that he *won't* be marrying. *Ever.*"

Now Constance understood all the stares and whispers.

The duchess's hair feathers shook with indignation. "Why is he doing this to me?"

Constance could also feel Phillip's temper start to rise. The heat of his expression should have seared the eyebrows off Lord Maven. Even the usually temperate Justin was taking insult. The twins exchanged a look, another of their silent communications.

However, what made Constance angry was the obvious relish the uncles took in sabotaging the marriage arrangement. For the first time in weeks she felt a surge of her old spirit.

Deciding to take matters into her own hands before there was an explosion of tempers, she said, "Your Grace, perhaps we should go to the card room? If there is a wager on the books, I believe I must at least meet Holburn for it to be valid."

The uncles all but sneered their opinions.

Constance didn't care. Her pride was up. If Holburn was anything like his uncles, she was ready to face public scandal and have her baby alone.

The dowager seized on the opportunity to escape. "Yes, I believe we should." She linked her arm in Constance's.

Phillip, Charlotte, and the others started to follow them, but Constance waved them back. If Holburn was as rude as the uncles, Phillip appeared ready to call him out. She could not let that happen. "This is a moment when I can acquaint myself better with the dowager, if you please?" She sent a silent plea to her sister.

The twins weren't the only siblings who could communicate without words.

And, fortunately, Charlotte understood. With a nod, she directed her husband to see about refreshments.

Once they were alone, the duchess confided, "My husband's brothers are greedy, greedy, *greedy*. And so disapproving. Can you imagine how difficult my life is with those dour-faced bastions of propriety lurking at my door? Don't worry. Holburn doesn't like them one whit. You won't have to deal with them often."

"Why are they so disapproving?" Constance asked.

"Because they worry that Holburn is going to spend all their money," the dowager replied breezily. "They fear if he dies, there will be nothing to inherit. As if Holburn cares about their wishes any more than he does mine. I will warn you, he can seem callous. He doesn't consider how his demise would affect *my* income."

Constance had given up searching for logic in the duchess's thinking. The card room was set up in the parlor. There were four tables with five to eight players at each. Almost everyone in the room was gathered around the table farthest from the door.

"Oh, dear, what is he doing now?" the duchess worried, and shouldered her petite self through the crowd.

Constance followed and had her first look at the man she would marry.

The duke was tall and lean. One would have thought him athletic except for the unnatural pallor of his skin beneath dark hair and the way his hand shook as he reached for a card to turn over. He was a handsome, elegant, dissolute man.

He realized his mother was there almost immediately. He looked up at her, his lids low over lazy eyes. "Mother," he said, deliberately pronouncing each syllable. "Have you come to watch me win money off of Gibbons?"

"Dominic, what are you doing?" his mother asked.

"Flipping a card," he answered easily. "High card wins two thousand pounds. That is Gibbons's jack on the table."

"Dom?" his mother said, but he shushed her.

"'Tis only money, Mother." He flipped his card and then his brows pulled together. "Pity. A king. I'm sorry, Gibbons. I had meant to give you money, not take it."

Gibbons rose from the table. "You'll accept my marker?" he said stiffly. He was a young man, and there was sweat on his forehead, as if the outcome of the cards had mattered a great deal.

"Of course," Holburn said negligently. "Does anyone else wish to play?" In spite of the early hour of the evening, he was obviously well into his cups. Constance's father had been a drinker, and she recognized the signs. It did not endear this man to her.

"Holburn," the duchess said, "there is some-one here you need to meet."

Almost as one, everyone turned to Constance and she could feel her face flame. Well, every-one turned save the duke. He kept his head low, his concentration on the cards his hands shuffled.

"Holburn," his mother chastised while the group gathered around him sent Constance sly, superior smiles.

Constance had seen enough. She turned on her heel and left the room. This man was not worthy of her.

She went out into the ballroom, searching for Charlotte, wanting to go home. If anything, Holburn had made her realize how deeply she missed Gordon—

Her steps came to an abrupt halt when she caught a glimpse of a familiar face coming toward her.

It was Fiona. And she was wearing the muslin and lace dress Constance had been in the night she was kidnapped. The gown had been carefully mended and washed so that only the most critical eye could see signs of wear. Her rich mahogany hair was styled high on her head. She wore no jewelry or adornment other than a fan she carried. She didn't need the fripperies. She appeared absolutely exquisite, a fresh, wholesome beauty in a sea of jaded appetites.

Coming to Constance's side, Fiona flipped open the fan to provide them a moment of private conversation. "I am so fortunate to have caught you alone. Come with me," she whispered before Constance could speak.

"Where are we going?" Constance wondered.

"To Gordon."

Constance couldn't move. "He's alive?" she said, almost afraid to dare to hope.

"*Yes,*" Fiona said, bringing her head close

to Constance's and giving her arm a squeeze. "Except that he *must* leave England as soon as possible. There are people who would have smuggled him out of the country by now, but he won't leave until he sees you again."

"Where is he?"

"First, is this true that you have promised yourself to another? It's all everyone is talking about this evening. They keep mentioning your name with the Duke of Holburn's."

"*No*, it's not true," Constance said. "Most particularly not now. Please, Fiona, take me to Gordon. I have so much to tell him. Or is he here?" she asked, struck by the even more amazing thought that he might be in that very room. She began searching the crowd with her eyes.

"He's not in these rooms," Fiona said.

"Then where is he?"

"There is a park across the road from this house—"

She talked to air. All Constance needed was a direction. Fiona hurried to keep up with her.

They had wound their way through the growing crush of guests and were halfway to the door, when Fiona's hand reached out and stopped Constance. "Don't take another step."

"Why?" Constance asked, alarmed by Fiona's

sudden paleness. It was as if all color had drained from her face and she'd gone as white as the dress she wore.

Fiona flipped open her fan, using it to whisper, "That officer over there . . . " She nodded in the direction by the door. "He's the man who led the attack on our camp."

Constance looked in the direction and was surprised to see Captain Jonathon Ardmore, the officer who had been at Madame Lavaliere's dance. His uniform was all brass and braid, and he sported a sling over one shoulder, the injured hand wrapped in bandages.

He saw Constance, his brows rising in recognition, and began moving toward her.

"Please," Fiona said. "I can't be near that man. His arm is injured because Tad bit him. Our brave dog almost tore his arm off."

She didn't need to say more. Constance turned around, ready to head in the opposite direction, and almost walked right into the Dowager Duchess of Holburn.

Worse, she had her son at her side. "His Grace wishes a formal introduction," the dowager said. "Miss Constance Cameron, this is my son, His Grace, the Duke of Holburn." Her words came out in a rush, as if she feared he'd bolt before she was done.

His sullenness did not endear him to Constance any more than his previous indifference. He bobbed the quickest greeting imaginable.

"What a pleasure to meet you," she shot back. "Now, if you will excuse me—"

Holburn blocked her way. "I would have preferred this one with the darker hair, Mother," the duke continued in a lazy, sensual voice, "over the one you've chosen." He referred to Constance. "I don't like blondes."

Before Constance could gather her wits to answer, Fiona stepped in. "And *I* don't appreciate arrogance," she replied, her refined Scots' accent giving the reprimand punch. "Moreover, if all you desire in your future bride, Your Grace, is hair color, let me inform you that Constance Cameron is not the wife for you. *You* lack the spirit."

"Who are *you*?" Holburn asked, sounding more intrigued than insulted.

"Yes, *who* are you?" his mother echoed, definitely insulted.

"Someone who doesn't have time for *you*," Fiona said, taking Constance's hand and pulling her toward the garden door. Constance glanced back and saw Holburn watching them leave, a speculative look in his eye. He completely ignored the dowager, who was so upset, presumably over Fiona's rudeness, that the feathers in her hair shook with her indignation. He started to follow.

"This way," Constance said, pulling Fiona's hand and ducking through a garden door.

The crowd in the ballroom had spilled out onto a wide terrace. Fiona and Constance navigated their way toward some stairs leading down into the garden. The ground was damp, so none of the other guests wanted to venture this far lest they damage their footwear.

"There must be a gate here someplace," Constance said as they moved deeper into the garden's shadows.

Fiona said, "*That* was the man your sister wanted you to marry?"

"He's a duke. Charlotte has a softness for one of us marrying a duke." But it wasn't going to happen. Not now that she knew Gordon was alive.

"That was my first London party," Fiona murmured.

A wistfulness in her voice caught Constance's attention. "Was it all you thought it would be?" she asked. "I personally have never been impressed."

Fiona shook her head. "Whether it is or isn't no longer matters. It's lost to me."

Constance pulled up short. "What do you mean?"

"I don't belong there any longer, Constance. I'm damaged goods."

"Not through any fault of your own," Constance replied with fierce protectiveness. "Do you hear me? Please, Fiona, reach inside of yourself and be proud of who you are. Let that sustain you instead of some nonsense about being untouched. The man who loves you will not care."

"How little you know of men," Fiona said.

The garden was much larger than Constance had suspected. They were walking in the silver moonlight toward the garden wall. A line of trees and shrubs provided privacy as well as foreboding shadows.

Constance stopped near the wall, protected from the sight of those on the terrace by a sheltering of evergreens. "I know enough to believe that any man worthy of your love will respect you for the person you are."

"If that was the case, courtesans would be wives," Fiona said.

Constance took her by the arms. "Please, Fiona, never give up hope. Never lose faith in love. Life makes no sense without it. And as soon as I find the garden gate, I'm going to your brother and I will never leave him again—"

A shadow against the shrubberies moved. Hands grabbed her shoulders, effectively cutting off anything else she was going say. Before Constance could make a sound, Gordon whirled her around and planted a kiss on her lips.

Nineteen

He was alive.

With a soft, glad sigh, Constance leaned against Gordon, reveling in the solid, very real feeling of him.

This was the man she loved. The only man she could ever be with. What had made her think she could marry another, even to give their child a father?

And he was happy to see her. Just when the kiss should break off, he'd come back for more. If she could have swallowed him whole, she would have. He wore coat and breeches—and this time even a neck cloth. The Sword of the MacKenna was on a belt around his waist. It bumped her hip as he gathered her close and kissed her more deeply. He smelled of the Highlands, the fresh, clean air and the magnificent forests.

At last they became aware of Fiona tapping them on the shoulder.

"Are you mad?" she whispered furiously. "Do you not realize where we are? Gordon, why didn't you stay over in the park?"

He ignored his sister's frantic questions. "I missed you," he said to Constance, a wealth of meaning in every word.

"I love you," she answered.

Gordon brought his head down for another kiss.

Fiona stopped him by placing her hand in the path between his lips and Constance's mouth. "Do you not hear me? We must leave now," she said, enunciating each word. "Ardmore is inside."

"Ardmore? That bastard—" Gordon let go of Constance. Placing his hand on the hilt of the sword, he said, "And what is this about you and another?"

"After that kiss, Gordon, do you truly think I could consider another man?" Constance said, pulling him back to her.

He would have kissed her again, but Fiona tugged on his coat sleeve. "Please, Gordon, don't be foolish. You must leave."

"I'm not going anywhere without Constance."

Constance melted in his arms. "Nor will I let you."

"So there is no duke waiting to marry you?" he asked.

"Even if there was, I'd let him wait," Constance said. "I've loved only one man in my life, Gordon Lachlan, and it's you."

"Please," Fiona begged, "do *not* kiss. We need to leave now."

But what truly helped her case was the sound of scratching close by and a whimper. "Tad," Gordon said. "Grace is holding him but he'll start barking if we don't go to him."

"Grace is here, too?" Constance asked happily.

"Aye, she's become the closest I have to a sister," Fiona answered.

"Which we won't be much longer if someone doesn't help me with this dog," Grace said in a harried, hushed voice from the other side of the wall.

They all laughed. Gordon sobered enough to say, "Are you ready, Constance? Will you leave with me now?"

"Where's the gate?" was her answer.

It was close by, hidden behind some shrubs. Gordon pulled back the branches and lifted the latch, but before he could let the women through, there was a male grunt and a heavy-sounding thud. A man cursed the garden's uneven ground. Constance recognized the voice.

"It's Colster," she warned.

Gordon started to swing open the door but Constance didn't move. She knew they were seen. Their light-colored ball gowns had to stand out in the moonlight.

She was right.

"Constance? Is that you? We've been looking for you everywhere. You disappeared from the ballroom. What are you doing out here?" he asked as he moved closer.

She moved to stand in front of Fiona and Gordon. "Please, Justin, keep your voice down."

"Why—" he started, then stopped as he recognized Gordon, who held the garden gate half open. "So the devil does live."

"'Tis good to see you, too," Gordon replied, his voice guarded.

Tad chose that moment to push his nose through the partially open gate. He sniffed and then shouldered the gate open, breaking free of an exasperated Grace so he could attack Constance with a glad, joyful run. Coming up on his hind legs, he embraced her with so much force, she fell back against Justin. There was a rope around his neck.

Grace followed him, blowing on her palm. "I'm sorry. I couldn't hold him, not once he heard Constance's voice."

"I'm glad to see you, too," Constance told the wolfhound, who had the good manners to come back down on all fours after his initial happiness was registered.

"Glad to see who?" Phillip asked. He was moving toward them, and would momentarily join their growing band beneath the protection of the trees. "Justin, did you find Constance?"

Gordon groaned his frustration while Justin said in a low voice, "I found her. She's here."

Phillip came closer and stopped dead in his tracks when he realized Constance wasn't alone. "Lachlan," he said coolly. "Are you mad?"

Gordon frowned his response.

"This is Fiona Lachlan, Gordon's sister," Constance said to fill the sudden silence. "And this is Grace McEachin."

"Scots," Phillip said, pressing his lips together with distaste. "Have you come to try and take Constance with you?" he demanded, not bothering to lower his voice.

"Yes," Gordon said. He held out his hand and Constance went to him. Tad moved around to nudge her hand and let her know he was there, too.

Phillip shook his head. "We can't let him, Justin."

"Yes, we can," Colster answered. "Do you not see, Phillip? They belong together with the same fierce passion you and Charlotte have."

For a long moment Phillip stood still. "But what of Constance? What life can he give her?"

"The only one I want," Constance said.

"I'm leaving the country," Gordon informed them. "I want her with me."

"Where are you going?" Justin asked.

Gordon's hold around Constance tightened. "Wherever a ship will take me."

"And the sword?" Phillip wondered. "What will happen to it?"

"I won't use it against the English, if that is what you are asking," Gordon said. "Colster's offer to the clan has been a godsend. Most of my clansmen are resettling on his lands. I don't want to disrupt their chance for peace. I'll take the sword with me."

Fiona stepped forward, her exasperation clear. "My brother must leave tonight," she said. "Please, Captain Ardmore is in the ballroom. He was the one who attacked our camp. If he finds Gordon, he'll see him hanged for the reward. But is my brother leaving? No, he insists upon standing here gabbing instead of fleeing to safety the way he should."

"Growing cranky, Fee?" Gordon wondered with that charm only a brother could exude.

She answered with a sound of complete exasperation.

It was Phillip who took charge. "She is right. You can't stay here. Almost every member of the government is inside." Tad had wandered over to give Phillip a sniff. He absently scratched the dog behind the ears as he worked the problem in his mind.

"I was going to leave by the gate," Gordon said.

"And go where?" Phillip countered.

"Portsmouth."

"How?" Phillip asked. "Do you have horses? Or transportation?"

"We'll manage" was Gordon's tight response.

"But you don't already have plans, do you?" Justin asked.

"I'll find a ship," Gordon said, hugging Constance close. "I'll see to both of us."

"It's been hard," Fiona said. "There have been those looking for Gordon to claim the reward. I tried to convince him to leave the country in Scotland, but he had to see Constance."

"Don't be a fool," Phillip said with his customary bluntness. "Accept help. We are two powerful men. Furthermore, Alex Haddon has a fleet of ships. If we work together, we can see you are safe."

"Absolutely," Justin agreed.

Constance couldn't believe her ears. "You would help us?"

"Of course," Phillip said. He shook his head. "I know I seem stiff to you. But I don't act on impulse and I take my responsibilities to my sovereign seriously. However, you are my sister by marriage. I would let no harm come to you or anyone you loved."

Constance crossed to Phillip and hugged him to show her appreciation. "I have been so unfair to you," she said. "I nursed a terrible grudge because of the way you hounded us after Miranda jilted you . . . but I was wrong."

"No, you were right," Phillip said. "I was nursing my pride. I felt it was all I had. However, Charlotte's love has changed me, as I see your love has changed Lachlan. If this is what you want, Constance, then my brother and I will help."

"We'll bring the coach around," Justin said. "No one inside must see you."

"But first we need to gather our wives," Phil-

lip agreed. "Wait here and we shall return."
With that they left.

In what felt like an eternity but was truly no
more than a half hour, the Duke of Colster's
well-equipped coach rolled to a halt before the
back garden gate. Constance, Fiona, Grace, and
Gordon climbed in to squeeze inside with the
two couples already sitting in the cab.

At a soft command from Justin, the coach began
to roll off, Tad running alongside the wheels.

Constance made introductions. Charlotte recognized Fiona's dress as the one she'd chosen
and sent to Constance at Madame Lavaliere's
academy.

"It looks much better on her," Constance assured her all-too-quiet sister.

"And Fiona adores the dress," Grace said.
"Even when the camp was under attack, she
made certain she saved it."

Charlotte didn't say anything but regarded all
of them with suspicion. Constance glanced at
Phillip. He, too, had noticed his wife's silence.

At the ducal mansion, a servant took Tad to
the kitchen for table scraps, while Constance
and the others went in search of Alex and Miranda. They found them in the back sitting
room, enjoying the fire in the hearth.

Alex recognized Gordon immediately. Constance hurriedly told him and Miranda what had happened at the ball.

"And now what?" Miranda asked when she finished.

"Now I'm leaving with him," Constance said.

At last Charlotte spoke. "No. You mustn't."

"Charlotte—" Constance started to protest, but her sister cut her off.

"I can't let you go with him," Charlotte said. "He doesn't have any idea what direction he is going to take. Or what he is going to do when he arrives there. It's too risky. Too dangerous."

"But she loves him," Miranda said. She had been sitting in a comfortable chair but now stood. "I won't stop her, Charlotte. And I will fight you on this issue."

"You would let her do something so foolish?" Charlotte demanded.

In the golden light of the room's many lamps, Miranda's face softened. "Yes . . . because that is what should have been done when I first announced I loved Alex. Instead, because of his Shawnee heritage, Father did everything he could to keep us apart." She rested her hand on her growing belly. "I won't ever come between two people who love each other, over fear of the future."

Charlotte began ticking off on her fingers all

her concerns. "He doesn't know where he is going. He has a price on his head . . . " And looking at Gordon, she asked him directly, "Do you have any means to even support a wife?"

"I have nothing save for the clothes on my back," he said proudly. "And a good education in law."

"He has nothing," Charlotte affirmed, ignoring his education.

"He has me," Constance said. "And *our* baby."

If she'd landed a punch in Gordon's face, she couldn't have surprised him more. He picked her up. "Constance? Truly?"

She nodded. His laughter rang to the room's high ceiling. She placed her hands on either side of his face and kissed him. She had to. Seeing him this joyful over her news was a blessing. Her heart brimmed with love for him.

But then he sobered and set her down. "Your sister is right. You need to stay here. I'll not have any danger come to you."

He would have turned and walked out of the room save for her grabbing his arm at the elbow and turning him around. "You have no right to make that decision," she told him. "This baby and I belong with you. And the baby will thrive. Look at my sisters and me. Our parents had nothing but we survived and we are stronger for it."

"You deserve better," Gordon told her. "Let me go and make a home for us and then I'll send for you."

"Wherever you are is my home," Constance answered, refusing to concede.

Gordon started to shake his head when help came from a surprising corner. "She's right," Charlotte said. The tension had eased from her face. In its place was sad resignation. "I misspoke myself. I worry for my sister . . . but Miranda is right. Constance doesn't remember our mother. I do. She was always singing. She radiated happiness. And Father was a very different man back then. A kind one."

She came over to Constance. "I want you safe. But I know I would follow Phillip anywhere. For a moment I forgot the example of our parents. I've been so focused on wanting the very best for you, I may have overstepped myself. I hope you forgive me," she said. "I raised those objections—"

"Because you are my oldest sister," Constance finished for her. She offered a hand to bring Miranda closer. Taking Charlotte's hand, she said, "The three of us have always formed an unbreakable chain because of our love for each other. It saved our lives that one night. And we've helped each other over the years, especially when Father would be so angry. I'm going with Gordon . . . but that doesn't mean the bond between us can ever be broken. It's just grown stronger because we've included more people to love."

At her words, Miranda and Charlotte turned to their respective husbands, taking their hands. The chain grew as Justin and Francesca, Grace and Fiona, were included.

"I'm going to miss you," Charlotte told Constance. It was a simple, heartfelt statement.

"And I you, but this is what I must do."

Alex spoke. Addressing Gordon, he said, "Where do you *want* to go? I have ships. I will have you out of London on the morning tide."

Gordon looked at Constance a moment before saying, "I want to go to America. I want to see this valley of Constance's. She tells me it is the land of milk and honey."

"And Indians," Charlotte added.

"But we will find peace there," Gordon predicted. "And a future."

With those words, he drew the Sword of the MacKenna from its scabbard. "Here," he said to Justin. "Take it. Protect and keep it from ever being used again in war."

Justin took the sword. "I shall see the matter done." Picking up a letter opener on a the side desk, he began working at the rubies in the sword's hilt. Prying one loose, he handed it to Gordon. "Take this. You've earned it. Let it be the beginning of your stake in America."

"I won't take it," Gordon said. "Give this to my clansmen who now claim you as chieftain."

"Constance has a dowry," Phillip reminded them. "A generous one. Do you other gentlemen wish it to go to Lachlan?"

"Yes," Alex said.

"I have always thought of Gordon as a brother in the clan," Justin responded.

"Then we are agreed," Phillip said, turning to Gordon. "I shall settle the funds in an account for you to draw on when you are ready."

"Thank you," Gordon answered.

Prying out the seven other bloodred stones, Justin said, "And what of the rubies? What shall be done with them?"

Fiona spoke up. "They belong to the clan."

Gordon nodded, and Justin said, "I shall see that the stones go to the others." He held the sword up. "It loses some of its power when they are missing, doesn't it? It becomes nothing more than metal." He walked over to the hearth and stuck the sword's blade in the fire. The smell of heating steel filled the air.

Gordon turned to Constance. "Let me have your left hand, the one that runs to your heart." Taking it, he said, "There will be no time for banns or parsons, but I handfast myself, Gordon Edward Lachlan, to you, Constance Cameron. I pledge my heart and my troth. And as soon as our ship docks, I shall speak these words in a house of God."

"And I pledge my heart to you," Constance said. "You will be the father of my children and I shall be the best of wives."

"Will you love me, Constance? Honor me? Obey?" Gordon asked.

For a second Constance almost said yes . . . but then smiled. "We'll have an ocean voyage over which to discuss the details. But, yes, I shall always love you, and with that love comes honor, my noble man."

"That's enough for me," he said, and kissed her. They took their time about it. When she'd thought she'd lost him, Constance had dreamed of his kisses. She would not deny herself now. It took Phillip clearing his voice to make them reluctantly pull away.

"We're handfasted," Gordon whispered. "Our hearts are joined."

"Yes," Constance agreed, her smile widening. No one and no cause would ever part them again.

Justin pulled the now hot blade from the fire. "Here is the Sword of the MacKenna," he said, his voice somber, respectful. "This sword was once used to encourage me to murder my brother. No longer." He swung the sword and struck it against the stone fireplace. The metal bent.

He turned and offered it to his twin Phillip. "Here's to peace," Phillip said, and brought the bent blade on the stone, crumpling it further. Phillip offered the sword to Gordon.

"Yes, to peace," Gordon agreed. He swung the blade so hard it bent at an angle, rendering it unusable, then said to Alex, "Would you like a turn?"

"I would." Alex held the sword out and said some soft words in Shawnee.

"What is he saying?" Constance asked Miranda, who shook her head.

Alex swung back the sword and brought it back against the stone, smashing the sharp edge of the blade. He faced them with the mangled remains of what had been a warrior's weapon. "This blade will claim no more lives," he said, and threw the sword into the fire.

For a long moment they watched the flames

lick and lay waste to the sword's leather and gold trimmings.

Then Alex said to Gordon and Constance, "We should leave."

"Let me pack a few things," Constance said, her excitement rising as she realized she truly was returning home, and with the man she loved. "It won't take long. I'll take items for Fiona and Grace, too."

She started to turn away but Fiona's voice stopped her. "I'm not leaving England."

The words had the impact of a pistol being fired in the room.

"You must," Gordon said. "You are my sister. I take care of you."

Fiona swallowed. Her eyes were huge. She clasped her hands in front of her as if holding them for courage. "I don't want to leave, Gordon. I won't go."

He studied her a moment and then drew a deep breath. "Then I shall stay here."

Almost everyone in the room disagreed with that idea. Not only was it too dangerous for him, but now, as Phillip pointed out, they were all implicated in the matter.

"There are people searching for that sword," Phillip pointed out. "If you stay here, we are all in danger."

Fiona spoke to her brother. "I have no desire to go to America. This is my home."

"But how will you survive?" he asked.

"We'll take care of her," Charlotte said, a suggestion that was quickly seconded by the others. "*Finally*, I'll be able to give someone a Season. And look at you," she said, taking in Fiona. "Why, if we put you on the marriage mart, we might snare a duke."

Both Gordon and Fiona shook their heads. He said, "I feel I must protect her."

His sister turned to him. "No, you must see to your own safety. You have a wife to take care of, Gordon."

"And a child," Miranda agreed.

"But what of you?" he asked.

"I must find my own way," Fiona said. "All will be well. Don't worry." She stood pale and defenseless, but resolute.

"She'll be safe," Justin assured him. "We will take care of her like one of our own. After all, you and I are still clansmen, of the heart if not by blood."

His words humbled Gordon. "What of you, Grace?" he asked. "Are you coming with us?"

Grace wrinkled her nose before admitting honestly, "I prefer staying here, too."

Gordon crossed to his sister. He took her in

his arms and hugged her, not wanting to let her go. "I shall worry about you every day."

"Don't," Fiona said, tears pooling in her eyes. "We always knew that one day our paths would part. It's the fate of siblings. Besides," she added, "I'm safer here than you will be with the Indians there."

Her honesty made them all laugh, including Alex. "It's not bad," Constance assured her.

"I nursed Brian's ear," Fiona said. "I'll take my chances here."

"We shall take care of her," Charlotte assured Gordon. "Francesca, Miranda, and I will find her a wonderful husband. She'll be the toast of the *ton*."

Constance gave Fiona a hopeful smile, realizing that she was the only one in the room who had noticed how pale she had gone at Charlotte's enthusiasm. Constance moved toward her. "Please, learn to trust again," she whispered.

Fiona's answer was a wan smile.

Gordon, still standing next to his sister, embraced her again. "You will write me."

"Of course," Fiona promised. "And I will have Tad," she said, showing some spirit. "He'll see me safe. He likes me better than he does you anyway."

"So you say," Gordon bantered back, but there was a sadness in his eyes.

Alex took charge. "Hurry and pack," he said to Constance. "There isn't a great deal of time to ready a ship."

In the end, Constance was ready in a ridiculously short amount of time. Within two hours they were dockside, waiting in the coach while Alex talked to one of his captains.

Her sisters and their husbands had all insisted on coming to see them off. Fiona and Grace had stayed behind. Fiona had claimed it would be too hard to watch her brother sail out of her life. Constance understood. Saying good-bye to her sisters was sad, but she was excited about the future. Her path no longer followed Charlotte's and Miranda's. Instead, she belonged with this man standing by her side. It *was* the fate of siblings.

As it turned out, there was a ship owned by another company preparing to leave on the morning tide. It was a sloop being delivered to a buyer in New York harbor. Alex used his influence to gain boarding for Constance and Gordon.

The first streaks of dawn were appearing in the sky as Constance hugged Charlotte and

Miranda one last time. She then put her hand in her husband's and they climbed the gangway.

As the sloop was set loose of its moorings, Gordon stood with his arms around Constance. She waved to her sisters until the ship rounded a bend and they could be seen no more.

For a second a stab of fear paralyzed her . . . but then her husband kissed her ear. Here, with him, was where she belonged.

Leaning back against his chest, she said, "You won't regret leaving. You can't imagine how beautiful the valley is."

"I don't need to imagine it," Gordon said. "Anyplace is beautiful as long as I have you with me. We are going to build a good life together." He swung her in his arms. "Come, wife," he said. "We have a lifetime of loving to start."

And that is exactly what they did. Down below, beneath the deck of a ship, nestled together in a hammock, two became one . . . never to be parted again.

Epilogue

Fiona and Grace were not up when Charlotte and the others returned from seeing Gordon and Constance off.

Charlotte didn't think a thing of it. It was well past dawn by the time she and Phillip turned in. She was weighed down by both fatigue and sadness. She'd spent her life looking out after Constance . . . and now her youngest sister was gone.

Phillip assured her that all would be well. She prayed he was right.

Several hours later a knock on the door woke her. Miranda, her voice frantic, said from the other side, "Charlotte, I believe Fiona is missing. And Grace and that big dog, too."

"Missing?" Charlotte repeated. She reached for a dressing gown, rubbing sleep from her eyes. Phillip was already rising, as concerned as she was.

They opened the door. An anxious Miranda waited.

"What makes you believe she is missing?" Charlotte asked, tying the sash of her dressing gown around her waist.

"Because she isn't here," Miranda said. "Francesca sent a maid up to see if Fiona and Grace needed anything. The maid returned to say their beds haven't been slept in."

"And that huge dog is gone?" Phillip asked.

"Yes," Miranda answered with a touch of impatience.

At that moment Francesca came up the stairs to join them. She held a note in her hand. "Justin found this in the Morning Room where we were last night." She handed the letter to Charlotte.

Please do not be alarmed. I cannot stay with you. I have no desire to marry and too much pride to be a burden. Know that I am safe. I have my friend Grace and Tad. Thank you for all your generosity.

Sincerely,
Fiona Lachlan

364

"Is she mad?" Phillip said. "A young woman alone can't survive in London. She has no idea what sort of scoundrels are out there."

"What possessed her of such a notion anyway?" Charlotte wondered.

"*We* did," Miranda answered. "Last night I heard her whispering to her friend that if we could do what we did as children, they could survive in London. I thought she was expressing worry over entering society and your new goal of finding her a husband. I had no idea she meant to go off on her own."

Charlotte could feel a headache forming. "We must find her. We were fortunate matters worked out for us the way they did. If I'd known then what I know now, we would never have left the Ohio Valley." She held up the letter. "I don't know what has possessed her to reject marriage."

"Perhaps she has something else in mind for her life," Francesca suggested.

"There isn't another option for a woman," Phillip answered. As the three women glared at him, he defended himself. "I'm being honest. A woman alone has very few choices in life."

"We must find her," Charlotte said. "She doesn't understand how dangerous London can be. Does she have any money?"

The others shook their heads. They didn't know. "She didn't take the rubies," Francesca said. "They were left with the note." She opened her hand to show she had them.

Surprised, Charlotte asked, "Not even one of them?"

"No," Francesca said.

A terrible sense of foreboding settled over Charlotte.

"Perhaps she means to return to her clan," Phillip said.

"I hope so," Charlotte said. "London is too dangerous for women alone. Not even we were foolish enough to attempt to survive it without some funds."

The others nodded agreement.

"I'll start a search," Phillip said, and left to join his brother and Alex.

But it came to naught. No one had seen two lovely women, one a redhead, the other with hair the color of a raven's wing, leave the house with a dog roughly the size of a deer.

It was as if the city had swallowed them whole . . .

And now a sneak peek at
A Seduction at Christmas,
Cathy Maxwell's
Avon bestseller
Available now wherever
books are sold

Fiona's Story

Wakefulness came slowly to Dominic Lynsted, Duke of Holburn, as it always did. He hated to open his eyes, dreaded having to drag his way through another day of his miserable, boring life—except this morning was different.

His gut hurt. There were many times it did. Excessive drinking was never good for one's constitution, but with the family he had, it was the only way to survive.

However, this time he felt as if his stomach muscles had been turned inside out. Or perhaps the pain seemed more distinctive because it was his *mind* that was sharper—

Dom was startled to realize *he was sober*. His mind was actually *alert*. He couldn't remember a time since boyhood when he'd been so aware of his senses.

He'd always meant to change his ways. Most people had little idea how much he'd thought about it . . . but in the end, it hadn't been worth the effort.

One thing was certain, being sober was not the heaven his irritatingly pious uncles had mournfully preached to him. He felt like hell. Like his body had been beaten black and blue and trounced on by a herd of goats . . .

Slowly, Dom opened his eyes and swore his surprise, uncertain if he was seeing everything correctly.

This was not his bedroom in Holburn House.

He opened his eyes again. The walls were a drab gray from years of soot. The room was tidy, but nothing could hide the squalor. The air smelled of a hundred different meals being cooked, and from someplace in the building a baby cried . . . while some man gave in to his morning hacking.

Dom was laying on a lumpy mattress on a bed in the middle of the room. Thankfully, the sheets were clean. He started to rise—and couldn't.

"What the bloody . . . ?" Each hand and each ankle was tied to a corner of the bed. He was literally spread out with just a sheet that came up to his waist.

He was also stark naked, a not uncommon state for Dom when he was in bed.

Whatever it was, he must have had way too good a time. No wonder he felt like hell.

And although he didn't mind playing games, he'd just as soon this one be over.

The curtain over the room's only doorway was pulled back. A young woman about his age entered. Her face was pale, her brown eyes dark with apprehension. Hers was a trim figure with big breasts and a tiny waist, exactly the way he liked his women. Her clothing was that of a shop girl, sensible and plain—and yet, she carried herself with the air of a queen.

She seemed familiar to him. The rich, cinnamon color of her hair that she wore tied back at the nape of her neck stirred a memory with him. They'd met before . . . although he'd never had her. He'd remember something like that, regardless of how much brandy flowed through his system.

Even tied to the bed, even feeling battered and bruised, his body sprang to life.

She noticed. A becoming blush stole up her cheeks. Her chin rose. "Your Grace, it's not what you think."

"And what do I think?" he wondered, unapologetic for his reaction. After all, he was a man, and she was the woman who had tied him to her bed. He was as certain of that as he was of his own name.

"What you shouldn't be!" she snapped. "You are my prisoner, Your Grace—"

"And happy to be so," he assured her. Perhaps being sober wasn't as bad as he had anticipated. Still, a little something would loosen them both up. "Why don't you fetch me a pint, lovely, and we'll start to know each other better."

Her nose scrunched in horror in the most adorable way. "Is that all you think about?"

"Pretty much," he assured her.

She stepped to the end of the bed, her eyes alive with indignation. "I'll not be serving anything stronger than cider to you, Your Grace. You are not the most pleasant person when you are in your cups, " she said, taking charge. "As for your circumstances, well, I had to do that for my own protection."

"Your protection?"

"You don't remember threatening to kill me?"

Dom frowned. A suspicious memory tugged at the edge of his mind, one in which he was not pleased with her. He could feel it now, and realized she'd had a hand at the pain in his gut.

"I saved your life," she said, as if realizing he was beginning to remember.

He looked at his bound right hand before lifting a skeptical eyebrow. "Oh, this must be a good story."

"It is, but I don't sense you are in the best of moods."

"Why should I be?" he replied, irritated. "I'm sober. I never take any news well when I'm sober."

"Then that is unfortunate," she said, "because I've decided to hold you for ransom."

"What?"

She nodded as if confirming the matter to herself. "I'm going to hold you for a fortune. And there will be no beer, no wine, no brandy, until you've paid."

"That's outrageous. You can't do that," he said, angered at such restrictions and enraged that she was dictating to him. No one told Dominic Lynsted what he could and couldn't do. Not even his mother dared order him.

"I can and I have," said this Scottish nobody. "I'll draw up a note for you to sign for your banker. Once that's done . . . I'll bring you a dram."

"Oh, I'll want more than a dram," he informed her. *"I'll want revenge."*

"That was exactly your attitude last night, Your Grace," she said, her eyes bright with concern in her pale face. "And why I had to tie you up. But have no fear. When the moment comes to release, I'll be long gone."

"We shall see, won't we?" Dom said.

Her response was to push aside the curtain, leaving him alone.

"Don't think you can turn your back on me." No one had never done that. At least not since his father's death. He always had his way.

Grace waited on the other side of the curtain, holding Tad back with a hand on his collar, her eyes huge with apprehension. "Fiona, what have you done?" she asked in a frantic whisper.

"The only thing I could do," Fiona said, her insides shaking at her own audacity. "We must have money."

"Couldn't we just ask him for some?" Grace said. "Explain about the men who tried to kill him and you?"

"Do you think he'd believe it? Or believe I wasn't involved, especially after I poured that poison in his drink?"

"No," Grace admitted.

"Well, then what choice do we have?"

The duke interrupted. "Fiona?" he said. "I heard you talking. I know your name. Come here, Fiona. Be sensible and release me . . . or you shall regret it."

"What now?" Grace asked her in a low voice.

Fiona picked up his neck cloth from the pile of clothing she had carefully folded and rolled it in a ball as she went through the curtain into the bedroom. Holburn was spread out on the bed, a handsome, virile specimen of masculine anger. "It's about time you listened to me," he said, every inch of him a duke.

Taking her courage in hand, she walked to the head of the bed, and as he opened his mouth to give her more advice, she stuffed his own neck cloth in it.

Then, without a backward glance, she left the room.